D1426847

THE ROMANCE OF MISS HILARY

AND OTHER STORIES

UNIFORM WITH THIS VOLUME

EVERY GIRL'S BOOKSHELF

Her Treasure of Truth. By H. Louisa Bedford.
Beryl's Triumph. By Eglanton Thorne.
Annie Carr. A Tale of Two Hemispheres.
Ellen Tremaine. By M. Filleul.
The Girls of Marleigh Grange. By M. M. Pollard.
Little Maid Marigold. By Eleanora H. Stooke.
The Mysterious Locket. By Ruth Lynn.
The Mistress of the Manor. By E. Kirby.
Anthony Cragg's Tenant. By Agnes Giberne.
The Heart of a Friend. By Florence Wilmot.
Brown Eyes and Blue. By Annie Mabel Severs.
Arthur Glynn. By Ruth Lamb.
Two Enthusiasts. By Evelyn Everett-Green.
The Faith of Hilary Lovel. By Evelyn Everett-Green.

LONDON : THE RELIGIOUS TRACT SOCIETY.

WITH MUCH CLATTER AND ADO, THE CREAKING VEHICLE
DREW UP.

[*See page 112.*

THE ROMANCE OF MISS HILARY AND OTHER STORIES FOR GIRLS

BY

E. EVERETT-GREEN, F. LANGBRIDGE, M.A.,
A. R. BUCKLAND, M.A., R. W. K. EDWARDS, E. A. GILLIE,
H. SMETHAM, MRS. MAYO, AND
OTHER WRITERS

LONDON
THE RELIGIOUS TRACT SOCIETY
4 BOUVERIE STREET AND 65 ST. PAUL'S CHURCHYARD, E.C.

CONTENTS

Contents

THE ROMANCE OF MISS HILARY

I

TOUCHING A TENDER SPOT

"DEAR me!" said Mr. Winter, in a tone of fidgety annoyance, as he raised his eyes from the deeply black-edged sheet of paper he was perusing. "Very sad, very sad indeed!"

"What does Aunt Hilary say?" asked his eldest daughter, Flossie, who presided at the coffee-urn; and Uncle Higgins looked up from his morning paper to hear the answer.

"Your poor grandfather's affairs have been left in a shocking condition. She says"—referring to the letter—"'The solicitor tells me that when all expenses have been paid there will be practically nothing left for me to live upon. The news has been a great shock to me, as at my time of life it is not easy to find the means of earning a livelihood.'"

"Then she is actually left penniless?" asked Flossie, arching her pretty eyebrows and screwing up her lips.

7

The Romance of Miss Hilary

"Poor soul! poor soul!" said Uncle Higgins.

"Women always are fools in such matters," said Mr. Winter; "I suppose I must write and ask her to come here, until she can find some sort of position for herself; though of what use she can be to any one I'm sure I don't know. It's a bad look-out."

"Here!" exclaimed Flossie, in blank dismay, ignoring the latter part of her father's speech. "Must Aunt Hilary come *here*? Why, wherever can we put her? We haven't room."

"Then you must make room," said the master of the house. "Where else is she to go, if not here, I should like to know? You must turn in with Maud, Flossie, and give up your room to your aunt."

Flossie made no answer, but her lips formed into a very decided pout. She was very fond of her own room, the only place in the noisy house where she could be quiet and alone.

When her father and uncle had gone to the City, and her little sister Maud had run off to the nursery, Flossie was sufficiently weak-minded to ventilate her grievances to her brother Jack, a shock-headed boy of fourteen.

"Why should we be inflicted with Aunt Hilary?" said Flossie, bursting with her private wrongs—"a poky old thing fussing about the house, as I know she will, and trying to be mistress! It's a shame I should have to turn out of my room. Of course, I'm sorry for her, and all that, but we can't *do* with visitors in this house. We're far too poor, and there are too many of us already. I'm sure it is bad

8

The Romance of Miss Hilary

enough to have Uncle Joe, with his old bachelor ways——"

"Oh! come now, Floss," objected Jack, balancing himself thoughtfully on the back of his chair, "where should we all be if it wasn't for Uncle Higgins? And you know he isn't such a bad old chap. Why, how d'you suppose you'd have got that swell dress for Robinson's party, and who'd have paid for your singing lessons, and——"

"Oh! be quiet, Jack," said his sister, with a gleam of compunction. "I'm sure I don't want to talk against Uncle Higgins. I know he has always been a sort of providence to us, and he is all we have to look to in the future. Still, if you had to cook for him, and to bear with all his faddy little ways, *you* would admit that he was fidgety."

"Wonder how long she'll stay—two months, d'you think?" hazarded Jack, returning to the former topic.

"Two *years* more likely," said Flossie, hysterically.

*　　　*　　　*　　　*　　　*

When Flossie said that Uncle Higgins had been a sort of providence to the family she spoke the truth. Mr. Winter was one of those men who never succeed in any undertaking. Uncle Higgins had come to live there on the death of his sister, Mrs. Winter, and being an old gentleman of a domesticated disposition, he esteemed it a privilege as well as a duty to be good to "poor Mary's children." Uncle Higgins was a prosperous man. He had begun humbly, but had now risen to the position

The Romance of Miss Hilary

of a large wholesale provision merchant, with an
extensive business and a steady income. He meant
to divide his money among his nephews and nieces
at his death, and in the meantime he kept the house
together, and acted the part of a beneficent fairy
godfather in the matter of giving presents. The
children were all fond of Uncle Higgins in their
own way.

Miss Hilary Winter shivered a little, partly with
cold and partly with nervousness, as the cab drew
up at her brother's door. It was a wet, drizzling
night, and the house looked dark and uninviting.
At the second knock, the door was opened by an
untidy maid-of-all-work. Miss Hilary, who had been
accustomed to superintend her father's house with a
delicate nicety of detail, felt a little shock of dis-
approval at the sight of the girl's coarse apron and
grimy face at this hour of the day. With a slight
sinking of the heart she asked timidly if Miss Winter
was at home.

"Yes 'm," answered the girl, civilly enough; and
then, to Miss Hilary's horror, she shrieked up the
stairs, "Miss Flossie, Miss Flossie, you're wanted."

Flossie's slim, graceful figure appeared on the
landing above in answer to this summons, and she
came slowly downstairs.

"How are you, Aunt Hilary?" she said, dutifully
presenting her cheek to be kissed. "Is this your
box? Susan, show the man where to carry it. Come
in and sit down, won't you, before you take off your
things? You must be tired with your journey."

"I *do* feel tired," said Miss Hilary, as she followed

The Romance of Miss Hilary

her niece into the dark little drawing-room, where the embers of a fire were feebly smouldering.

"Dear me!" exclaimed Flossie, in an annoyed tone, "it's just like that girl. She has let the fire almost out, and never lit the gas!"

She struck a match sharply as she spoke, and then gave the fire a vicious poke, which almost extinguished it.

"Never mind, my dear," said Miss Hilary, with a timid attempt to soothe her niece's ruffled temper.

Flossie was ungraciously silent. She chose to consider the remark patronising, and there was a tacit resentment in the curve of the wilful, rosy lips, and the defiant upward motion of her pretty chin, which Miss Hilary was quick to recognise. She was tired, cold, and dispirited, but she was humbly anxious to conciliate the niece of whom she had often heard, so she called her scanty stock of fortitude to her aid, and persevered with gentle interest.

"And so you are Flossie. Deary me! how you have altered since I saw you last! Then you were a tiny child just learning to walk, and now you are quite a grown-up young lady. I had no idea I should find you so tall and womanly; I thought of you as quite a little girl still. How old are you, my dear?"

"Nineteen," answered Flossie, frigidly, "and I have kept father's house for the last three years." ("I'll have no mistakes made on that point," she thought.)

The Romance of Miss Hilary

"Really!" Miss Hilary's eyebrows went up in mild surprise. "You are very young for so much responsibility. When I was your age I should have been far too inexperienced. But girls are so advanced nowadays."

Flossie was not expansive on the subject.

"Won't you come upstairs and take off your things?" she said; "tea will be ready in a few minutes; and I dare say you will like to wash."

Miss Hilary followed her niece into the bedroom which had been grudgingly prepared for her reception. It looked bare and uninviting enough. A clumsy black iron bedstead stood revealed in all its naked ugliness of outline, unsoftened by any of those dainty white draperies in which Miss Hilary's soul delighted; the narrow strips of Kidderminster carpet, economically disposed about the floor, added to the bare and unfurnished appearance of the room; but it seemed to the stranger a haven of refuge, which she hailed with a sigh of relief.

When Miss Hilary at length descended, and, acting upon the advice of the grimy domestic, found her way to the basement of the house, she was introduced to her other nieces and nephews, who each held out a limp, dirty little hand and submitted, with an air of sheepish resignation, to be kissed and patted on the head.

It was a terrible trial to Miss Hilary to find herself thus suddenly thrown into a position of helpless dependence. She was proudly determined not to be a burden upon them for any length of time; but in the meanwhile she wished that they might

The Romance of Miss Hilary

look upon her kindly, and she was nervously anxious not to prejudice them against her.

"I am so ready to love them," she thought wistfully ; "surely they will give me a little love in return."

Poor Miss Hilary! As she sat down to the evening meal for the first time in her brother's house she faltered under the consciousness that six pairs of merciless eyes were fixed upon her in keen and critical scrutiny. It was almost more than she could bear. All her timid affability deserted her ; she felt the habitual old-fashioned frigidity of her manner settling down upon her, and was powerless to resist it. She sat through the meal in stiff silence. No one showed much interest in her beyond a few formal questions as to her journey, and all the kindly, natural inquiries she had been planning to make herself died upon her lips. She sat with her little figure primly drawn to its fullest height, her hands, encased in beaded mittens, sedately folded before her, her lips frigidly compressed into their most uncompromising lines, and her heart surging in a passionate, impotent protest against the harsh impression that she knew she was creating.

She was grateful when the meal was at an end, and Flossie rose and suggested in an uninviting tone that they should go up to the drawing-room. Flossie wondered wearily of how many tedious evenings this was to be the forerunner, as she watched Miss Hilary choose the most uncomfortable of the stiff-backed chairs, and producing from her pocket an ugly little leather housewife, commence busily tatting. Flossie had thrown herself listlessly upon the couch, from which she was criticising her aunt's proceedings with half-closed eyes, when Miss Hilary, with a desperate attempt at friendliness, looked up and spoke:

"Do you tat, my dear?"

Flossie indignantly construed this innocent question into an implied reproach of her idleness.

"No," she answered, flippantly, in her clear, ringing young voice, "I don't do anything useful. I'm afraid girls have sadly deteriorated since your young days, Aunt Hilary."

Jack, who had buried herself in a book at the further end of the room, looked up and giggled. A dull, painful red rose in Miss Hilary's cheeks, but she answered the words, and not the tone.

"You do yourself injustice, I am sure, my dear," she said; "you told me yourself that you were the housekeeper."

"Oh!" Flossie answered, carelessly, "the house keeps itself."

Miss Hilary looked at her pert, pretty niece with an involuntary tribute of admiration. She put down her tatting for a moment, for a sudden mist rose before her eyes; when it cleared again the door was opening to admit a new-comer.

"Oh!" said Flossie, "here is Uncle Higgins. You haven't met him yet, have you, Aunt Hilary?"

* * * * *

Uncle Higgins made straight for Miss Hilary, holding out his hand from the other side of the room. He was a hopelessly commonplace man in appearance, with grey whiskers, a bald head, and large, bluntly-cut features. He was of a big, stout build, and looked flourishing, but there was nothing ostentatious in his bearing.

"How are you, ma'am?" said Uncle Higgins, shaking Miss Hilary's hand like a pump-handle; "hope you ain't tired out with your journey?"

It was the first cordial greeting she had heard; it went straight to her heart.

"I am well, I thank you, sir," said she, dropping an old-fashioned curtsey, "and not over-fatigued."

Jack's and Flossie's eyes met, and Jack subsided behind his book.

"Come," said Uncle Higgins, with unwonted officiousness, "you all seem very quiet here. Can't you give us a little music, Florence?"

Flossie rose with an obedient sigh. As Uncle Higgins had paid for her singing lessons, it was impossible for her to refuse. After a great deal of searching she found the song she wanted, and, sitting down at the jingling old piano, trilled out a brilliant little song with a good deal of taste and style. Unfortunately it was lost upon her hearers. Uncle Higgins, as was his custom whenever "a little music" was the order of the evening, had retired into a big arm-chair in the corner, peacefully reposing with his handkerchief over his face. It was one of his "ways," and therefore did not create surprise. Aunt Hilary was placidly counting her stitches in a half-audible voice as Flossie ceased, and flung off the music-stool.

The Romance of Miss Hilary

"That was a very pretty song, my dear," she said, mildly ; " but what was it all about ? "

This was rather a searching question.

"Oh," answered Flossie, vaguely, " it's a serenade, you know. He tells her that her eyes are like stars, and all that—they always do."

"Indeed ? " said Miss Hilary.

She was not asking for information ; her interjection was politely mechanical, but to Flossie's uneasy conscience it had a satirical sound. She plunged about in her mind for a change of subject.

"Don't *you* play or sing, Aunt Hilary ? " she asked, never doubting the answer.

Miss Hilary's heart fluttered. Here was the opportunity for her to develop those "social qualities" that she longed to possess ; yet it was a terrible effort to rise to the occasion. She cleared her throat nervously several times before she answered.

"I am not accustomed to performing before an audience," she said, growing pale at her own temerity, "but there are several little things I used to sing to your poor grandfather——"

"Oh, pray let us hear them ! " cried Flossie, reopening the piano. They were going to find Aunt Hilary amusing, after all !

She rose, trembling in every limb, and walked to the piano. Her unaccustomed fingers stumbled through a few notes of prelude.

"What shall it be ? " she said, with a little gasp. " I can sing ' The Last Rose of Summer,' or ' I dreamt I dwelt in Marble Halls,' or ' Ben Bolt '—— "

The Romance of Miss Hilary

"Let us have 'Ben Bolt,'" said Flossie, interrupting the simple repertory; "it's quite a new song —to us."

Miss Hilary began. The thin, reedy voice, cracking on the higher notes and wheezing out the lower, was even funnier than the listeners had anticipated.

"'Oh! don't you remember sweet Alice, Ben Bolt,
Sweet Alice, with hair so brown?'"

quavered Miss Hilary plaintively, the antiquated little curls bobbing in time to the tune. Jack was in convulsions; even little Maud tittered; while Flossie, with her handkerchief pressed to her lips, tried to frown down the other culprits.

But suddenly their merriment was checked in surprise. Uncle Higgins was sitting up, with the handkerchief off his face; but he was not looking at the culprits or thinking of them. His mind had gone back, far back into the past; and there was a dimness in his old eyes as he rose and walked across to the piano.

"Thank you, ma'am," he said, as the last discordant notes died away; "you have given me such a treat as I haven't had for many a long day. My mother used to sing that song when I was a bit of a lad, not near so old as Jacky here. You've made me see her again, as plain—— 'Sweet Alice, with hair so brown.' She had brown hair, and I always used to think of her when she sang it. Ay, she was a sweet woman, and a good one— there ain't many such nowadays. How does it go ? " and he crooned to himself, in a low, unmusical growl—

> " ' She blushed with delight, if you gave her a smile,
>   And trembled with fear at your frown.'

Ah! that was just my mother—a tender, sensitive creature as ever was ! "

He was talking more to himself than to Miss Hilary, and she was listening to him with tears in her eyes.

II

MISCHIEF BREWING

SOME days had passed before Mr. Winter deemed it necessary to discuss the future with Miss Hilary, and then it was she herself who introduced the subject. She watched her opportunity, and when, after tea, the usual dispersion of the family took place, she followed her brother, with a beating heart, to his private den. In answer to Mr. Winter's impatient "Come in" she slid apologetically into the room ; but she was alarmed to find he was not alone. He and Uncle Higgins were evidently engaged in discussing "business," of which mysterious occupation Miss Hilary had a truly feminine horror. With a deprecating murmur she was about to slip away again, when Uncle Higgins rose and handed her his chair.

"Oh ! " she said, in a flutter, "I did not know I was intruding. I thought you were alone, James,

The Romance of Miss Hilary

and I could take the opportunity to have a talk with you ; but any other time will do."

"No, no," said Uncle Higgins, "you ain't interrupting *us ; our* business can wait."

Mr. Winter frowned: perhaps he did not altogether agree with this view of the matter.

"Well," he said, ungraciously, "no time like the present, I suppose. What have you to say, Hilary ? No, don't go, Josiah," as Uncle Higgins was delicately preparing to take his leave; "we shall have time to go into that matter again, I have no doubt."

In response to this not very encouraging invitation Miss Hilary spoke.

"I wanted to consult you, James," she began, in a low tone, "about the best course for me to pursue in procuring a—a situation."

The poor gentlewoman brought out the distasteful word with an effort.

"I am very ignorant in such matters," she went on, "and I am afraid my qualifications for any position are very limited, but I would conscientiously do my best in whatever I undertook."

"What have you thought of ?" asked Mr. Winter, tapping the desk with a paper-knife, as though to hurry on the conversation.

"I thought, perhaps, some position as housekeepe or companion," faltered Miss Hilary.

Her brother interrupted her fretfully.

"Ah ! it is not so easy to get those things as you imagine. There is too great a demand. You know nothing of the world, Hilary."

The Romance of Miss Hilary

" I wish I knew more," she answered, meekly. " I am afraid I am very unfitted to battle with it."

Uncle Higgins cleared his throat and walked to the window.

" If you had known a little more of the world," pursued Mr. Winter, warming to his subject, " you would not have allowed yourself to be left in such a dependent position. You have had the control of the house in your own hands for the last ten years, I suppose ? Why didn't you limit the expenditure more ? You ought to have moved into a smaller house, dismissed some of the servants, and dispensed with the carriage."

" I had no idea," murmured Miss Hilary ; " I never had anything to do with money. It never struck me that we were living beyond our income. Father would not have liked me to interfere——"

" But it was your *duty* to interfere," Mr. Winter interrupted. " You knew how childish my father was becoming ; if you had been at all a business woman, you would have insisted upon looking into the expenses."

" Come, come," urged Uncle Higgins, in a deprecatory growl from the other end of the room, " we can't expect the ladies to understand business."

Miss Hilary had been sitting perfectly still throughout the interview, her hands clasped as in a vice, her lips pressed so tightly together that the blood had deserted them, never raising her eyes from the ground ; but now, at Uncle Higgins's words, she suddenly lifted them. They had the expression of a hunted animal. He could not resist their mute,

The Romance of Miss Hilary

pathetic appeal. He came forward and joined in the discussion.

"Don't you worry, my dear lady," he said ; "we shall find something for you in time, and in the meantime you're among friends. We'll put an advertisement in the papers for you, and see what that will do ; but you mustn't think too much about it, must she, James? She must look upon this as a little holiday."

"Oh, sir!" exclaimed Miss Hilary, with a gasp, "you are too kind."

The unexpected kindness had entirely unstrung her. She took his hand in both hers, and clutched it nervously ; then, fearful lest she should be betrayed into tears, she hurried from the room.

"Don't you think, James," suggested Uncle Higgins, diffidently, "that it would be better to leave the past alone—kinder, and more brotherly, eh?"

Afterwards, when he was alone in his own room at night, he paced up and down in unusual restlessness. The unconscious appeal in Miss Hilary's eyes haunted him. All the latent chivalry in his nature had been awakened in her defence. His heart was wounded for her sake.

"Poor soul," he muttered, "poor soul—poor, desolate creature!"—he heaved a deep sigh. "There are the children to be remembered," he said ; "no, no, it is out of the question ; I must not think of it."

*   *   *   *   *

"Oh!" said Flossie, "it's too ridiculous for anything."

The Romance of Miss Hilary

It was one of those evenings when the breakfast room was considered sacred to Flossie and her sweetheart Hugh ; and its two occupants were sitting side by side before the fire, in a confidential attitude, discussing the affairs of the nation.

"What is so ridiculous?" asked Hugh, absentmindedly.

"Why," said Flossie, with some impatience, "Aunt Hilary and Uncle Higgins! He has got it into his head that we don't treat her kindly—though I don't know what business it is of his ; and so he has constituted himself her champion—Mr. Josiah Higgins, knight-errant to the rescue!—that sort of thing, you know. It's *too* absurd to see them bobbing and curtseying each other, with, 'I thank you, sir,' and, 'Not at all, ma'am!' I've laughed until I'm tired, and now I am really beginning to think it a serious matter. If we don't alter our tactics, he will marry her before our very eyes, purely out of pity for the poor ill-used old soul—and, presto! all *our* expectations will be scattered to the winds."

Hugh had listened to this speech with more attention. He was a quiet, serious young man, slowly making his way through the hospitals. He was thoroughly good-hearted, and somehow Flossie's last speech hurt him.

"I don't like to hear you speak like that, Flossie," he said, so gravely that she opened her blue eyes wide in surprise. "*I* know you don't mean what you say, but even then I don't like to hear you say it."

Flossie could not find it in her heart to lower Hugh's ideal of her.

The Romance of Miss Hilary

"I don't think I *do* quite mean all I say," she said, resting her head on his shoulder, with a charming, penitent smile, which carried irresistible conviction along with it. "My tongue runs away with me sometimes. But, Hugh," she added, conscience prompting her, "I'm afraid I am not quite so good as you think me. I'm not at all a pleasant-tempered girl, *really*. It is quite true I haven't been as nice as I might be to Aunt Hilary. I've been very naughty and impatient. I know: but I will try to be better, for your sake. I'll be as sweet as honey to her —and ask her to teach me how to tat to-morrow— *there !* "

"And," said Hugh, not perfectly satisfied even now, "will you do another thing for my sake ? Don't talk as if you really cared about your uncle's money. Why, Flossie, if it was for his happiness that he should marry Miss Hilary, you'd be the first one to tell him to do so."

"Should I ? " said Flossie; "perhaps I should." And she ended the discussion with a kiss.

*　　*　　*　　*　　*

The next day the house was unusually quiet. Uncle Higgins, on the previous evening, had informed them that he should not be at home for several days, as he was very busy "stock-taking," and should sleep on the premises. Jack, whose holidays were drawing very near their close, after a few days of uneasy loafing and grumbling, seemed suddenly to have discovered an occupation for himself, and had mysteriously disappeared.

"He is after some mischief, I have no doubt,"

thought Flossie, complacently; "but as long as it keeps him out of the way this last day or two, I don't much care."

Aunt Hilary thought that evening that she had never seen Flossie so attractive, bending quietly over her darning, with a gentler expression and a softer light in her eyes than usual. Miss Hilary's heart quickened with new hope; instinctively she knew that the girl was more approachable to-night than ever before, and she addressed her with a cheerful confidence at which she herself marvelled. Flossie did not repel her advances: a kindly, tolerant influence was at work within her, and she was surprised to find at the end of the evening that in pleasing Hugh she had pleased herself also.

III

A COMFORTABLE COUPLE

By Miss Hilary's plate, on the breakfast-table next day, was an envelope, directed in big, sprawling characters. This in itself was an event, for Miss Hilary had few correspondents, and the sight of it quite fluttered her, especially as she did not recognise the hand-writing.

"Dear me," she said, as she broke the seal with trembling fingers, "it must be an answer to my advertisement. I had hardly hoped for one so soon."

She held the letter up close to her short-sighted

eyes. Flossie was watching her with a newly-awakened interest. Miss Hilary turned red, then white, and suddenly crushing the letter into her pocket, she rose from the table.

"I feel a little faint," she gasped—"no, don't come"—as Flossie prepared to follow her—"I shall be better directly."

As she left the room Mr. Winter looked up for the first time.

"Some fresh bad news, I suppose," he said, in his tone of personal injury; "some people are born to be unlucky."

"I don't think it was *bad* news somehow," answered Flossie, thoughtfully, knitting her brows with a puzzled expression. "I should have said— Now, Jack, what is the matter with *you?*"

Jack, with a very red face, was apparently choking over his coffee, while Maud, with mistaken zeal, hammered his back with both her small fists.

"Nothing," said Jack, in a muffled, choky voice. "Maudie, leave me alone, will you?"

Flossie looked at him with sudden suspicion, born of past experience. "That boy's been up to something," she thought, "and I'll find out what it is."

But as soon as breakfast was over Jack adroitly slipped from the room, and for the time being evaded her questions.

"There's a mystery somewhere," said Flossie to herself; "I'll go up to Aunt Hilary, and see what I can make of her."

She found Miss Hilary quite composed; "her

faintness was only temporary," she said, "but she had thought it better to remain quietly upstairs."

She had been writing, and when the girl entered was putting on her bonnet and cloak.

"I am just going to the post," she explained, as Flossie expostulated.

There was some indefinable change in Miss Hilary. Her eyes were brighter and softer: she had been crying, but they had not been tears of sorrow: a tender radiance was diffused over her face, which softened the uncompromising lines and restored for a moment the grace of her past youth. A fugitive smile trembled on her lips, a rosy, youthful blush tinged her withered cheeks.

"No, no, my child," she said, in answer to Flossie's expostulations, and the girl fancied that there was a thrill of new tenderness in her voice; "the air will do me good. I will not trouble you with my letter, thank you."

As she was leaving the room she turned suddenly, and taking both Flossie's hands, squeezed them with agitated eagerness.

"You will love me a little, won't you, Flossie?" she said, with wistful eyes; then she pressed a hurried kiss on her niece's white forehead, and was gone.

* * * * *

Flossie felt dazed. What had happened? Her mind reverted to the absent Uncle Higgins; was it possible that he had any part in the mystery?

It was later in the day when she at length succeeded in encountering Jack. She fancied he

looked ill at ease, and cornered the suspected mis-
creant at once.

"Now, Jack, what is it?" she said.

Jack was overcome with somewhat nervous
merriment.

"What a joke!" he said, "and I've got it all
to myself. I thought I'd tell you, but you seemed
rather crabby this morning. You'd grin, though, if
you heard it. Where's Aunt Hilary?"

"I don't know: I haven't seen her since she
returned from the post," answered Flossie. She
noticed Jack's face suddenly lengthen. "What's this
fine joke?" she went on, sternly, for she was beginning
to feel anxious. "You had better tell me, Jack.
Where's the fun, if you keep it all to yourself?"

"Well," said Jack, "promise you won't tell. I
expect it will come out some time, but I shall be
back at school to-morrow, and well out of it all—
only I didn't reckon on her being in such a hurry to
answer—I told her not to."

"She—*who?* Jack, tell me quickly!" cried Flossie,
impatiently.

*　　　*　　　*　　　*　　　*

Ten minutes later Miss Hilary was sitting quietly
in her room, when a hurried knock came at the door,
and Flossie, without waiting for the permission to
enter, flew into the room. Her eyes were wild and
dilated; she seemed transported out of herself. She
threw herself impetuously on the floor by Miss
Hilary's side.

"Oh, Aunt Hilary! how shall I tell you?" she
gasped.

The Romance of Miss Hilary

Miss Hilary was fluttered, but not alarmed. She had her own private reasons for excitement, which she thought might offer some explanation of Flossie's conduct.

"My dear," she said, very gently, though with a little inward quaking, "it is I who should have told *you* before; but I intended you should all know of it shortly. I——"

"No!" cried Flossie, in an agonised tone, laying her fingers on her aunt's lips, "you must not—you must not say another word. Oh! *how* can I make you understand? Aunt Hilary, *dear* Aunt Hilary, that letter was not from Uncle Higgins at all. It was Jack who wrote it, that bad, wicked boy—for a *joke!*"

"What!" said Miss Hilary.

She rose to her feet, pushing Flossie away from her. She stood for some moments quite still, unconscious of her surroundings, dazed by the suddenness of the blow which had been struck at her; but slowly a full consciousness of her position surged back into her brain.

"God help me!" she said, in a reverent yet anguished voice. For the first time in her simple, prosaic life Miss Hilary rose to the height of tragedy. Flossie looked at the antiquated little figure, which had appeared so ludicrous in her eyes, with a sense of awe. It was invested with the dignity of strong indignation, with the sublimity of passion.

"Oh!" she said, turning her white face to where Flossie still crouched in self-abasement, "may God forgive you, and save you from such bitter humiliation as that you have brought upon me!"

The Romance of Miss Hilary

Flossie could not answer her. The depth of the accusation touched her also : it was her own example of ridicule and raillery, which, acted upon by another, was bringing this terrible retribution.

"From the first," Miss Hilary continued, eloquent in the force of her indignation, "you have looked upon me as an object of contempt and indifference. I expected no more—I asked no more—but you might have spared me this open ignominy, this crowning insult. Do you think that because I am old, and dull, and uninteresting, therefore I am beyond feeling ? Ah! why have you done this ? You, who have youth, and beauty, and love—all that makes life precious—could you not at least have left me my one possession, my self-respect ? "

"Aunt Hilary!" cried Flossie, in a piteous attempt at defence, "you *can't* think I was a party to this. Oh! I know I have been cruel and thoughtless, but I am not so bad as that. Is there *nothing* I can do—nothing to show you how wretchedly I feel about it — how miserable I am for your sake ? "

At the first words of sympathy and compunction Miss Hilary faltered. She spread out her hands feebly before her, as if groping her way to the seat she had left ; then, suddenly, the strong tension of her emotion was relaxed, and, covering her face with her thin fingers, she began to weep in a pitiful, helpless fashion, which was infinitely more touching than her wrath had been.

"Oh!" she moaned, "why—why did I answer the letter ? "

The Romance of Miss Hilary

Flossie drew near, and laid her hand on Miss Hilary's shoulder with a gentle, caressing gesture.

"It will be easily explained," she said; "don't cry so, dear. Uncle will understand at once. He is always kind and considerate—it will be as if nothing had happened."

Miss Hilary looked up almost fiercely.

"Do you think I shall stay here and meet him?" she asked. "*Can* you think such a thing? No, I must not give way like this; there is so much to be done, and I must leave the house to-day. Flossie, you asked if you could help me. Help me now to get my things together. I am so foolishly unnerved I hardly know what I am doing."

"But where can you go?" asked Flossie, in amazement.

"Where?" Miss Hilary drew her hand confusedly across her brow. "I hardly know. There are some people in Manchester who would receive me for a week or two, I dare say. Yes, I will go to them."

"You must not!" cried Flossie; "you don't know what you are saying—you must not go. What will father say—what will uncle say if you go? Dear Aunt Hilary, have some pity on us, and stay."

Never in all her life before had Flossie been so thoroughly in earnest as now in this excited appeal. She threw her strong, supple young arms impetuously round her aunt's little figure, clinging to her gown, as though to keep her by main force. Miss Hilary recognised the warmth and sincerity in Flossie's face and voice with a pathetic attempt at a smile.

The Romance of Miss Hilary

"No, Flossie," she said, "you ask too much of me. Put it to yourself. Could *you* stay, in my position?"

The girl made no answer. She loosed her hold of her aunt's gown, and, rising from her kneeling posture, left the room without another word.

*   *   *   *   *

Once outside the door, Flossie snatched her hat and jacket from the peg in her bedroom, and ran fleetly out of the house, buttoning her jacket as she ran. An inspiration had come to her; she would go to Uncle Higgins herself. She had the vaguest idea of what she intended to say to him; but she felt that, in some undefined way, he alone could set everything right. She ran all the way to the station, and was fortunate in just catching a train. It was not a long journey, but to her restive fancy it seemed hours before the train reached the City terminus. She knew her way to her uncle's warehouse, and hurried through the busy streets, looking neither to right nor left, pushing aside all obstacles with a mechanical impatience. On reaching her destination she breathlessly mounted the flights of stone steps until she reached the landing where she knew her uncle was generally to be found. The door of his private office was closed, but Flossie boldly turned the handle and entered.

He was sitting at his desk, with a blank sheet of note-paper before him, and his head resting dejectedly on his hands. He looked older and more feeble than Flossie had ever before seen him. As she entered he said sharply, though without looking up—

The Romance of Miss Hilary

"Didn't I give orders that I was not to be disturbed?"

Then he realised his mistake.

"Flossie!" he exclaimed.

"Yes," she said, "it is I. Oh! uncle, you must help us. Aunt Hilary——"

"I was just writing to her," he interrupted, in a troubled voice. "Some vile trick has been played upon her. I never wrote the letter she received."

"I know, I know," Flossie broke in; "it was that wretched Jack. But, uncle, never mind that just now; you must come with me at once. She has taken it dreadfully; she says she shall leave the house directly—you must come with me and stop her."

"But," said Uncle Higgins, staring with a stupid, dazed expression at the sheet of paper before him, "how am I to stop her? What can I say?"

"What were you going to say—there?" Flossie pointed to the pen and paper.

"I was going to tell her," said Uncle Higgins, simply, "that though I did not write the letter, it is quite true that I love her; but that I'm not free to offer her marriage, because, because——"

"Because what?" asked Flossie, imperiously. Her lips were parted in her eager interest, and there was a strangely exultant expectation on her face.

"Because," he said heavily, "there are too many claims upon me. What would become of you, my child—of you and the others? Who have you got to look to but me?"

The Romance of Miss Hilary

"We have ourselves to look to," cried Flossie, with generous ardour; "it is right we should learn to be independent. Oh, uncle, be guided by me! Do you think we are so selfish, so horribly mercenary, as to let you sacrifice yourself and poor Aunt Hilary for our benefit? You have no *right* to do so; you have her to think of, as well as yourself. If you could but have seen her as I did to-day, there would be no need for me to plead for her. If you knew how unhappy she is!"

*　　*　　*　　*　　*

Uncle Higgins faltered visibly. He laid his head down on his folded arms again.

"If I only knew where my duty lay," he said, in a husky, uncertain voice.

"I will show you," Flossie said; "only come with me."

She reached his coat and hat as she spoke. The impetuosity of her enthusiasm infected him; he could not hold out against it; he submitted himself to her guidance like a child.

"Bless you, my dear!" he said; "you have a generous heart."

*　　*　　*　　*　　*

"To think," said Flossie to Hugh that evening, with a beautiful, whimsical smile—"just to *think* that you were right, and that it is *I* who have made the match after all!"

OLD ANNE'S PALACE

I

A PLAIN, HONEST SOUL

THERE was nothing about Old Anne to interest a casual observer. She was but a little withered body, with pale eyes and a sharp voice, in which she talked bad grammar. Yet there was an expression of humorous shrewdness on her wrinkled face.

I do not suppose Old Anne had ever been a pretty girl, and her hard days had begun early. She had had many little brothers and sisters, whom she had dragged about in her girlish arms. Most of them died — poor little things ! — but Anne never forgot their names or confused their identities. She used to tell the children about little brother Bob with the blue eyes, and Sister Sally with the squint, and the twins who took the scarlet fever. Then Anne's father and mother died, too, and her work in life was changed from baby-minding to tending her grandmother, who lived with another old woman, who was nearly blind and a little " off her head." Of the latter Anne always spoke with a profound reverence, seeing that the poor old body had had a brother who was a "real officer," and that her own manners were " always genteel."

Old Anne's Palace

The two old women lived long. Anne was twenty-six years of age before first the boarder and then the grandmother departed. Their little pensions died with them; the current "quarter's money" and the sale of the ramshackle old furniture barely paid for the funerals. Anne went in debt for her own mourning: a humble haberdasher of whom she had made her little purchases was willing to "trust" her. Anne always proudly remembered it; and his faith was justified, for he was repaid out of her first year's wages as a general servant.

Anne must have been nearly thirty-five when that happened to her which, I think, she always felt was a most strange and wonderful thing. She got married! I do believe Anne had never thought of such an event as among the possibilities of her existence. Her husband was a respectable working shoemaker, and they set up housekeeping on the third floor of a house in a quiet city court. Anne's face always softened when she thought of those days. I think the husband must have been a good Christian man. She never spoke much of him directly, but once, when the affairs of some neighbour were being discussed, Anne volunteered the observation :

"No woman need think herself so awful bad off, if she's had a real good man for a husband!"

If Anne had thought it wonderful to find herself a wife, what must she have felt when she became a mother! This happened twice. The little baby boy lived a few months; the little girl reached the age of five years. Then they were taken away,

Old Anne's Palace

and the great, cold world was as if they had never been—but not the mother's warm heart. One day, when they had been dead nearly thirty years, Anne suddenly showed us their two little pairs of shoes ; she had them in the corner of her box. She showed them to my cousin, who was then grieving bitterly over the loss of a first baby.

"You'll cheer up by-and-by, dearie," she said. "Don't you be afraid when you feel you can. Don't you fancy you'll forget. No, you'll never forget. There's some things it would be well to forget ; but not them that's dead. I reckon the angels will have brought up them children by this time better than I could, but I don't believe they'll be too fine for their old mother."

Anne must have been quite fifty before she became a widow—too old for service. Besides, I don't think she could have borne to break up "the little home," which remained the sole witness of her wifehood and motherhood. "The little home" of such as she is not a house, not even a room— it means a bedstead, and a chest of drawers, and a little table, and some chairs and china, and perhaps a bird-cage and one or two pictures. Anne had straightway to leave the rooms which she and her husband had occupied ; she had to go into one poor, broken attic in a ruinous house. But she kept all her "sticks."

Then began that standing miracle of life whose secret is known to so many elderly women of the type of Old Anne! She was also ready to do "charing," and her energy was really wonderful!

Old Anne's Palace

She did a little sick nursing, too, among her poor neighbours, and was not to be despised as a reliable "sitter-up" by people of much greater pretensions. A sentinel would not be less likely to fall asleep at his post than was Anne on her vigils.

But when one reflected that there was always the "rent" to pay—that the wages of her work could scarce cover the expense of the day—and that there were often weary intervals between her jobs, one could not but ask the question, "How did she manage to get along?"

I was a favourite with old Anne, and in the course of time I managed to insinuate my wonder on this head into the conversations we often had in the kitchen of our house on the servant's "evening out." Anne parried my hints by a general statement that "people was very kind." But I had to take this with a grain of salt, for, in other colloquies, it came out that her pittances often reached her grudged and scrimped, and were sometimes cruelly delayed. Perhaps one could see something by certain sidelights. Anne would say that she thought most people "ate a great deal more than was good for 'em; if they knowed what some could thrive on, she'd think they be ashamed." Every time I had occasion to visit her I noticed her room grew emptier. At last the change was so manifest that Anne faced it boldly.

"I'm not so young as I have been, an' I need my strength for summat else than keeping clean a lot of sticks I've no use for, and never shall have. I thought I couldn't have parted with 'em onst.

Old Anne's Palace

When he died they seemed to be his things that I couldn't give up. But I've had 'em now to myself for so long that they're just mine, and I can do what I like with 'em."

I wonder when Anne first began to turn tremulous regards on her future? I first discovered this carking terror after she had an attack of bronchitis, from which she made a rapid recovery, but after which she was never quite the same. It slipped out thus :—

"I thought the Lord was going to take me; and then I wished I had not repined so much, lest I'd live to have to go to the workus."

Nevertheless, with returning health, the "repining" returned too, and the secret having been once divulged, Anne seemed never able to resume her proud reserve. She "fretted" without disguise. As for the duty of believing that all things are in the hands of a loving Father, who will not forget any of His children, Anne not only knew this without our reminders, but inculcated it upon herself vigorously, alternating her bewailings over her apparently inevitable lot with bitter self-reproaches at her own "rebellious proud-heartedness."

"It's no use a-saying to myself 'the workus—what's the workus? If it's not shame that's brought ye there, there's no shame in being there.' That's all true enough, I dare say. But it's no use. The workus is a bad thing, and everybody ought to be afeared o' comin' to it. Why, when I was a girl I knew a man that was so desperate afraid of it that he just did anything to make money, ground the

Old Anne's Palace

faces o' the poor, he did, and slaved himself nigh to death; and yet, though he got ever so rich, he never could get a sort o' fear out o' his mind. And when he'd made millions, an' was an old man getting silly, he actually took a fancy he was on the parish, and he went along wi' them paupers that get the loaves and doles given to 'em, and his sons paid the guardians to give 'em to him, just to humour him. An' he thought his own grand house was the werry workus itself. Now doesn't that show what a thing it is to be afeard of, when the fear o't will work so on a man's mind, and is it any wonder that it frets a poor old woman like I, who knows I must come to it unless I dies first?"

"Ah, it feels bad, it does," said Anne one day to my brother; "it feels bad to know there are them will look at ye, and think either that God does not keep His promise after all, or else that you are not one of those the promises are given to. For doesn't David say, 'I have been young, and now am old; and yet saw I never the righteous forsaken, nor his seed begging their bread'? An' I reckon as there wasn't a workus in his time; that's the way of begging bread nowadays. It's getting bread from those who don't give it to you out o' love. But I'll just keep about as long as I can, and maybe I may die sudden some night."

It was pitiful to think that this was the hard-working woman's brightest hope—a longing to escape from the world before her experience should seem to belie those Divine promises in which she strove to trust. It was pitiful, too, to see how she struggled to maintain her strength, and how strenuously she denied its decay. Sometimes, in an earlier stage, she had been apt to speak about being tired and not so young as she had been. But now the cry was that she was fit as ever for a good day's work, if people would only believe it!

There were few persons interested in Anne who had any power to aid.

Those who had loved her were in heaven, "and maybe, up there, they doesn't see whether you're in the workus or not, but only whether your heart's right or wrong," said Anne. "It's God alone who knows everything, and that's a comfort, for what would my man do, if he thought his wife was a pauper?"

II

TRANSFIGURATION

ANNE'S reconcilement with the trial which seemed inevitably approaching was deepened in a very strange way. An old neighbour who had married a man who kept a little public-house fell ill, and was unable, as usual, to mount guard over her untrustworthy bar attendants and her boozing customers. Her illness was likely to be prolonged. The woman thought of Anne—her unimpugnable honesty, her strict temperance, her venerable years, even her sharp tongue and "high" temper, all made her an acquisition for such a place—if only she would fill it. The woman offered Anne a home in the tavern, with

40

Old Anne's Palace

"plenty of good living," and a stipend beyond what she generally earned, "when everything had to come out of it."

Vague rumours of some undefined good fortune having befallen our friend reached our ears. We wondered that we did not get a visit from her. We called at her room, to ask if it was true, but Anne was out. We had to remain curious for a day or two longer, when old Anne walked in, her usual serene, impassive self.

"What, you've heard all about it?" she asked, with her dry, quizzical smile, as we greeted her with eager inquiries. No, we had heard nothing—except that "somebody" had offered a comfortable home in return for certain services, and we had thought, "What a blessing——"

Anne interrupted us. "Humph," she said. "D' ye know where it was to be? No. Well, then, it was at the 'Noah's Ark'—with all the beasts inside, I reckon. I own it was a temptation. Says I to myself, 'There, Anne Evans, God does not mean ye for the workus, after all!' But thinks I, presently, 'Would God keep you out o' the workus, Anne, by putting ye into the very place that has a chief hand in the filling of workuses?' And that didn't seem to come right. And then I thought, 'Maybe He might mean ye, Anne, for a grain of salt in the 'Noah's Ark.'" But then that would have to work by driving its custom away, and that wasn't what I was to be hired for. An' it's like my imperence to count myself a grain of salt, anyhow, and I reckon if I dropped myself down there, I'd be o' the sort that

Old Anne's Palace

has lost its savour. If I'm only thinking o' being a grain o' salt, I can be that in the workus as well as anywhere else. But there's a deal o' the old Adam in us, an' it dies hard, it do. I lay awake all night afore I could give up the idea. An' I can tell you, miss, I did feel easy in my mind when I washed my hands o' the whole affair, with civil thanks to the poor body who had meant it kindly!"

There was never another word of complaining anxiety. Anne seemed to have risen above her dreaded calamity. I think I caught the thread of her feeling.

"The workus can't be worse than the Cross, an' Jesus took that, and the shame and reproach o' it. But He knew, ye see, that He could have had all the kingdoms o' the world and the glory o' them, if He would just have fallen down and worshipped the devil. He'd had His choice, you understand."

It was on a Sunday evening about this time that I happened to meet Anne coming down the steps of her church. The lined old face was radiant.

"We've had a grand sermon," she said. "From the text, 'Casting all your care upon Him, for He careth for you.' I can't think how He's going to care for me. But I reckon that's not my part of the bargain, and it will be real interestin' to watch what He will do."

There seemed no further perceptible failure in Anne's strength at that time. But presently we noticed in her a curious change of another sort. Every day became a "fine day" with the old woman. It might be hail, wind, or fog, but she now greeted

42

Old Anne's Palace

us with the uniform phrase, "Fine seasonable weather." Once or twice she explained that she was "watching the glorious sunset," when we found her gazing at a dull, leaden sky. Presently she puzzled and alarmed us by telling us of the "kind ladies" who came to see her in the night; she could listen to the rustling of their silk dresses as she lay in bed, and sometimes they sang to her. She spoke not only as if she believed what she was saying, but as if it was the most matter-of-fact circumstance in the world.

Next the landlady of the house where Anne lodged called upon us. She was really alarmed for her. It appeared that sometimes Old Anne would wander out alone for hours, and though she always came back quite fresh and cheerful, the landlady began to fear lest some day she would not come back at all. At other times Anne slept long beyond her usual hours, and so alarmed the neighbours that they had gone into her room uninvited.

It was plain that Anne must be at once put into some safe keeping.

Old Anne's long-dreaded evil day had overtaken her at last.

My cousin undertook to conduct the old woman to her sad destination. It was but a very bare little room which was to be left now. We brought a cab for Anne, and said we were going to take her for a drive.

"Eh, I never thought to be a carriage lady," said Anne. "I'll not know how to behave when the people looks at me."

Old Anne's Palace

She took a childish delight in the drive, and exclaimed with pleasure when she saw the flowers in the workhouse lodge.

"This is to be your new home, Anne," said my cousin, gently leading her in. "All these good people will take care of you and look after you. See, what a grand dining-room! And there is your nice, clean little bed."

Tears were streaming down Old Anne's furrowed face. "To think it's all mine—mine!" she said. "And I, that used to pray I might be able to keep my own little attic, while the Lord was preparing a palace for me! Please God I won't put upon my servants. I knows how servants is put upon. And I hope He'll keep me humble."

Yes, Old Anne was in the long-dreaded "workus" at last; but thus it was transfigured for her. She lived there for several months, in greater physical comfort and rest than she had ever known in all her toilsome life, while the golden mist drawn over her mind saved it from any of the pain it must otherwise have encountered. All the "fancies" of her second childhood were bright and cheerful fancies.

"I'm so glad to see you," she would say, when we visited her. "I never thought I'd have such a place as this here to welcome you to. I've often wished to do you all honour—but my life was mostly take, and no give. That's over now, though. Ye see, I likes to have a lot of poor folks in my house. I allays thought it seemed selfish to have big places with nobody in 'em, while others is crowded. It's a

44

Old Anne's Palace

little noisy here, sometimes, but what harm, poor souls?" And then she would prattle on about her husband and her children, as if they were living and moving around her. I never saw a sad look on her old face again.

She died in the night. When we stood around her coffin, to take our last look on the old face upon whose commonplaces a strange, glad dignity had settled down for ever, my cousin Mary said softly:

"So He giveth His beloved sleep."

"Her delusions saved her from a great deal, poor body," said the Union doctor, who accompanied us.

"There's a mystery about some delusions," mused Tom. "They are so like revelations. Light comes in through cracks, you know."

A HEART OF LOVE

I

THE DEAR BOY

DAVID DUNBAR had been only a few months in his first charge in the busy Northern town ; but he had succeeded in winning the hearts of most of his flock. His greatest enemies could find nothing worse to say of him than that he was too impulsive, and—that he was not married !

The congregation did not know how much of the success of their young preacher was due to the sister who guided both himself and his house so well, yet so unobtrusively, that the guiding hand was never seen.

Among his most ardent though secret admirers were a certain Thomas Johnson and his sister. Something in the seeming loneliness of this couple, and their affection for each other, appealed to the young minister's heart ; and, wishing, if possible, to break through the reserve and shyness that cut them off from their fellows, he took the opportunity one evening of telling the shrinking clerk that " he would take tea with them the following day, if that was convenient."

Thomas happened to be unaccompanied by his

46

sister that evening, and the minister's proposal was so sudden, so unexpected, that it fairly took away his breath, and for a moment he could do nothing but blush and stammer. For he and his sister looked upon the minister of St. John's as such an important personage, and his office as such an exalted one, that the idea of entertaining him in their own home, and at his own request too, was a very unexpected honour indeed.

"I heard him refuse an invitation to a grand party at Mrs. Brunton's only the other day," said the clerk, in an awed whisper, to his sister, when he rushed home to tell her the great news; "and to think he should actually offer to come and have tea with us!" His sister was equally overcome, for she, with Thomas, had watched the minister's triumph in the church with wonder and pleasure, and had looked upon those who talked and laughed with him in quite a familiar manner as standing upon an exalted and unattainable height of bliss.

"Are you sure you understood him aright, Thomas?" she inquired, anxiously.

"Of course I am."

"Well," said Miss Johnson, drawing a deep breath, "I shall never have courage to talk to him, Thomas; I shall be silent all the time."

"I'll tell you what to do; you must show him your album—that is what people do with their visitors—then you need not talk so much."

"Why, what a boy you are for thinking of things!" said Miss Johnson, in admiration. "I shall just do that, and you can do the talking, Thomas, for you are not stupid, like me—but I shall see and have a nice tea for him," and the little woman began planning it on the spot.

The minister succeeded in finding the house without much difficulty, and had scarcely begun to mount the stairs when he saw the clerk coming down to meet him.

"We live on the top flat," explained Thomas, apologetically. "I am sorry you have so far to go."

"Oh, don't mention it," returned the minister, cheerfully; "it is nice to be near the sky." They stopped at last, however, and found a plain little woman waiting for them.

"My sister, Mr. Dunbar," the clerk announced, solemnly; for this was the first time his sister had been introduced to the minister, and Thomas was anxious that the meeting should go off well. She made a low curtsey, and her brother watched with admiring eyes, for he was proud of this performance. She had learnt it from a dressmaker who had once been employed in "high families," and her brother said "she did it just as good as a duchess."

"Come in, please," Miss Johnson said, in a soft prim voice, smiling rather nervously, "I am proud and glad to receive you here. The dear boy told me you were coming, he did."

The room which they entered was not large, and a good deal of the space was taken up by a round table laid for tea. The floor was covered with a flowered carpet, carefully laid so that the worn parts were hidden as much as possible by the furniture, which was heavy and old-fashioned.

A Heart of Love

The walls were covered with heavily-framed pictures, and the mantelpiece was loaded with vases and china figures.

As soon as the minister was seated on the sofa, Johnson, after a mysterious whispering with his sister, disappeared, and Mr. Dunbar was left alone with his hostess, who was sitting nervously wondering what she should do next; then, noticing that his eyes were fixed on a large photograph on one side of the mantelpiece, she remarked :

" I dare say you are wondering who that is." (In truth he was wondering how any one could like such heavy gold frames.) " It is my father, he was a clerk, like Thomas."

She looked long and proudly at the picture, and her eyes were moist as she turned to her visitor.

" He was a very good man was my father, and the dear boy takes after him—I am afraid in health too, but then he may outgrow it; I hope so, the dear boy ! He and I are the only ones left out of six now." Then remembering her brother's suggestion, and afraid of being drawn into a lengthy conversation, she said :

" Do you like looking at photographs ? I have got an album ; it used to be mother's, so I prize it, I do—there it is ; " and she produced a cardboard box, out of which she took a plush-covered album, worn and faded, to be sure, but still treasured carefully. It was quite full, and she had something to say about each photograph, and the minister led her on till she almost forgot her shyness.

A Heart of Love

The last one was that of a broad-shouldered man, with an honest, kindly face. "That is an old friend of ours," she said, touching the photo caressingly; "he used to live near us in the old home, and was often with us, but now he is in America. We hear from him sometimes; he is a kind man, he is;" and with a sigh she closed the album, and wrapping it up carefully replaced it in the box. Then she drew her companion's attention to a photograph of her brother on the mantelpiece.

"Is it not the image of him?" she said, gazing at it with beaming face. "I tell him it is almost as good as having him by me, to see it there on the mantel. He is a dear good boy, I can tell you, sir, but he is not capable of looking after himself in the least. He is not strong either, you know, so I am sure I do not know what he would do if he was left to himself. I always hope that I shall be spared to look after him till he gets a wife, although he always says he will never leave me. But young things never know their own minds, and he has not seen much of the world yet, so I am saving up for him, that he may have a little nest-egg whenever he feels inclined to marry. But there, I do believe I hear his step; he *has* been quick; I hope he has not been too hurried," and she went out to meet him.

At the last moment, as she had glanced at the tea-table, she had had doubts as to the abundance and quality of the repast, and had sent Thomas out to procure "something specially nice." She

50

now arranged the contents of the bag on a plate, and a few minutes afterwards announced that tea was ready.

It was a cheerful meal, for the minister was so bright and friendly, and had such a way of making every one feel at ease, that the shyness of his host and hostess finally disappeared, and Thomas, strengthened by his sister's presence, actually went the length of making one or two jokes. The hostess was too anxious as to the success of the tea to eat much herself, but she kept a sharp eye on the plates of her guest and her brother.

"You have made a very poor tea, Jenny, I am afraid," remarked Johnson, as he craned his neck to see over the bead-work cosy.

"Poor tea? What nonsense you do talk, to be sure! Why, I am quite ashamed of my appetite."

When the meal was ended, Miss Johnson proceeded to clear the table, while her brother showed the minister some views. She was carefully putting the remaining queen-cakes into a paper bag, and, as she laid them in the cupboard she murmured to herself, with a smile: "They will just do for the dear boy's lunch to-morrow; it will be such a nice little treat for him."

Her brother did not hear her: but the visitor did, and was glad he had gone there that night.

By the time a red cloth had taken the place of the white one, the photographs were finished, and Miss Johnson poked the fire and placed chairs near it—although it was not cold—choosing the draughty side for herself.

A Heart of Love

"I am sorry we have no piano," she said, seating herself. "I dare say you will be accustomed to music; I am very fond of it. But we have a harmonium," and she uncovered a diminutive instrument, which had served as a sideboard. "Mr. Winter—he that is in America—got it cheap once, at a sale, and gave it to me. It is little, but good."

"Won't you play something on it?" said the minister, noticing that her fingers caressed the keys. Miss Johnson flushed, then paled.

"Well, really, I think not; you see, I never had any lessons, and just know a few simple airs out of an old book of my mother's. I would be ashamed to play them to you, who knows something about music, I have heard."

"Why, you play them quite nicely," interrupted her brother, while David assured her he was no connoisseur. "She sings, too," said Thomas, gazing steadfastly at the opposite wall, as if he did not dare to meet his sister's eye after such boldness.

"Thomas, how can you?" exclaimed she. "You know I never sing, except when I am by myself, or when you tease me to."

But when the minister again asked for a song, saying that he found quiet music conducive to thought, she no longer liked to refuse him; and taking out an old song-book, she very nervously began "The Last Rose of Summer."

To the listener by the fire the scene was very pathetic—the room looking dim and shadowy in the fading light, the thin clerk in rusty black, who stood by his sister and watched her with such lovingly

A Heart of Love

admiring eyes, while the quaint, old-world tune floated through the room like the scent of some brown and withered rose, which had once been young and fresh.

When the last notes died away the performer turned round with a blush that recalled her brother's. "I made several mistakes," she said, apologetically; "but I was so flustered. I have never sung to strangers before."

"Please sing something else," said the minister. "Sing another song like that."

"Really, I am sure you are very kind; I am fond of singing myself, but I am afraid it is no treat to you," returned Miss Johnson, turning over the leaves of the music-book, and wondering all the time how she had the courage to sing at all; but, as she explained to her brother afterwards, "The minister had such a way with him that I don't believe a baby would be afraid of him."

So, after clearing her throat, she began "Those Evening Bells." David Dunbar wondered, as he heard the plaintive strains, why she chose such sad songs, and if all in the book were the same. When it was finished there was silence, and the singer did not move from her place. The silence was broken by Thomas, who was of a very practical turn of mind.

"I think, Jenny, we had better have a light," he remarked, as if the idea had just struck him; instead of which, he had been pondering over it since the song ceased, and, indeed, ever since he had heard the words, "Within the tomb now darkly dwells."

A Heart of Love

"To be sure," said Miss Johnson, shutting the harmonium promptly. "How ridiculous to be sitting here in the dark! and I do declare I should not have thought of it but for you; but you have such a head, dear boy."

Thus stimulated, he lit the gas.

"I fear I must be going," said the minister; "I have some work to do to-night."

His friends received the news with regret, and timidly ventured to hope that he would come again.

"We would consider it an honour," the little woman gasped, when the minister assured her not only that he would come again, but that he would bring his sister. Thomas was too overcome to say anything, and hastened to bring in Mr. Dunbar's coat and hat. When he had overcome his surprise and emotion, he insisted on seeing his guest home, saying that the way was somewhat intricate and difficult to find; and the minister, afraid of hurting his feelings, yielded, although he would have preferred a quiet walk by himself.

He opportunely mentioned Miss Johnson, however, and his part of the conversation was practically over, for at his sister's name the clerk's tongue was loosed, and he seemed as if he would never tire of singing her praises. "She is so unselfish, you know," he summed up, for they were nearing their destination, "so very good to me. I do not know what I should do without her; I am just afraid she might sacrifice too much for me, and if so, I would never know; but I am saving up a little for her secretly, if ever she should want to marry."

At the last words, like a flash, the minister remembered the last photograph in the album.

II

A GOLDEN SECRET

It was not till several months had passed that the minister was able to visit the Johnsons again; and by that time his sister had begun to rival him in Miss Johnson's affections, and was almost worshipped by the clerk.

The hottest summer days were over, and the minister had returned from his holidays with tanned cheeks and a new tenderness in eyes and manner. One of their first duties, he told his sister, before they got into the eddy of winter work, was to visit the Johnsons. A note was accordingly despatched, warning Miss Jenny of their intentions; and the next evening saw them outside the Johnsons' door, where they found their hostess waiting.

Miss Dunbar thought the little woman was looking pale and tired, but put it down to the hot weather, and the black dress she was wearing. She was attentive as ever to her guests at tea-time, but ate next to nothing herself; and Thomas, too, was so much taken up with watching Miss Dunbar's plate that he had not much time to give to his own.

After tea the minister took Thomas out for a

A Heart of Love

turn, and Miss Johnson and her guest sat by the window. The little woman knitted in silence for a time, and her companion noticed again how pale and small she seemed. At last she looked up and said, "Do you know much about hospital nurses, Miss Dunbar?"

"Why, yes, a little; they are usually very good, brave women. Why do you ask?"

There was a little pause, then the knitter answered:

"I had a letter from a nurse in Liverpool the other week—such a kind letter as I have had from no one before, except, perhaps, my father; my mother never was away from home."

Miss Dunbar waited quietly, for there must be something more coming, she knew, and she was right.

A flush crept into the pale cheeks, and then Miss Johnson went on hurriedly, "I wanted you to know the end of—my friend, Miss Dunbar, for I think you are the only person who understood how it was with us."

Here the speaker's voice trembled a little, and she laid down her knitting. "I told you he had gone to America—well—he came back a few weeks ago, and wanted to take me—by surprise—but he failed, poor fellow! This is the letter I got which told me about it."

Miss Dunbar took the letter from the trembling hand and opened it, wondering if this were another broken love story. The writer of the epistle must have had a very tender heart, for the news was broken gently and the story told very kindly. It

A Heart of Love

was that of a man who, having worked and slaved for years, had succeeded at last in making a "tidy sum for some one at home," and who, full of joy and hope, had landed in Liverpool, hoping to bring great pleasure to a patient woman's heart next day. But he had been fallen upon the night after he had landed by some who had heard his story, but felt no pity for him, and, in spite of his desperate defence, he had lost nearly all his money, and been carried almost dying to the hospital. His greatest wish had been to have news sent to "Jenny," with the assurance that it was in no drunken brawl that he had fallen.

The minister's sister read on, and the tears welled in her eyes. Miss Johnson had certainly not posed as a martyr when she had told Miss Dunbar the simple outlines of the only romance she had ever had. "He asked me to marry him," she had said simply, when they were looking at the album together, "but, you see, I could not think of leaving Thomas."

But her listener had been able to read between the lines of the simple tale. She knew so well herself how such stories of love and loss might be filled in, and now, as she thought of a distant Highland churchyard, and glanced at the signet ring that seemed so heavy for her own slim finger, a great pity filled her heart.

She laid her hand gently on the rusty black sleeve; and there could be no doubt of her sympathy as she said, "I am so sorry; I am so very sorry, for I understand."

A Heart of Love

Her companion had taken to her knitting again, and the needles flew more quickly; then she said, "I think it is a beautiful letter, and when I think of that nurse, I always bless her."

"I am glad you showed it to me, for now I know something of your friend, and revere and admire him."

The knitter's pale face flushed, and she dropped her work. "I got the money mentioned, and I would have liked to get a big photograph of him to hang on the wall, but then I thought Thomas might not like it; it would be like making him equal to father, and it might have hurt the dear boy's feelings; besides, you see he does not understand. So I just kept the Post Office order; I would rather not part with it, for it is the only thing of his that I have got—except a piece of hair the nurse sent."

The words were said wistfully, and Miss Dunbar had not the heart to suggest that in all probability the money order had never been in the man's hands at all.

"One thing I am very glad of," her companion went on. "I was in time to send money for his—his burial. For in hospitals and such-like places I do not suppose much care is taken; I could not spare enough to go myself, but I took the liberty to write the nurse about it. I was rather troubled about it, for I did not like to tell Thomas. But it was not depriving him of anything, for it was money I had saved for my own—I did not want him to have the expense of it. You do not think

A Heart of Love

it was wrong my not confiding in Thomas, do you, Miss Dunbar? I did not want to trouble him, that was all." The pale blue eyes anxiously sought the dark tender ones opposite her.

"I am sure you did right; you certainly did not injure your brother in any way." She would have added more, but at that moment the minister and his companion returned. "It came on to rain, so we had to return," said Thomas, cheerfully; "but perhaps you will sing something, Jenny: the minister wants you to." For David Dunbar had told his sister that Miss Johnson must be prevailed upon to sing to them, to complete the visit.

But Jenny looked up appealingly, "No, dear boy," she pleaded. "I really cannot sing to-night; I think I have a cold or something, but I know I cannot sing."

"Can't you really?" put in the minister. "I should like to hear one of those songs again." His hostess looked distressed; she did not wish to refuse her visitor anything, yet she felt sure she could not get through a song that night. But Miss Dunbar noticed her embarrassment, and interposed:

"If you have a cold, it will be bad for you to try; I will sing instead, though I can't manage your songs, I am afraid."

Her offer was gladly accepted, and in a few minutes her sweet voice rang through the shabby room, while the harmonium gave forth music that had never been heard in that place. The clerk stood transfixed, never taking his eyes off the singer's face. It seemed to him almost as if he heard an angel

A Heart of Love

singing, and for a time was sharing the heaven where she belonged. Miss Dunbar sang song after song, hoping that she was soothing one sore heart, as she had often soothed her own.

When the singing was ended, and the other listeners had given her their thanks, Thomas still stood speechless. His sister could not understand this apparent want of manners, and gazed reproachfully at him. But the glance was in vain, and his sister did not like to follow it up by reproof. She could not bear to shame him before such visitors. But when they had taken their leave she could remain silent no longer: "Thomas, dear boy," she said reproachfully, "how could you be so rude as to forget to thank Miss Dunbar for her music, when she sang to us so sweetly?"

"Forget to thank her, sister!" said Thomas. "I shall never cease to thank her all my life. To think, just to think that she should sing away in this room of ours! I had never hoped for so much happiness. Jenny, Jenny, I have never seen a woman like her."

His sister looked at him first in wonder, then in anxiety. At last she laid her hand upon his arm, and said gently, "She is much above us, Thomas, dear boy, and——" here she hesitated, but looked at her brother, and went on firmly, "and will marry a clever minister, like her brother."

"You need not tell me that, Jenny," said the clerk. "I know that she is as much above me as the stars are above the earth, but nevertheless a man may watch them from afar, and reverence and

A Heart of Love

love them, and thank God for letting him see such bright and beautiful things. This room will never seem plain or mean any more, since she has condescended to sing in it;" and poor Thomas, who had never risen so near to poetry before, and whose stooping figure had never held so much dignity, left his sister, and went into his own room.

Miss Dunbar, on a flying visit to Liverpool, made time to go and see the "friend's" resting-place, and called the following day to describe it all to Miss Johnson. And when that little woman, by exercise of the strictest economy, saved enough to make a journey to Liverpool, was it not Miss Dunbar who offered to go with her, because she trembled at the mere thought of the strange busy city? It was the same lady, too, who—as Miss Johnson told her brother on her return—had not been ashamed to walk down the gayest streets with her, and had taken her to lunch in the "grandest place in the town."

On one occasion, when Jenny had been telling of some new kindness done by the minister, Thomas said doggedly, when she had ceased her eulogy:

"All the same, Jenny, I think the minister's sister is to him just what you are to me, and that is—the best part of him; although she keeps herself in the background, and makes him appear everything——"

Jenny was so overcome by this speech, and so taken up with trying to convince the "dear boy" that she was the most selfish person in the world, that she quite forgot to speak in defence of the minister.

But, in spite of her impartiality, she yet regretted one step which the minister took, and bemoaned it to Thomas. That was his marriage. There were many in the congregation who rejoiced when, some two years later, he brought home a shy young stranger. But not so the Johnsons. "We'll never have such another as Miss Grace," Miss Johnson said, sighing, when she heard the news. The little woman made so bold as to go to the station to see the minister's sister depart, and waylaying her in a quiet corner, timidly offered her some flowers tied up with white ribbon.

"Thomas suggested them," she said, but did not add that he, too, had ordered them at the best florist's in the town, and had doggedly declared that he did not mind the cost so long as they were as pretty as possible. "He sent his respects, Miss Dunbar, and his best wishes for your happiness," added the little woman, with a break in her voice.

Then had come the crowning grace from that splendid friend of hers, for Miss Johnson had seen the stately head stoop and had felt a kiss upon her brow. It was so wonderful that she could not take it in, and had only been able to gasp out, "God bless you," and then had turned away with a sob.

"The flowers are very sweet," said her brother's wife, as she joined Miss Dunbar, "but what a plain, insignificant little woman it was who gave them to you!"

A Heart of Love

"God sometimes puts large souls into insignificant bodies," replied the minister's sister, as she laid the flowers on the rack. "He has given that little woman a very great soul."

The bright face of the young wife grew grave for a moment: "I shall never learn to know people as you do, Grace," she said, shaking her head. "I do not understand how you manage. I am never able to sympathise with people and get their confidence like that."

"All things come with time; you have not had opportunity enough yet," said Miss Dunbar, brightly; but she might have added, nor yet loved enough, nor—suffered enough! That night the insignificant little person knelt long in her mean room, praying with an overflowing love in her heart for "the only woman that had kissed her since her mother died."

This woman had one virtue, which raised her for ever above the commonplace—she loved much, and that not herself.

A BRAVE WIFE'S SACRIFICE

EVERYBODY said that Mrs. Halkett was "close," and so perhaps she was. It is hard for two people to be generous on the large sum of fifty pounds a year, and that, when rates were paid, and parish claims met, was the exact income of the Rev. Theodore Halkett. Mrs. Halkett realised that a person must either look on the cheerful side of things, or go mad. She had elected to do the former, and it was well for the broken-hearted man whose happiness was the aim of her life. Every year found him thinner, more despondent, less fit to grapple with life; but practice makes perfect, and Mrs. Halkett could still turn a smiling face to the world. She was stout, and past fifty, this valiant woman, but she laboured with a cheerful countenance. Love makes hard things easy.

The husband and wife used only three rooms of the big house, but even so, work accumulated, and the disused apartments gathered dust. Once a week a woman came from the village, and then she and Mrs. Halkett worked one as hard as the other; but whereas Mrs. Gunn partook of tea and pork in the kitchen, Mrs. Halkett, who also only enjoyed meat when it was provided at some other person's expense, had tea and bread-and-butter in the dining-room.

Mrs. Halkett had always been too busy in her home to do much in the parish. Only the Sunday after her daughter Theodora's death, she went bravely to the old harmonium, and played with trembling fingers the chants and hymn tunes, and she had done it ever since. But this was a matter of course to the rustic mind, and to no one but her husband was that stout figure on the music-stool a type of patient heroism.

When the rector chanced to look out of his study window on this particular summer morning of which we are writing, and saw her toiling behind the mowing machine, all the chivalry of his nature was roused. He put on his rusty black hat, and hastened into the garden — a meagre, shabby figure, with the bowed attitude of habitual dejection.

"Anna, Anna," he called, "what are you doing? Come in at once!"

"The grass was so long, Theodore, and the daisies are coming up so fast."

She tried to laugh, but after all she was tired, and his summons was a relief. She seemed to realise all at once that she could not have done any more if she had tried. She laid her hand on his arm, and they went in together. His study was comparatively cool, and with a tenderness which touched her—for its exhibition was rare— he drew forward his armchair for her, removed the large unbecoming hat she wore, and began to

A Brave Wife's Sacrifice

fan her with the old dry-as-dust pamphlet he had been reading when he observed her.

The rector was a very neat old gentleman, and when one came to look at him it was possible to understand that, in his young days, he had been attractive enough to win the affection which he found no difficulty in keeping. He was ten years older than his wife, and his face was now drawn, and aged, and wrinkled, but the features were well cut, the eyes very blue, and the white hair fine, and still abundant. His hands and feet were small, and there was about him a certain daintiness that evinced itself in the scrupulous care of his person, and the cleanliness of his frayed linen, and the way he wore his threadbare coat.

"Now, Anna," he said, "you must rest for the remainder of the morning."

Mrs. Halkett shook her head and laughed. "Certainly I shan't do any more mowing, Theodore, but resting, you know, is a luxury. I am going to mend your cassock, which is in a disgraceful state, and this afternoon Mrs. Gunn is coming for a half day, as she only had a short time on Saturday. You know I always put away the ornaments when she is here during my absence. Her capacity for breaking is so wonderful."

"Are you going out this afternoon, dear?"

"Yes, yes, Theodore. Had you forgotten? It is Mrs. Bigdows' 'At Home.'"

Mr. Halkett heaved a sigh. "Then the pony will be wanted?"

"Yes."

A Brave Wife's Sacrifice

"We must go, I suppose, dear?"

"Oh, certainly," said Mrs. Halkett, with alacrity, for this was the first of the series of summer garden-parties, and she had been expecting it with great longing. It was pleasurable excitement to take the long, slow drives behind the old pony, which were impossible in winter, and to go seven miles to shake hands and exchange salutations with, perhaps, thirty other people, and to enjoy a good tea without feeling that cake was an extravagance. And then there was the drive back, the delight of having some one to talk about besides themselves, in retailing to her husband the little bits of information she had gleaned, and the arrival home just tired enough to find sitting quiet a pleasure, and the approach of bedtime welcome.

Accordingly, after their early dinner, the dilapidated pony was taken out of the stable, and Mr. Halkett had to harness it himself, and put it into the funny green box on wheels, with a broken step and an obstinate handle, which did duty as a carriage. Pony and trap were both very old, and the uninitiated might well expect each journey to be the last, but when the Rev. Theodore took the reins and spoke in an encouraging voice, the grey horse bowed its head and ambled gently and uncomplainingly along at the rate of four miles an hour on a level road, but, as one might expect, with a little less celerity when there was a hill to mount; while the old trap, though it creaked and jolted at every revolution of the wheels, remained intact, and bore without injury the strain of Mrs. Halkett's by no means despicable weight.

The sun poured down upon them, and the pony

A Brave Wife's Sacrifice

had need of the bough with which its head was decorated to save it from distraction, so persistent were the flies in their attentions. Mr. Halkett kept flicking his whip, to save the animal, and grew hot in the process, and Mrs. Halkett sat serenely under the shelter of her old black parasol, smiling in pleasant anticipation, and remarking from time to time how agreeable they would find it driving back, when there would be less sunshine, fewer flies, and a possible breeze.

When in the cool of the late afternoon they returned to the rectory, Mrs. Halkett found Mrs. Gunn loitering about before the door which was the means of communication between the kitchen and the sitting-rooms. The expression of Mrs. Gunn's face was not reassuring. It somehow reminded Mrs. Halkett of the day when she had thrown out among the empty boxes in one of the out-houses a present her mistress had received of a dozen glasses, and only discovered too late that the box which she had thought contained nothing but straw made an ominous crash when it was flung to the ground.

"Is anything the matter, Mrs. Gunn?" she asked.

The charwoman made a significant gesture. It was evident she did not want Mr. Halkett to hear what had occurred, and with a sinking heart Mrs. Halkett followed her into the kitchen. Then Mrs. Gunn pointed to a black object flung across a chair.

It was Mr. Halkett's cassock, which his wife had spent the latter part of the morning in mending and sponging. His cassock, did I say? No, for there was no longer a cassock, but only a frayed, scorched remnant of one.

"Mrs. Gunn!" exclaimed Mrs. Halkett, aghast.

Mrs. Gunn herself, though not easily subdued, seemed troubled by the mischief she had done. She trembled, and fidgeted with her apron strings. She was on the verge of tears.

"What will my husband say?" sighed Mrs. Halkett, and there was sadness as well as dismay in her voice. She could not bear to think of any annoyance coming to the man whom she cherished with an almost motherly love.

"Oh, ma'am," said Mrs. Gunn, "I'm that upset. It all came of trying to be useful. I see it damp, and I thought as I'd air it and hang it against the fire, and then I went to dust the setting-room, and the next thing I knew there was a smell of burn, and I run in, and it was scorching and had catched light. I pulled it off, and it's a wonder and a mercy as I wasn't burnt to ashes myself, and I throwed it on the hearthrug and rolled it up, and it isn't every one, ma'am, as would have had the presence of mind; but when at last I returned to look at it, I saw that it was regular spoilt, and even with a surplus on top I don't see however it could be of use to any clergyman, as you may say more than half burnt away."

Neither did Mrs. Halkett, and it was with a very heavy heart that she took the damaged garment and bore it away to her bedroom. She had no reproaches for Mrs. Gunn. She was only filled with an instinctive desire to keep the news from her husband as long as possible. It was an old cassock, for he had worn it for many years, but he could not afford a new one.

Mrs. Halkett threw it on the bed, and then proceeded to change her dress, for to keep on her best attire was an unheard-of thing. She took the very greatest care of it. Her husband had given her the material for that dress years ago as a birthday present; that was in the days when he was able to give her presents. She valued it because it was his gift. It was a good material, for Theodore was one of those whose gifts are always the best possible. It had stood the test of much wear, and it had been cleaned and cleaned and turned and dyed an astonishing number of times. It had been grey at the beginning, then violet, then, if I mistake not, purple, and it was still making a very creditable appearance in the world in its present state of blackness. It had been trimmed and retrimmed, and made and remade—it had gone with lace, with beaver, with jet. It had given employment to Mrs. Halkett's mind and fingers, and she saw still further possibilities for it, with the aid of a certain beaded flounce in her possession.

In short, this dress represented to Mrs. Halkett all the little recreations and amusements of the last decade, all the innocent vanities which few genuine women quite outgrow. She could still enjoy her husband's appreciation of her resourcefulness, as shown in the changed attire, which she manifested to him. But neither of them foresaw what the ample and wonderful gown was yet to do.

A Brave Wife's Sacrifice

When Mrs. Halkett, her mind full of her husband and his loss, turned to the bed, to take up the dress she had laid there, and hang it in her wardrobe with the white sheet, to protect it from possible dust, she took hold of the cassock by mistake. And then she observed that the material of which the dress was made, bore a very similar aspect to the garment she was holding.

She was not a woman who reasoned much. Ideas which came to her were generally the result of intuition. She stood quite still, irresolute, still holding the ruined cassock.

She remained so a long time, then she went slowly to the wardrobe, and hung the two up together.

"Anna, Anna," called her husband.

"I am coming, dear," she answered, in the tone a mother uses to a child that cannot do without her, and she hurriedly fastened the hooks of the faded gown she wore of an evening, and went down to the homely meal.

She was very silent, in spite of herself, and absent-minded, and her husband rallied her on the absence of conversation, and asked her if after all her outing had tired her.

"I don't know," she answered. "Perhaps. It was certainly very hot."

"The horse goes slower every year," said Mr. Halkett. "Long journeys try one's nerves, I think."

After supper they strolled out arm-in-arm to the hay-field. The crop was a poor one, but it would suffice for the horse's needs.

A Brave Wife's Sacrifice

"I do not think I shall sow it again," said Mr. Halkett. "I think it would pay me better to let Brown have this field, with the rest of the glebe. If we have to give up keeping a pony, we must."

Mrs. Halkett said nothing. She looked over the meadow, which was bereft of yesterday's waving grass; the sun had set, and the oncoming twilight made everything seem monotonous in colour. There was a great stillness, and somehow the whole scene depressed her. Life seemed to stretch before her a grey, dreary, changeless vista. Then Mr. Halkett spoke again. He was answering his own thoughts.

"There is a better world than this, Anna," he said.

The tears sprang to his wife's eyes.

"Yes, dear," she answered.

"And, at any rate," he added, "we are together here."

"Yes, dear," she said again. And they turned and went in.

All night Mrs. Halkett lay awake. A larger sacrifice would have been easier to make, but there was very little to glorify the cutting up of an old black dress. And this was what she felt she ought to do. It might be possible for her husband to do without a cassock, she was aware, but she could not imagine him, who was so particular as to all points of detail, contenting himself without the garb of his office.

On Sundays and on Saints' Days he always wore his cassock from morning till night. He would miss it. Possibly, through some charity he might obtain another, but it would mean delay. And she knew

A Brave Wife's Sacrifice

how he shrank from advertising his poverty. If she made him a new cassock, he need know nothing about the accident till it was repaired. A long course of necessary economy had made her very skilful with her needle, and with the old one as a model she was not afraid of being able to make a very creditable garment. There was a great deal of material in the dress, and it had big turnings. Her husband was not a tall man, and she could contrive. She made all her measurements in her head as she lay in bed, and, so to speak, rehearsed her dress-making.

But her heart was very heavy. She knew she could no more afford a new dress than he a new cassock, and that meant that she must for this summer at any rate refuse all invitations. She would not be able to go to Mrs. Pittman's to-morrow, for she must certainly set to work at once. She could not go to Mrs. Graham's on Saturday, nor to the annual flower show.

It was very childish surely for a woman fifty years of age to mind things of that sort, but she cried a little, as she lay there awake, at the prospect of renouncing these passing vanities. Still, she made up her mind to do so, and in the early dawn she fell asleep.

The next day her husband had to go to a clerical meeting in the neighbourhood, a sort of semi-social, semi-ecclesiastical function of quarterly occurrence. For once, Mrs. Halkett was glad of his absence. She sometimes, when she had much needlework to do, sent for lame Gussie from the village, but on this occasion no one must help her. It would never do for the village to know how the rector came by a new cassock, and, moreover, she had a feeling she would like no one to touch it but herself.

And so, with a sinking heart, and a hand that trembled, she set to work at the business of unripping a seam, but, the first and hardest step taken, she gained courage. Bravely she continued her self-imposed task, and gradually she became interested in it.

It was not a very congenial employment, one would think, for a hot summer's day, but Mrs. Halkett sat on amid her pile of black stuff. The scissors snipped, the machine whirred, pins were everywhere, and the work progressed. Only about four o'clock in the afternoon she had to check the too ready imagination, which showed a vision of Mrs. Pittman's shady lawn, a plate of strawberries and cream, and the pleasant sound of friendly voices. But she sternly put it away from her, and worked with renewed energy. She had only a few days to make the cassock in, for it must be finished before the end of the week, and she had, as a rule, too many domestic duties to be able to give one thing her undivided attention. By-and-by, as she went on, she became interested in what she was doing, and took pardonable pride in her skilful workmanship, and when at last she laid it by, weary though she was, she felt almost happy. Every sacrifice has an abiding element of joy, and to Mrs. Halkett the giving up of that old silk dress was a great renunciation.

That night she slept well, and in the morning prepared to go on zealously with her work.

A Brave Wife's Sacrifice

About ten o'clock her husband came to her, as she was washing the breakfast things.

"Anna," he said, "I think the horse is ill. It is lying in the stable. I cannot get it up."

"Theodore!" said Mrs. Halkett, in consternation, and followed her husband to the stable.

There a pathetic sight awaited them. The faithful animal lay trembling on the ground, its legs helplessly flung out, and the tears actually streaming from its eyes, at the effort it had lately made with its master's assistance to rise to its feet. The fresh hay the latter had put for it was untouched, but when Mrs. Halkett, bending down, pushed the pail of water within its reach, it drank eagerly, then let its head fall again.

"I think it has had a stroke," said Mr. Halkett. "I will go round to Gray's and see Reynolds. Perhaps he will look in on his way back from work."

Mr. Halkett departed, and his wife returned to the house, every now and then running out to look at the poor dumb servant, to whom she had become so attached. Every time it regarded her with eyes which said as plainly as words, "Don't try to make me stand," and Mrs. Halkett patted it, and spoke to it. Once she made a remark to it, which might have struck an onlooker as ludicrous, but it comforted her, and perhaps after all the animal understood. It was when she noticed how painfully its ribs showed at the rise and fall of its breathing.

"Tom," she said, "you should have had corn if we could have afforded it."

At noon the labourer who had the care of Farmer

A Brave Wife's Sacrifice

Gray's horses, looked in. His investigation did not last long. He glanced uneasily at the rector and his wife, who were anxiously watching him, and shook his head.

"'E wo'ant do any more wurk," he said.

Mrs. Halkett turned aside.

"Then he had better be put out of his misery as soon as possible," said the rector. "Will you see about it, Reynolds?"

"That I will, sir," said Reynolds, "and a'm thinking Brown to Ulby would give a shilling or two for t'body of him."

"No, no," said the rector, hastily, "let him be buried somewhere in the place."

He did not join his wife. He felt as if he could not bear to talk just yet about what had happened. He went out on to the meadow, where lay poor Tom's provender for the coming year. Perhaps he got a little comfort from the thought that he could sell it, and make a few pounds, but the lack of a horse was a great deprivation, nevertheless. It made them virtually prisoners. For himself he minded little. His life was bounded by the parish and his study. But poor Anna, who had so looked forward to her summer outings, what would she do? Well, perhaps, if the hay sold as it stood, he could afford to hire a horse and trap now and then. He determined to go at once to his tenant, and see if he would take the field of hay.

When they were sitting at their early dinner they suddenly heard the sound of a shot being fired. Mrs. Halkett burst into tears.

A Brave Wife's Sacrifice

"Oh, Theodore," she said, "I am sure there is a heaven for horses."

In the afternoon the rector went out, and she set to work on her cassock with feverish energy. She actually now found comfort in it. She was genuinely glad she had given up her dress. After all, if she had kept it she would have found no opportunity to wear it. She never wore her best apparel on Sundays at church, because her work at the organ made it shiny. And certainly, she reflected, her husband had gained something. The new cassock was in far better condition than the old. When all the new button-holes were made and the new buttons she had ordered sewn on, it would look quite nice. On the whole, she was well satisfied, and rather looked forward to telling him about Mrs. Gunn's mishap.

At tea-time Mr. Halkett informed her that he had disposed of his field of hay.

"Brown will give me ten pounds for it," he said, "and I am to let him have the meadow in future. It is just as well, for I shall not be able to keep another pony."

"The money will be a great comfort to us," she said. "You need some new shoes, Theodore."

"Yes," he answered. "Well, I can get them now. I have asked Brown to drive me into Burtown when he goes on Saturday."

Mrs. Halkett was not sorry to hear of this engagement. She would have a chance to finish her cassock in peace.

She worked at it steadily on Saturday afternoon, and had only just finished when her husband came

A Brave Wife's Sacrifice

back from Burtown. He seemed in very good spirits. Perhaps the little outing had done him good. He chatted to his wife about the incidents of the day, repeated things he had heard and seen which might amuse her, and seemed altogether more like his old self than the solitary recluse he had of late become.

"Brown is a capital fellow," he remarked, presently. "He has more kindness in him than any one would suspect. And he says that, as we have been so unfortunate about poor Tom, he will let us have a pony and trap and a boy now and then, if we want to go anywhere. He seems pleased that I have let him have the field."

He had expected Mrs. Halkett to show her satisfaction, and was a little disappointed at her saying only :

"Oh, I think we had better make up our minds to stay quietly at home this summer."

"Certainly not, Anna. I shall pay him for anything I have, of course, so you need not mind accepting his offer."

"Oh, it isn't that," said Mrs. Halkett, and prepared to change the subject. But her husband kept her to it.

"You have something on your mind, Anna ; what is it ? It isn't like you to make objections."

Mrs. Halkett looked down. She knew he had been thinking of her happiness, and she did not like to disappoint him. However, she would have to tell him sooner or later.

"The fact of the matter is, Theodore, I really have no dress to go out in."

A Brave Wife's Sacrifice

"There is the redoubtable black silk," he said, laughing.

"I can't possibly wear that any more, Theodore."

"Why not?"

Mrs. Halkett rose. She spoke cheerfully, but there was a suspicious tremble in her voice.

"I will fetch it and show you," she said.

When she returned she had two garments flung over her arm. One she held out to him silently.

"Why, Anna," he exclaimed, "what are you thinking of? You have brought me my cassock."

"No," she said. "This is your cassock." And with a dramatic gesture she spread wide for his inspection the poor scorched remnant.

Then, as he gazed at it in dismay and bewilderment, she briefly told him what had happened to it.

"And this?" he inquired, touching the one he held.

"That," answered Mrs. Halkett, with something between a laugh and a sob, "that is my old silk dress. I hope it isn't wrong to have used it for such a purpose. But it was all I had, and for the last few days I have been a clerical tailor."

Down went both the cassocks on the floor, for the husband and wife were clasping each other's hands and looking into each other's eyes, as if they had been young lovers instead of elderly fogeys.

"Anna," said Mr. Halkett, "you are the best and cleverest and most unselfish woman in the world."

"That is nonsense," she answered, smiling. But it did her good to be praised, all the same.

A Brave Wife's Sacrifice

"I should like to scold you for what you have done, but I can't. And indeed, on the whole, I believe I am pleased you have destroyed that old dress. It may make you appreciate a little present I bought for you to-day."

"Oh, Theodore, I hope you have not been wasting money on me!"

"Certainly not. But the giving should not be all on one side."

And letting go her hands he left the room, returning almost immediately with a brown paper parcel.

He stood by while she opened it, enjoying her unfeigned interest.

And for a moment the cloud of poverty was lifted from them both, for a moment they saw themselves freed from the dreariness of constant isolation; for a moment they knew again the pleasure of giving and of receiving, as Mrs. Halkett with an exclamation of delight, removed from their wrappings the shimmering folds of new black silk.

FOR THE LOVE OF GOD

"FOR GOD SO LOVED THE WORLD"

"FOR His sake come over and help us in Aschenthal. The cholera is with us, one doctor gone, the other dead.—PASTOR BRAUN."

It was a curious announcement to appear in the little German paper, and the reader's eyes surveyed it several times before they wandered away to the green hill-slopes, from behind which the cry had come.

"For God so loved the world." Here, in the quiet German valley, amid limitless beauty, there seemed little doubt of that, and disease and death appeared utterly out of place.

"It is sudden destruction," murmured the young man; "for a week ago it was far up the river."

The face—where the sun had not yet quite tanned the cheeks made pale by study—grew more thoughtful, and, laying the paper down, he stepped out through the window into the garden.

Half an hour afterwards his mother entered the room he had left, and after a glance round in search of her son did as he had done—took up the paper.

"Actually a newspaper again!" she said to

For the Love of God

herself, smiling. "John will be glad to see it, although it won't give much news."

She glanced over it carelessly, till her eye caught the strange heading : "For God so loved the world." She read it over once—twice—wonderingly ; the third time, her face paled, and she looked round anxiously. "He must not see it," she whispered ; "there is still time." The next moment she pushed the paper into the stove, and had scarcely closed the doors again, when her son entered the room. She glanced quickly in his face as he bade her "good-morning;" but it was the same as ever, strong and quiet, with the sparkling blue eyes lighting up the whole, and she felt at rest again.

They were the only visitors in the quaint little German inn, but neither had tired of each other's company. Indeed, that morning, with eyes sharpened by fear, the mother looked still more lovingly at her companion, marvelling anew at her possession of such a son—so brilliant, yet withal so simple and tender. There was no lack of conversation over their coffee, and their laughter floating out through the open window made even the stolid servant girl in the kitchen smile from sympathy.

"Now, mother," he said, gaily, as they rose from the table, "be my companion for my smoking stroll ; it will add to the pleasure of it all ;" and the mother went gladly, rejoicing that he had not remembered to ask for the newspaper.

"We must leave here as soon as possible," was ever her thought, as they strolled backwards and forwards. At last there came a pause in the talk,

For the Love of God

but the mother, wondering how best to introduce the subject of their departure, scarcely noticed that they had walked the length of the garden twice without speaking.

"Mother." She started at the abruptness in his tone. "Mother, when do we go to fetch Beatrice?"

She looked up brightly. "Just the subject I was going to begin on, John dear. I think we might leave here to-morrow. She will only miss a day of school, and it will be nice to have her with us."

"Yes, I think so," replied her son, absently; then throwing away his cigar half-smoked, he drew her arm through his, and covered her small trembling hand with his firm one.

"Mother dear," he said, and his voice was very tender, "I have a little plan for this afternoon to talk to you about. In a little town on the other side of those green hills——"

"John!" there was such agony in the sudden cry, that the son stopped alike in his walk and his speech.

"Not that, John—not that!" she cried, holding tightly to his arm with both her hands. "Not to the cholera town—you are not really strong yet, after all your work—you know what Dr. Carroll said. John, John, I *cannot* let you go."

He stooped and kissed her gently, and was silent; indeed, she left him no time to speak, but went on nervously, with a catch in her voice. "Think of your career, John, just opening up to you, so full of promise, so brilliant. Think—think of me—it was so

83

For the Love of God

hard without your father, and now—you are so like him, and I have seen so little of you lately, and now—now, when we are to be together—I had planned so much for the future—oh, John! think of me."

The firm lips quivered, and pain drove all the sparkle from the blue eyes. It was the first time in his life the firm, brave little mother had ever said, "Think of me," and it made it doubly hard to resist her pleading now.

"Mother dear," he said at length, "do you think I could ever forget you? That made the decision all the harder. But what have I studied for, if not to be able to relieve pain? What would any doctor do, but go over and help them? I would not be worthy of my calling, if I lingered when I heard that call. Doctorless—think of it—and the cholera there!"

"But there may be others there now," she urged. "Surely some German can answer the call. You are English, the people have not the same claim on you. Besides, it may not be so bad yet, it has come so suddenly."

"The cry was desperate, mother, and I am nearest—there is not even a doctor here. Others may have their own work to do, and I am free——"

"But wait till to-morrow," urged the mother again; "the news may be better then; wait till to-morrow, John."

He shook his head.

"And let them go on dying without my help? By to-morrow both you and I, mother, must be

For the Love of God

away from here. Ah! I know that yours is the harder part—a mother's so often is; but then," he added, cheerfully, "there is no reason why I should die: others have done the same, and lived."

His mother shook her head. "If he goes, he dies!" her heart told her, but her lips refused to answer. Then he took both her hands into his, and looked down into her pale, drawn face.

"Mother dear," and she raised her eyes to meet the smile that won all hearts, yet kept its chief sweetness for "the mother," "you have always been first in urging me to duty, and if a knight goes off without his lady's 'God-speed,' he goes with a heavy heart."

There was silence between the two, while the bees hummed about the flowers, and a blackbird's clear call came from the neighbouring wood. Then a shower of white blossom fell upon them from the tree above, and the mother drew her hands away from the strong grasp that had held them.

"Give me a little time, John," she said, with a smile that was more pitiful than tears; "a lady must have time to work her knight's banner."

*   *   *   *   *

The evening sun was gilding the tree-tops, as a carriage crept slowly up the winding road leading over the hill. The driver sat stolidly on the box, and the mother and son sat silently behind. They had tried to talk cheerfully and naturally all the way, but now they had grown still. Perhaps the mother was trying to gather courage for the end.

For the Love of God

At the bend of the road the driver halted, and the two descended.

"Be here again in an hour's time," said the young doctor, as he turned with his mother into the footpath that led through the birch-wood that covered the top of the hill. Still they moved silently, the mother leaning on the son. They stopped once, near the summit, and looked back at the valley through a break in the trees. The evening sun added to its glories, and made it seem to them a little paradise.

"It is very beautiful," said the son, softly. "We must try to come again."

"Yes," said the mother; then her lips closed tightly, to hide their trembling.

They had only once before come so far, and then the day had been dull, so that the sudden glimpse of the next valley that met their eyes on emerging from the wood was like a revelation.

"It is more beautiful even than the other side!" exclaimed the young doctor, eagerly, forgetting his errand for the moment. But the mother could not forget; her eyes had fallen first on the town lying below, and the slow river running through it—the river that was carrying death with it.

"John!" she cried, suddenly, "let me go, too; I could help to nurse—I will go, too."

The brightness died out of the son's face, as his mind and eyes were drawn back to the present.

"Poor Beatrice!" was all he said, and the mother understood. But this time she could not keep back the tears or control her quivering lips.

86

For the Love of God

"It is time I was going, mother dear," he said, gently, throwing one arm round her. "'For God so loved the world'—you know the rest. My dearest little mother, good-bye."

Then the mother clenched her hands fiercely, and forced a smile into her face.

"It is a coward-hearted lady who has never a smile for her knight," she said, with white lips. "God-speed!"

He stooped and kissed her vey tenderly, then turned away quickly and descended the hill, the sunlight streaming upon him as he went.

Behind, in the shadow of the trees and the chill of coming evening, watched the mother till the son's form was far out of sight. Then the tender pity of Him who long ago had "set His face steadfastly to go to Jerusalem" enwrapped her.

* * * * *

On a certain hillside above a fair German valley, just where the full beauty of the view breaks upon the climber, stands a simple wooden cross. At it, and the words rudely carved there, visitors look and wonder and speculate. But few, if any, of those who hazard guesses as to its origin, connect it with a simple stone in the acre of God below, whereon the same words stand: "For God so loved the world."

A BROTHER'S KEEPER

I

A MUSCULAR CURATE

THE Darells had a remarkable pedigree, and next to no money. But neither the presence of the one nor the absence of the other troubled Dunstan Darell. For he had a stout heart and sound body. There was enough (by home economy) to send him to Cambridge; but the last fields of the old property were mortgaged to the hilt, and at the death of his father he knew that there would be little or nothing for him and his brother.

For himself he cared but little; for Athelstan he cared much. His own tastes were simple; his own work he had already chosen. But Athelstan's tastes, boy though he was, were not simple, and Athelstan's future would have to be his concern when their father was gone. Their mother had died years before, leaving the memory of a gentle, trusting spirit, whose simple reliance on God and life of sweet unselfishness had corrected, in a way, the dreamy, unpractical tendencies of her scholar husband.

At last Mr. Darell also died, commending, with his last breath, Athelstan to Dunstan's care. His

A Brother's Keeper

sons buried him, and then realised that they were alone in the world, with few friends and fewer possessions. Dunstan had only just been ordained; Athelstan had been offered work by the agent of the great landowner who called the countryside his own, where Darells had once held it.

Athelstan liked country life, and thought this was the very opening for him. He drew a cheerful picture of the time to come, when he should have succeeded " Old Hicks," the agent, and have become a prosperous person.

"And then, old boy, I'll save money, and buy some of the lands back, and we will have you down here as vicar of the parish."

And so they parted; Athelstan setting out in jaunty self-confidence for his new home hard by, Dunstan taking the next train to town.

Dunstan's first and only curacy took him to a poor parish in West London. Into its stormy life he plunged with zest. He won the people's hearts because he was not afraid of them, because he was always natural, always polite, and always manly, because the children liked him. They would not come to church, even for him; but they sent for him when they were ill or dying; they graciously allowed him to admonish them after their misdeeds, and console them in their sorrows; they borrowed his money freely, and a few, very few, in moments of moral exaltation, even paid him back. In their way many of them loved him; he was to some the only person who had ever spoken to their better natures.

It was Dunstan Darell's lot early to bask in

A Brother's Keeper

the smiles of authority. The bishop heard of him, and in a curious way. It was in the days before suffragans began to be as common as blackberries, and the great diocese of London was under but one prelate. Now the bishop had a relative who bored him with requests to be shown some of the worst parts of the diocese. The bishop at last sent him down to Mr. Motherby.

The stranger penetrated alone into those dismal wilds. Now the misguided inhabitants of the parish had a contempt for strange clergy. They respected their own—that was natural enough; but there was no feeling in favour of others. When, therefore, the stranger drew near to the vicarage, in the gloom of a November afternoon, he was suddenly confronted by a burly ruffian, who seized him by the throat, and began, with a skill born of long practice, to rifle the stranger's pockets.

But even whilst he was fingering a well-filled purse Dunstan Darell burst upon the scene.

The robber had but a week or two before come out of gaol, and had then expressed, in terms of improper warmth, his gratitude to the curate for succouring his "missus an' kids" during his short period of seclusion.

He dropped his prey, as Dunstan took him by the collar, and with a hasty "Didn't know as the genelman was a friend o' yourn," disappeared round the corner.

When the visitor, later on, told the story to the bishop, the prowess of the curate was duly honoured.

A Brother's Keeper

So in his fifth year Dunstan got a living.

It was a neglected parish. His predecessor had been an able man, dowered with a fatal gift of fluency. He should have been a preacher only, for at the common duties of the pastor amongst his people he was a brilliant failure.

Dunstan Darell was neither fluent nor fashionable ; but he loved the poor, and loved work.

Before he had been in his new district three months, the forces of good and of evil knew that a new power was in their midst.

But sorrows of a new order began to thicken. There was bad news of Athelstan. For a year he had done well; then he was less content and less satisfactory. Finally he had married, and not wisely. He had chosen the only daughter of a manufacturer. She would have had money, but that within six months of the wedding her father became bankrupt, and shortly afterwards died penniless ; and Mrs. Athelstan Darell had not been reared to face poverty, although people said her father had begun life as a mill-hand.

The result was soon felt by the elder brother. Athelstan's "borrowings" became every quarter more numerous and larger. Then, just as Dunstan was about to declare that they must cease, came the news that Athelstan's services were no longer required on the estate he had served from his schooldays.

Thus it was that just when Dunstan Darell was earning golden opinions in his new parish, family sorrows were falling thick upon him.

A Brother's Keeper

Three months passed before Athelstan found a new occupation. It was in the office of some auctioneers and estate agents, well-known in the country. He owed the opening rather to his name than to any character he had gained as a worker. His income was smaller; but then Dunstan always had something to spare—Dunstan, who wore shabby coats and a contemptible hat; Dunstan, who lived with the simplicity of an anchorite, and even then was never sure of getting a meal in peace.

Dunstan went down to see his brother, who received him joyfully, assured him that he had turned over a new leaf, listened patiently to his exhortations, and borrowed a five-pound note, "just to clear off one or two little things that were troubling Lucy."

Before six months were passed, it was clear that Athelstan's promises were of little value. The requests for help became as regular as heretofore. There were signs that the new place, as he himself put it, "was not all one could wish for." And the lonely man in his London parish felt the strain of this increasing anxiety, for he was never inclined resentfully to cry, "Am I my brother's keeper?"

But, whatever the strain, his daily work had to be done.

II

A PAINFUL INTERVIEW

IT was whilst Dunstan Darell's anxieties about his brother were at their height that he received an

A Brother's Keeper

offer of lay help in his parish from a Mr. Marmaduke Smallpiece.

The bearer of this name was, as he informed the vicar, an Experimental Philanthropist.

"I've some ideas as to influencing the lives of the poor," said he, "by bringing them into contact with the cultured. I am told your parish is an excellent field ; may I settle in it?"

"You are a Christian man?"

"I accept all the articles of the Christian faith ; but I should describe myself rather as a philanthropist than a religious worker."

He had money to help the poor, and he wished to learn. Therefore he came. Short, dark, thin-lipped, sharp-nosed, eager-eyed-curiosity was written in large letters all over him. Page, the curate, laughed at him ; Dunstan Darell, like a conscientious vicar, tried to draw out his best qualities.

It was toilsome work. Smallpiece, in social intercourse, soon made it known that he set great store by ancestry and connections, rigid respectability, and the things that make for advancement. It was his joy, in moments of confidence, to show to acquaintances a genealogical tree, from which it was clear that he had an undoubted descent from two kings of England. In agreement with this he had, in an exaggerated form, the common middle-class faith in the supreme advantage of a University degree.

"Is he a gentleman?"

"Has he been to the University?"

These were two questions Smallpiece invariably

asked when men came up for discussion. If it was a question of personal appearance, especially in its bearing on character, he added one more—

"Has he got a refined face, like me?"

It was not until he had been unsuccessful in carrying out a gigantic scheme for a poor man's club and dwelling-house that a halfpenny paper disclosed to the world the painful fact that Smallpiece's father had been "The little Boy's Tailor" in a western town. The genealogical tree must have come from the heraldic stationer.

But this is anticipating.

Smallpiece early entertained grave doubts as to the soundness of his vicar upon what might be called the social side. The Rev. Dunstan Darell had jested upon pedigrees, spoken of remote ancestors as "great rascals, some of them," and even used disrespectful language as to the value of a Cambridge pass degree.

Sore from this treatment, Smallpiece had sought consolation once in Mrs. Page's little drawing-room.

"Strange," he said, "that the vicar never says anything about his family."

"Why should he?" said Page, the curate; "there are hosts of other things to talk about."

"Of course; wonder, though, is he a man of good family?"

"No notion; he's a good worker, any way."

"Not quite the same thing," said Smallpiece, judicially.

"Of course not," said youthful Mrs. Page. "But

perhaps his friends are all dead; I often think some
people may find that convenient, don't you, Mr.
Smallpiece?"

"Well—er—it's a great privilege to have one's
kith and kin with one; but I myself suffer from that
loss. My poor father——"

"Yes, yes," broke in Mrs. Page, with ready
sympathy, "but that does not matter to you; you
are buoyed up by remembering that roll of ancestors
behind you."

"Of course. It's a great privilege to be a man
of family. I often feel that. But I shouldn't like
to misconstrue the vicar's silence, and yet still, you
know—er——"

"Exactly," said Mrs. Page; and with no more
comfort than this, Mr. Smallpiece went his way.

But the suspicion which he had divulged to his
friends grew within him, and he was always on the
watch for evidence which might confirm the theory
he had formed. Indeed, he often found the subject
a pleasant relief from dabbling in the affairs of boys'
clubs, men's clubs, and kindred organisations, and
from intimating generally how much better everything might be done if his own ideas could be well
carried out by everybody.

At last an opportunity arrived for confirming his
suspicion that there was a skeleton in the vicarage
cupboard.

There had been a parish ceremony. Sir Titus
Stukeley, a city knight who loved good works, had
been laying the foundation-stone of a building meant
to house a club. The chief guests had returned to

A Brother's Keeper

the vicarage drawing-room, where Mrs. Page was pouring out tea.

The parlourmaid came in quietly with an announcement for the vicar.

"Some one wishes to see you, sir."

"Ask him to sit down in the parish-room—or, better still, to be there at ten to-morrow."

"He wanted to see you at once, sir."

"Yes, they all do. Is he the usual sort?"

"He told me to say that a relative wished to see you, sir."

Dunstan smiled a little uneasily.

"Put him in the study, Mary; tell him I will come when I can."

Had any one followed this dialogue? The maid spoke quietly; the drawing-room was large.

Moreover, Sir Titus had been telling one of his stories, and the clerical hearers were exhibiting the strange interest proper for the occasion. Mrs. Page had cut in, as the story ended, with an enquiry about Sir Titus's teacup.

But Mr. Smallpiece had followed the incident, and caught enough of the conversation to feel warmly interested. When the vicar's parlourmaid spoke of "a relative," Smallpiece, while edging his chair a little nearer Sir Titus, that he might not lose one word of the story the benevolent knight was telling, listened with all his might for the vicar's directions to the maid.

It was odd, surely, that something like secrecy should be observed, especially as Mr. Darell's countenance fell at the news. Clearly something was wrong.

A Brother's Keeper

Mr. Smallpiece presently withdrew to the house of a frugal widow, where he rented the drawing-room floor. His presence was felt in those rooms. The arms of the House of Smallpiece were painted on the wooden chimney-piece. The arms of the college at which Smallpiece had graduated were displayed upon a banner-screen. The arms of the University, emblazoned upon a tin shield, hung amidst some photographs of Cambridge.

At these emblems Smallpiece would gaze with some complacency when he returned to his room, but on this occasion he entered in a brown study, and for a moment stood twiddling his hat in his finger. Then a sense of loss dawned upon him.

Where was his umbrella?

He must have left it at the vicarage.

Without a moment's delay he turned, sped down the street, and knocked at the vicarage door.

He was at once admitted.

"I think, Mary," he said, in his most conciliatory manner, "I left my umbrella behind me. No—" after a survey of the stand—"I don't see it here; I must have taken it in with me to the vicar's study." And then with a light step he crossed to that door and knocked.

"Come in," said the vicar. And with the utmost alacrity Mr. Smallpiece entered.

He described the scene afterwards with a good deal of gusto in Mrs. Page's drawing-room.

"There was our dear vicar in his usual chair, with a look of most beautiful patience on his face, and there was his visitor sitting opposite to him.

A Brother's Keeper

A very shabby person, I assure you; and not at all
the kind of relative that a person of—er—birth and
education ought to have."

"But how can they help it, Mr. Smallpiece
Why, there is Lord Amstel; before his two brothers
died he was in America. They say he was a
butcher—actually sold chops. Now suppose he
had come over from America to see his brothers in
those days?"

"Very awkward for the brothers, I'm sure; but,
as I was saying, the vicar's visitor looked most
peculiar. Of course, I could not scrutinise him too
closely——"

"Of course not——"

"But I took him in, so to speak, whilst looking
round the room for my umbrella."

"Horrid nuisance that umbrella of yours must
have been," said Mrs. Page, with an ill-concealed
yawn.

"Most provoking; for it really wasn't in the
vicar's study after all, so that I troubled him for
nothing."

"Stolen?"

"No; most curious thing, just as I got back to
my rooms, I noticed it behind the door!"

"How very odd!" said Mrs. Page. "And who
was the visitor, after all?"

"I really don't know. Of course, if one were
possessed with that detestable curiosity to which
common people are a prey, I might have forced the
vicar to explain. But he seemed occupied, and I
withdrew as soon as I could."

A Brother's Keeper

"Quite so."

A few minutes afterwards Mr. Smallpiece took his leave.

As he passed down the street he came upon a little boy, who, with nose flattened against a window-pane, was trying to follow some pleasant incident in the room within.

"My boy," said Mr. Smallpiece, poking him in the back with his umbrella, "don't you know that such curiosity is ill-mannered and wrong?"

"G'arn!" said the boy, as he slunk off.

"Just like the manners of the poor!" exclaimed Mr. Smallpiece, resuming his walk.

III

A LIFE SACRIFICED

DUNSTAN DARELL'S visitor was his brother Athelstan; Athelstan in shabby attire, and with a dejected air.

The visitor began the conversation, assuming, though with obvious effort, something of his old jaunty way.

"Sorry to see me, I dare say," he said, as he took his brother's hand.

"It must be your fault if I am," said Dunstan, "but I hope you don't think so."

"Well, I wouldn't trouble you, Dunstan, really, but the fact is, things have gone all wrong with me most awkwardly."

A Brother's Keeper

"Really? You haven't written for some weeks. What has been happening?"

"I've had a little difference with Newton, Bowles and Co., and I left them—let me see, just a month to-day."

"'A little difference.' What does that mean?"

"Well, I had a few words with Newton. A trifling sum was at the bottom of it; a really absurd sum for all the fuss that was made; but you know what people of that sort are."

"But why didn't you write and tell me you were going?"

"Well, I went a little suddenly at last, and I rather thought something might turn up, so that I should have another place in mind before bothering you with these trifling details."

"Hardly trifling, I fear. But what have you been doing?"

"Well, as we were getting rid of our furniture— I told you of that, didn't I? No? Well, I thought it would be costly stuff to carry about, and of course we can get along in furnished lodgings for a time; so we had a sale. Wretched prices you get, I can assure you."

"But where have you been?"

"Well, I thought we might spend a week with William and Belinda—Lucy's sister and brother-in-law, you know—at Bath. They couldn't very well get out of having us, for they spent their summer holiday with us last year. But they have no policy you know, and very little feeling. I assure you that

A Brother's Keeper

a day or two after I got there they wanted me away again. That little brat Arthur——"

"Why a brat?"

"Well, young Arthur blurted out at the dinner-table, 'Oh, Uncle Athelstan, you're going soon, aren't you? Mother says she hopes you will.'"

"Trying," said Dunstan, with a faint smile.

"And then William began to preach to me about missing good chances, and Belinda reminded me that she had to work to keep things together. So I thought I would run up to town and see you."

"I have heard nothing from them."

"No; I suppose they thought I should tell you everything."

"And now you are here, what am I to do?"

"Well, amongst your friends you might know some one who could find a place that would suit me."

"And until then?"

Athelstan shrugged his shoulders.

"By-the-by," continued his brother, "where is your wife?"

"Ah, I meant to have told you. The family are in some lodgings—poor but clean—in Shepherd's Bush."

"And the funds?"

Again Athelstan shrugged his shoulders.

Dunstan sighed, and after more thought promised to hold a family consultation with his brother and his wife at their lodgings.

In the meantime inquiries showed that Athelstan's conduct had obviously made his continuance in the service of Newton, Bowles and Co. impossible. Nor was it likely that they could speak of him in such language as would smooth the way to another place.

Dunstan Darell did not cherish any delusion as to the ease with which his brother might be reformed. He had seen only too many cases in which men, fallen from honesty and sobriety, had told themselves and him that their future should know no more disgrace, that they would cut themselves off from the past, that the exercise of self-respect and self-control should save them from any renewal of the old mistakes.

Dunstan had watched these light-hearted attempts of frail humanity to reform itself, and had verified in their experiences the theological fact that man cannot save himself. There would be no change of life in Athelstan until there was change of heart. How he pleaded with him! And how lightly Athelstan put it all aside!

Athelstan was not a penitent; his brother's exhortations utterly failed to move or guide him. He was conscious of no spiritual need, and he had at least enough regard for the truth left to refrain from playing the hypocrite.

"My dear fellow," he would say, "you can't think how I feel all that you say; but I assure you that it will be all right."

"I wish I could think so," Dunstan would sadly reply.

"Well, wait and see. Anyhow, I don't think anybody could have a better chance than I have with a brother like you to care for me."

A Brother's Keeper

In the meantime Dunstan had to keep Athelstan and his family, and to inquire far and near for some situation within his capabilities. Athelstan also bestirred himself, examining with great ardour the advertisement sheets of the papers, and occasionally applying in person for some situation, but invariably arriving an hour or two after it had been filled up.

It was Dunstan who at last found the place. He went to that eminent worthy, Sir Titus Stukeley, and told him all the facts, and asked for his help.

There were people who said that Sir Titus was a humbug—that he "made a good thing out of his religion," and some day would "astonish his pious friends." Dunstan knew that the man's religion was true, before the story of Athelstan's career had reached its end.

Sir Titus promised help, and in a week it came. Athelstan was to go down to Manchester. The place, indeed, was a small one, but, if well served, would lead on to something better.

In a fortnight Athelstan started, Lucy and the children following a week later. He was happy and confident. No doubt, he condescendingly admitted, it would be trying at first; but he was bound to succeed, and success meant a good deal. He understood that large fortunes were often made at Manchester; it was not impossible for one of them to be made by him; and then he would see that Dunstan should not suffer for his kindness.

Lucy had heard something like this before, and smiled faintly. Dunstan hinted at the peril of self-confidence, and the need of care. Athelstan took it all in good part, and left for the station, with the air of a prince setting out to take possession of a kingdom.

For a month or two all went well, and letters were full of contentment. Then they grew less frequent; then they ceased.

Dunstan felt the anxiety keenly, and when the silence had extended to months, he caught a cold, and fell ill.

But, sick as he was, the silence was unendurable, something must be done. It was broken by a letter from Sir Titus. Athelstan, after repeated inattention and unpunctuality, had quarrelled with the manager of the Manchester branch, and had been summarily dismissed. Where he had gone was unknown.

The vicar sent for his curate, and told him the whole melancholy story.

"What I most fear, Page," he said at its end, "is that he may not have the courage to face me again, and so may drift away from me altogether."

Page smiled; perhaps he knew human nature better than his vicar did.

"I think he will come back to you." That was his verdict.

The vicar sighed gratefully, and turned upon his pillow.

Day succeeded day, without news of the prodigal, until an eventful afternoon, when Mr. Smallpiece begged the favour of an interview.

Dunstan, much better, was sitting up in his study; only waiting until a sunny day should justify the doctor in letting him out.

A Brother's Keeper

"So sorry to trouble you," said the philanthropist, "but a curious thing happened this afternoon, which you ought to know; although of course, as you will easily understand, I am very far from assuming that the facts really concern yourself."

"Pray go on," said Dunstan.

"You know, my dear vicar, that I am an Experimental Philanthropist. Well, my friend Ricardo Mill, who is deeply concerned about the struggles of the poor, asked me to view with him a little property in the Borough, which illustrates in a very striking way the amazing conditions under which some of the poor live. It was a miserable slum. We examined several tenements without any objection from the lodgers. Mill manages them so well, you know, and I myself was able now and then to offer a suggestion or two, in the way, er——"

"Of helping the worst cases," put in Dunstan.

"Well—er—yes, in my own style, of course. But, as I was saying, they were all very respectful, as the poor should be to men of higher station who are interested in their struggles; but there was one exception."

"Really," said the vicar.

"Yes, one fellow—with the remains of education and refinement still just visible about him—refused to let us enter his room, said his wife wasn't very well, and he didn't want to see strangers."

"Poor fellow!" began Dunstan.

"Well," continued Smallpiece, lifting his eyebrows disapprovingly at this comment. "I endeavoured to explain to him the advantage to the poor of allowing

A Brother's Keeper

inquirers to learn their ways of life, when this impertinent fellow rushed out at me, threatened to throw Ricardo Mill and myself downstairs, said he had been born a gentleman, and that if we had been we should have known better—such impertinence, you know. Then, when I ventured to explain that I was an Experimental Philanthropist, he said he had a brother a clergyman who was worth fifty such Experimentalists—as of course *you* would be, my dear vicar, for I thought I caught your name."

"What was he like?" asked Dunstan, rising eagerly from his chair.

"Ah," said Smallpiece, "I am bad at seeing resemblances, but I could not help being struck at the extraordinary likeness between this violent person and a caller who was in your study one afternoon when I was looking for my umbrella."

"It must be Athelstan—my brother. The address, if you please."

Mr. Smallpiece gave it.

Ten minutes later he was in Mrs. Page's drawing-room explaining to her the painful fact that the vicar had a brother who was not only a scoundrel and a drunkard, but a man so far lost to good as even to threaten an eminent person like Mr. Ricardo Mill with personal violence.

"Oh, I *am* so glad!" cried the little woman, with characteristic fervour.

"*What!*" cried the caller, "glad that a ruffian living in one room should threaten a——"

"No, no; not that, of course; but glad that the vicar has found his brother."

A Brother's Keeper

The vicar, very much against the urgent plea of his housekeeper, had, on Mr. Smallpiece's departure, wrapped himself up, sent for a cab, and left for the Borough. An hour later he returned with Athelstan, Lucy, and the children. Athelstan was apologetic, but still hopeful. He had been in fault; he was a wretched fellow; but all would yet be well. Lucy was tearful, but anxious for the health of her brother-in-law.

Indeed, that anxiety was only too well-founded. Dunstan had braved an east wind, and his bronchitis was hanging about him.

By the evening it was necessary to send for the doctor, who was lost in amazement at the foolish act of his friend. Pneumonia was dreaded, and pneumonia came. Before the prodigal had been forty-eight hours under his brother's roof Dunstan was dead.

There was little opportunity for converse, but Dunstan was so concerned for the welfare of his brother that the careless prodigal was utterly broken down. Dunstan had laid down his life for him; here was love indeed. Beside his brother's body he vowed himself to a new life—no longer in his own strength, but in that of the Christ who died that such as Athelstan Darell might live indeed.

Dunstan's possessions did little more than bury him; Athelstan had still to face the world. It was the oft-maligned City Knight who came to his aid. Sir Titus approached, thought he saw hope in Athelstan's contrition, and promised him "another chance." It was taken, and though something of

A Brother's Keeper

the old self-confidence would now and then break out, Athelstan persevered, and won his employer's confidence fully. He never made his fortune; he never came to high place in the firm; he remained in a post of mediocrity; he never restored the fortunes of the family. But he was happy, and useful. If over him there lay the shadow of his brother's death, there was still the brightness of the new life into which by this path God had led him. For himself he kept green the memory of his brother, as the memory of a hero who had died a hero's death; but other people were less exacting, they merely said that Dunstan Darell "went out too early after bronchitis."

HER TRUE LOVE

I

" FEW places of the size of our village have the high privilege of possessing so many single gentlemen of means," chirruped Miss Joy. " And I assure you, ladies, I've taken care to impress the fact upon my niece Jessamy in my letters."

"When do you expect your dear young niece?" asked Mary Armytage, the sweet-eyed, silver-haired elder sister who mothered the good vicar.

"Any day, my dear. It might be this very evening. And I'm sure I can count upon your sympathy, ladies. A young girl is a heavy responsibility, particularly where there are so many single gentlemen."

At that moment Jessamy Joy was craning her round, white neck from side to side to admire the scenery, as the lumbering old omnibus which met one train a day toiled up the steeps to the pert little township.

"I don't go *inside* that stuffy old ark!" had been Jessamy's first thought, when she emerged out of the station, and eyed the venerable vehicle all over. "I'm the only passenger?" she queried. "Well, then, I am coming up beside you."

"Be you, missy?" Bates, the old driver, who was a match in all points for the antique vehicle, stood up

as straight as rheumatism would permit, to stare
admiringly at the tall, slender figure of the young
stranger. "I'm agreeable," affably chuckled the old
coachman, as he assisted the girl to clamber up to
the box seat and prepared to follow her. "But you
bain't the only passenger, missy. If I ain't mistook,
there's that little Mr. Grigsby comin' up with us.
I know'd as he was expected to-day, and folk do
make a p'int o' suitin' theirselves to the 'bus."

Jessamy, from her seat above, looked calmly
down at the approaching dapper figure which
stepped briskly forward to enter the 'bus, and a pair
of honest blue eyes met hers, with a faint gleam of
surprise in them.

"Evenin', Mr. Grigsby, sir. All right!"

There was a crack of the whip, a volley of
encouraging expletives to the scraggy pair of horses,
and the 'bus rumbled off.

"Perhaps—do you think that gentleman wanted
to sit up here? Am I in the way?" asked
Jessamy.

"Little Mr. Grigsby sit up on the box seat!"
said Bates. "Oh, bless you, no, missy! He's a
keerful gentleman, and prefers the inside o' the
'bus in the evenin' air; though when it comes to
November, he's out with the 'ounds three times a
week. We all has our weakness, and Mr. Grigsby,
he has a tidy huntin' seat, though you mightn't think
it to look at him."

"The evening air is delicious!" said Jessamy,
drawing in a long breath of it, and feeling disdainful
of anybody who feared its freshness. "I've come here

to live with my aunt, Miss Joy. I suppose you
know her?"

"Sartain; a well-respected lady she be," said
Bates; "though I ain't one to put my trust in
wimmen-folk; the Psalmist enjines us not to——"

"I thought it was princes, not women," mildly
corrected Jessamy.

"Evenin', sir, evenin' to you!"

Bates ignored the reproof, by volubly greeting the
occupant of a high dog-cart behind a horse, with
silver-mounted harness, that overtook and passed the
lumbering coach.

"Good evening, Bates." There was a friendly
nod and a prolonged gaze, the first for Bates, the
second for the passenger perched beside him.

"That there's the major's nevvy, Mr. Algy Binks,
a gay young spark, but over-free with the whip,
same's he was a woman, axing your pardon, miss
—but ladies does spile the best horse going with
the whip."

Jessamy nodded vigorously in assent, and thereby
won the heart of old Bates for all time.

"Who's the major?" she asked.

"Major Binks, missy, of the Little Hall, one of
our gentry up yonder"—pointing with his whip.
"He's an uncommon peppery gent, but free enough
with his money, I will say. There's some as think,
'specially hisself, that Mr. Algy will be the major's
heir." Old Bates interrupted his local history to sing
out cheerily: "Here we are atop! You've got to
Bury-cum-Easter, missy; and there's Rose Cottage
with the big wooden gate. Woa!"

Her True Love

With much clatter and ado, the creaking vehicle drew up. A short, roundabout figure, surmounted by a lace cap and a cunning, upright pink bow that thrilled in unison with its wearer's every thought, stood at the gate nodding like a mandarin in greeting.

"Welcome, dear child! Welcome, Jessamy!"

"Is that my Aunt Letty?" Jessamy had never so much as seen Miss Joy before.

"'Tis so," began Bates, touching his hat to the little lady. Then, before Jessamy could spring down, a hand was outstretched to help her, and a pair of blue eyes again met her own.

It was the inside passenger, little Mr. Grigsby; and presently, after Miss Joy, having kissed the newcomer on each cheek, had introduced him, he was lifting his hat with an old-world grace, and elaborately bowing, while Jessamy Joy demurely curtseyed.

II

JESSAMY JOY had not been long at Bury-cum-Easter before she knew as much if not more about her new surroundings than Aunt Letty herself. The tall, active, springy girl, with her sweet face and silver tongue, had made friends and slaves of everybody, from Major Binks at the Little Hall, her devoted admirer at first sight, to Bates, whom she called her oldest friend.

"She be the sunshine o' the place," declared the latter, proud of the young lady's unfeigned interest

Her True Love

in his bees; for Bates was a beekeeper of some renown.

"What's the matter, Bates, this morning?" a bright brown head, under a picture hat of straw, shot round the corner of his cottage to say.

"Why-a," answered Bates, who stood brooding pensively in the misty heat of the summer morning over his bees, "why-a, missy, there've been a swarm!"

"You don't really mean it, Bates!" Jessamy was alert with excited interest. "When, where, how? Are you glad?"

"Glad? Ah, you don't know the old rhyme, missy, that's clear—

> "'A swarm o' bees in May
> Is worth a load o' hay;
> A swarm o' bees in June
> Is worth a silver spoon;
> But a swarm in July,
> 'Tisn't worth a fly.'"

"And this is the first of July. Oh dear!" sympathised Jessamy.

"Oh, good morning!" she turned round, startled, to add, at the sound of approaching footsteps.

It was little Paul Grigsby, with a girlish blush on his honest face.

"Good morning, Miss Joy. Don't you be down, old chap," he turned to say cheerily to Bates. "These ancient rhymes were made to fit in with the old style, not the new. We are not out of June yet by twelve days."

"Well, a-well," rejoined Bates, regarding the

speaker respectfully, "I allus do say as you be a wonnerful wise genelmun for your size, Mr. Grigsby, sir!"

Jessamy laughed outright, and Paul, no whit disconcerted by the personality, beamed at the compliment to his wisdom. Then the young folk wandered off. And Bates raised himself straight, to watch their retreating figures, the girl's slim and stately, her companion's short and trig.

"They ain't no sart of match, they two," he decided. "They wouldn't run in double harness, nohow. Missy, she be so rarely tall for a woman, and he be so tarrible shart. No, 'twon't do!"

So thought somebody else.

Mr. Algy Binks, in all the glory of lightest summer tweeds, whitest spats, and shiniest patent-leather toes, lent a sudden transfiguration to the homely scene.

"There goes another string to missy's bow!" chuckled old Bates, as the new-comer picked his way fastidiously, in the wake of the strikingly ill-matched pair.

Somehow, when Algy caught up with the two, the July day's beauty suddenly died out for Paul Grigsby. He had been secretly pluming himself, as he walked on tiptoe and on air by Jessamy's side that he was beginning to make some way. Ruefully the modest little personage regarded his splendid rival, and shrank into himself a still smaller man. He had best take himself off; he was only in the way of this supremely well-assorted couple; and he slipped behind, unnoticed by the two,

Her True Love

who wandered on, Jessamy, for one, quite oblivious that the little gentleman had forlornly dropped away.

It was the beginning of the end, Paul disconsolately told himself. And as the summer days sped on, and Algy Binks still lingered at the Little Hall, all Bury-cum-Easter began to take the same view.

"Well, well!" sighed the major, "we must all give way to youth. My Algy's a fine young fellow; no woman could resist him."

"Oh, Aunt Letty, I love the life, the free country life. I shall never want to leave it!" cried the young girl, ecstatically.

"Well, dear child"—Miss Joy's pink bow thrilled in her lace cap—"you've but to hold up your finger to be asked to stay all your life long in Bury-cum-Easter!"

"Why? Do you mean—do you really mean, Aunt Letty, that you would have me stay with you? Do you like me, then, a little?" The girl's dewy, fresh face bent close down over little Miss Joy's, and her innocent eyes widened.

Miss Joy looked back into their clear, child-like depths before she spoke, and then it was only the last part of the girl's speech she replied to.

"Could I help liking you, loving you, Jessamy dear?" The little spinster gently pulled down the bright brown head to kiss the warm red lips of the girl.

Her True Love

It was a brilliant summer, and Algy Binks made its unexceptionable fineness an excuse for his incessant descents on the Little Hall. London was over-hot. Far more congenial to his idle nature was it to wander through the meads, and up and down the hills around, in attendance on so fair a maiden as Jessamy, carrying her sketch-book and little Miss Joy's camp-chair.

"'Tis a pratty sight, look, they two young things!" cried Bury-cum-Easter, approvingly. One person, however, held another opinion. Little Mr. Grigsby retired to his trim, well-appointed red-brick mansion much as a weather-wise snail withdraws itself in its shell when the clouds are unpropitious.

For the first time in the honest little gentleman's life he made personal acquaintance with the tender passion.

The whole world, the face of Nature itself, had been changed for Paul Grigsby. His old life of pampered, coddled ease fell away from him, and he emerged from his dead self a new and stronger-natured man.

With vain longings had his soul swelled within him, in the desire that he might do something to prove to the whole world his knightly devotion. To win a smile or a word from Jessamy's sweet, warm lips would be guerdon enough, he told himself fervently, for any sacrifice. To win herself, Paul

Her True Love

humbly felt was as impossible as if she were of the blood royal.

New chapters of an unexpected romance were opening for the simple-natured little man. While he ruefully spelled them out, Jessamy, like a human butterfly, revelled in the summer sweetness of the country life, unconscious of the upheaval her coming had caused in the primitive community. It was pleasant enough to the young girl to have Algy Binks at her beck and call. Not that she had any particular favour for Algy, but as well him as any other, for Jessamy was fancy-free.

Again and again came the major's nephew to the Little Hall, and on each visit his friendship for Aunt Letty's niece gained ground.

"You ride, Miss Joy? You will hunt?" Algy had said in his assured manner, when the summer had fled, and November was next door.

"Hunt! Oh no. I don't even ride!" Jessamy blithely laughed.

"But you will let me teach you to ride?" Algy was fired with new-born anxiety to begin.

"No, no; I've neither habit nor horse——"

"You will allow me to supply the last deficiency?" eagerly put in the voice of little Mr. Grigsby, who happened to be present. He grew ruddy with the thought that he might possibly be of some use.

"Thank you. But indeed I should not care for it at all." Jessamy secretly rebelled at the notion of being a pupil of Mr. Algy Binks. "I can stick on a pony with anybody," she added; "and that's all I shall ever be in a position to attain. So where would be the use of trying to teach me?"

And the girl was firm. But when hunting fairly set in, she was ready enough to be driven by Mary Armytage in the vicarage governess-cart to the meet, to see the hounds throw off.

IV

BOTH Algy Binks and little Mr. Grigsby hunted. The latter was a quiet, steady horseman, who got over the ground in an industrious fashion, quite distinct from Algy's showy, conspicuous, unequal style.

"I—I shouldn't ride that new mount the major has got to-morrow, if I were you, Binks. I d—don't much fancy her," nervously stammered Paul Grigsby, one dusky afternoon when Miss Joy's drawing-room was full, and the subdued rattle of tea-cups and the tinkling chink of silver spoons were giving the usual satisfaction to the beaming hostess.

"You wouldn't what?" Algy, standing on the hearthrug, looked down from his superior inches at the honest face raised to his.

"I shouldn't ride her." Paul grew bolder. "She's new to the country and new to you—and the ground will be lumpy after the rain."

The little man spoke earnestly, even anxiously. Deep down in his heart was an undying jealousy of his handsome rival, but Paul was not the sort of man to let his likes and his dislikes jostle against his duty.

Her True Love

"When I want your advice I'll ask for it," said Algy, crisply, and secretly furious at Paul's interference.

A pair of shy eyes in the corner, where Jessamy sat pouring out cups of tea, flashed a glance of indignation at the speaker, which Algy would scarcely have relished, had he intercepted it.

"Well, you can't say I've not warned you, anyway," Paul retorted, good-humouredly ignoring the open insolence of Algy's tone and words. "I don't see why you should run the risk of breaking your neck on the back of an untried animal like that new mare. If you can't get a better mount for to-morrow, I'd rather lend you one of my two."

"You would! Perhaps you would go further still. Perhaps you'd do a bit of brag, by offering to ride the new mare yourself, to show off?" Algy said, with an unlovely sneer; and Jessamy bit her full, tender lip with her white teeth.

"N—no," Paul considered; "I never could myself see any great valour in being reckless," he said, thoughtfully.

"Ah!" began Algy, at white heat, "your idea of valour, I take it, is the sort that runs away, and lives to fight another day——"

"Mr. Grigsby," softly called out Jessamy, instinctively throwing herself into the breach, "I want you to give me your opinion about Dandy's paw. I believe he must have trodden on a piece of glass."

Paul, who loved all animals almost as well as

119

Her True Love

humans, wheeled round, and on his knees carefully examining the terrier's wounded paw, speedily forgot Algy's insulting words.

Not so Jessamy. Uneasy doubts of the fine, town-bred lover, who already had half-declared himself, stirred in the girl's heart, and her speaking face was clouded over for that night.

V

IT was twenty-four hours later. The day had been a typical hunting one, with "a southerly wind and a cloudy sky," but it had been rounded by a tragedy. Up the winding hill road toiled a mournful procession which halted half-way, to deliver its burden at the Little Hall.

In spite of Paul's friendly warning, Algy Binks had persisted in riding the new mare, the stranger in the major's stables, and his heart throbbed with pride over the success of his obstinacy, as the day wore on. It had been a tame run so far, and the mare had had but smooth sailing ahead.

"Don't put her at this, whatever you do!" energetically shouted Paul Grigsby, who looked and was another man in "pink." The "field" was making blindly for a grim obstacle, as he turned his head to warn his rival. "It's a rasper as black as your hat. Do be advised, Binks! There's a gate further down!" he called out, with the best intention, over his shoulder. But Algy's blood took fire instantly.

"Then use it yourself, you coward!" he half

Her True Love

screamed, a mad flicker of fury in his eyes. Setting his teeth, he put his quivering, nervous animal at the "rasper," following Paul's lead.

The latter's horse, a seasoned hunter, went over like a bird, but behind came a rushing and crashing, a terrific smash; then a hideous thud on the clay, as the frightened, rearing animal failed to clear the obstacle, and fell heavily backward, plunging madly.

It was a horrible moment until horse and rider were disentangled.

Foremost among the helpers was Paul Grigsby, who had hastily dismounted and scrambled through from the other side. Tender as a woman, without a thought of danger for himself, the little man, risking many a kick from the madly alarmed animal, strove to draw his rival's senseless form from out of peril. There was not a grain of selfishness or craven fear in Paul Grigsby's composition, mean of physique as he was to human eyes. That it was the rival who had ousted and cheapened himself by small, ill-natured wit and open insult, Paul utterly forgot.

"He is frightfully injured!" said a voice, as at last the mangled, unconscious figure was separated from further peril. "Best wrench off the gate yonder, and carry the poor fellow home, while somebody rides to Bury-cum-Easter for Duchesne or O'Kell."

So they carried home the silent burden, and over the Little Hall gathered a pall of speechless gloom, while the issues of death hung in the balance.

Her True Love

VI

It was some days after the accident in the hunting field. To the relief of everybody, a London physician, the owner of a great name, had come down, and given forth his *fiat* that Algy would live—live as a cripple, probably; time alone would decide. The external injuries were grievous enough; his hearers shuddered, as the big man detailed them calmly. Still, they would not necessarily have a fatal result, and the blandly delivered verdict was a hopeful one.

In private consultation with his brethren the mighty medicine-man unbent much further.

"Patch him up between you," he said. "You'll have your work cut out for you, but with patience a good deal may be done. That poor fellow will live; not that he will be particularly glad, for he is frightfully disfigured. The torn-off ear is a bad business—very bad!"

A couple of days later, when Algy had crept so far out of peril as to have his external hurts tackled, the young Irish assistant-doctor had made a startling proposition to the assembled group, who out of the dusky gloom stared at him as at a raging madman.

"Come, come, O'Kell, we can't have any fool-hardy tricks and experiments here!" sternly said Dr. Duchesne.

"But I assure you," burst in the Irishman, fervently, "the thing's been done over and over again by distinguished French surgeons!"

122

Her True Love

"Pooh, pooh!"—the major had recovered himself—"I might have guessed it was some foreign cannibal notion. No decent Englishman would lend himself to——"

"Ah, just so, major!" the elder doctor struck in, to ward off a slap at the sister isle. He did not relish his colleague's toes being trampled on—save by himself. "In this case, I confess I don't see my way, O'Kell, at all."

"You don't, sir! Then I do. And, gentlemen, I appeal to you, one and all, to help me. If you refuse—well, thin, it's harrts of stone that's inside of ye! I appeal to you," he reiterated. "Which of you will come forrward?"

"I never heard such an extraordinary request in the whole course of my life. Really, it is hardly to be called decent!" sententiously said the vicar, shuffling first one foot and then the other in abject embarrassment.

"My own opinion, exactly," struck in the major's stentorian voice. "A most improper, I may say profane, proposition!"

"I—I—wish to say that I should be most happy to place myself at your service, O'Kell!" unsteadily stuttered Paul Grigsby, speaking for the first time. His face was chalky-pale, and his voice vibrated with nervousness.

"God bless ye, Grigsby! You're a prince! God bless ye, I say!" almost shouted the excited Irishman, springing forward to shake hands so violently, that the little gentleman, already highly strung, was thrown off his equilibrium. "There, there, Grigsby!

Her True Love

I didn't mean to knock you over, me bhoy! Excuse me, but it was too much for me. It's proud I am to call you me friend, sir! I'd have bared my arm willingly, and helped myself to a slip of my own skin with all the pleasure in life. But I couldn't do both—be the operator and the material too. Oh, but it's going to be the pride of my life ; as pretty a case as ever was known ! "

VII

WHEN little Mr. Grigsby's offer was known, Bury-cum-Easter rose in a ferment of excitement. To think that in a Christian land such a proceeding should take place! To beg the skin off your bones was hitherto unheard of.

"God bless little Mr. Grigsby for a brave, good man!" murmured gentle old Mary Armytage.

"Amen!" assented the vicar, with fervour.

"He's a splendid boy, Grigsby is!" Young O'Kell brimmed over with an enthusiasm which was perhaps excusable on his part, seeing he had successfully performed a brilliant plastic operation by means of the slip of flesh taken from generous Paul Grigsby's arm. From all sides resounded loud praises. But one voice was silent, and Jessamy Joy thought the more, for saying so little.

Perhaps it is in the hour of grave peril that some of us get best acquainted with our own natures. Jessamy suddenly felt herself to be a woman, no longer a heedless girl. She looked life in the face steadfastly. Her heart told her that Algy Binks in his grave danger was to her but a sick man lying half-way between life and death. She was sorry for him; but that was all. Oh yes, she must be heart-whole. But was she?

VIII

THE weeks fled by. Christmas came and went. And with it came the slow knowledge to Jessamy that she had not any heart at all, whole or otherwise. It had, all unconsciously, been given away to another's keeping. And its keeper was a worthy one, little as he dreamed of his own good fortune. Paul Grigsby was much too humble to move one step nearer, and Jessamy sighed helplessly in secret. Her one shy pleasure was to listen greedily to the chorus of praises Paul's name never failed to evoke.

Winter was bleak enough on the hill-top. Jessamy, her life-spring loosened, took to cowering over the cheerful wood fires of Rose Cottage, or to crooning dismal ditties at the old-fashioned piano.

"You will be all right when the summer comes, Jessamy," wistfully said Aunt Letty.

"Yes, oh yes, Aunt Letty, when the summer comes."

"Why, my dear, I do believe that's little Mr. Grigsby coming in at the gate! What a stranger he is! Now we shall have tea at once, and hot tea-cakes. Delightful!" Aunt Letty cried out fussily, and Jessamy's startled blush had not ebbed away when Paul entered, with a new spring in his step, a new light in his face.

"I—I have brought you some news," at last Paul

Her True Love

blurted out, constrainedly. "I was at the Little Hall this morning, and there was a letter from Mentone—from Algy."

"Ah, yes! Poor Algy! what does he say about himself? Is he really mending, do you think?" asked Miss Joy, anxiously.

"I don't know about mending. He doesn't say. But—but he is going to be married," jerked out Paul, and then he carefully stared into the blazing fire until his eyes watered.

"Going to *what*?" Miss Joy's cup slipped from her fingers on to the tray, making a loud clatter, and Paul's heart stood still. Not daring to remove his eyes from the fire, he did not doubt but that Jessamy had fainted.

"Going to be married," he mumbled.

"To be married!" echoed Miss Joy, her voice rising *crescendo*-wise in her astonishment. "Who on earth is he going to marry?" she excitedly demanded.

"A rich American. A—a widow with a large fortune," replied Paul, in a thin flat voice. What a fool he had been, not to break the thing more gently! Ah! What was that? A peal of girlish laughter and a volley of barks from Dandy broke out in unison. Paul sprang to his feet. Yes, she was positively laughing—and it was genuine laughter! There was a rush of joy to the little man's heart, and the pulses in his head beat like hammers.

How many cups of tea Paul swallowed after that he never knew.

"There's just light enough for me to write a note or two, and tell people the news, if you'll excuse me,

Her True Love

Mr. Grigsby," Miss Joy suddenly jumped up to say. Writing little notes was a pet hobby of the spinster, but to indulge it satisfactorily it was imperative that she should be alone. So, slipping away to the dining-room, she left the young folk to themselves.

An hour later, when she returned, Jessamy was half-weeping, half-laughing. Paul Grigsby, on his part, was stammering haltingly and talking volubly by turns. Thus the two came forward, hand in hand, in the firelight to little Miss Joy, with the shy story they had to tell.

"Oh, my dears!" Up went the little spinster's plump white hands, and the pink bow vibrated in her lace cap. "To think it should have come to this! Oh, Jessamy! Oh, Mr. Grigsby——"

"Say 'Paul,' do say 'Paul,' now!" Was that assured voice, brimming with happiness, little Mr. Grigsby's? Impossible!

"Oh, my dears!" Miss Joy, suddenly realising all that it meant, if she were to begin calling Mr. Grigsby "Paul," fairly broke down, and sobbed aloud; while Dandy, who had been for the past hour silently watching proceedings with one alert eye, as he lay curled among the frilled cushions on the couch, barked snappishly. All this emotional business was beyond his ken; it therefore must be quite unorthodox in a respectable family.

"Oh, my dears!" The English language seemed to fail Miss Joy, and she dabbed her face with her handkerchief. Then, in attempting to kiss Jessamy, she found she had kissed Mr. Grigsby, who was nearer her own height, instead.

Her True Love

"Earthquakes are nothing to this!" cried the little lady, horror-struck; and the pair of lovers had forthwith to pat her on the back, to "bring her to." In truth, the drawing-room of Rose Cottage had never before witnessed a like commotion, and in the end the notes written to announce Algy Binks's engagement were never despatched. A wedding nearer home effaced the matrimonial bargain the major's heir had achieved for himself.

"Every man of us, we're all willing to be your bridesmaids, Grigsby, me boy!" the assistant went so far as to generously declare, in Irish fashion.

As for Algy Binks, who had done so well for himself, he could afford to be ostentatious. Out of the grateful fulness of his heart, he sent the bride a string of pearls to adorn her white throat.

*　　*　　*　　*　　*

Before the June roses were over the worthy Bates had the honour and glory of driving up to the hill-top, in their own smart new carriage, the happy couple, on their return from the honeymoon.

"Inside passengers both, this time," chuckled the old man. "Well a-well, 'tain't by their outsiders we've got to judge folk," he murmured, irrelevantly. "Now I deesay that there lovin' couple a-settin' behind me thinks theirselves perfect, for all she's so tall and he's so shart. But there, look see, 'tis the hearts that are spliced in true love. And little Mr. Grigsby, he's got a lion's heart in him, for all his shartness; while she's that sweet and wholesome— there! God bless they both, I do say!"

A CUP OF HIS WIFE'S TEARS

I

THE PURTIEST LASS IN THE GLEN

AND sure, Tim Logan is the foinest flute-player annywhere, barrin' that he niver blows a breath down the instrument. There's a power of music inside of Tim, an' bedad, if he wanst tuk down the flute that's been hangin' on his wall these twenty years, there's no tellin' hwhat wouldn't happen.

"What does he do for a livin'?" d' ye say? Faith, he kapes a cow. That's his cottage, across the glen, fornenst the crag, wid the pig in the doorway. An' if ye went across there, Tim 'd show you his flute maybe, for mighty proud of it he is, and kapes it shiny and bright, but if ye axe him for a chune, faith, ye'll be to whustle for it.

It's thrue enough hwhat I'm tellin' yez. Tim could be the greatest musician in Ireland—let alone the adjacent counthries—at this moment, if he chose. There was niver a song but it'd come thricklin' and tinklin' like melted silver entirely. Och, the likes av it was niver heard, and little wonder that the purtiest lass in the glen married Tim, for Tim and his flute and the moonlight 'd persuade a princess, though Biddy had the pick of the bhoys and the polis for

A Cup of his Wife's Tears

miles around. An' when Tim had thravelled over the gap every moonlight for three years to serenade Biddy, she gev'm the sign, and Father Mulcahy married 'em a week afther.

Well, Biddy and he lived like a couple av fairies for some months, and every avenin' Tim 'd take down the flute and discoorse most beautiful. An' Biddy 'd sit and watch him, for he had a lovely smile on the face av him whin he was playin', not like one av these furrin fiddlers as scowls over their music. And Tim tuk to makin' chunes out of fancy, and played his flute to Biddy all as one as a mavish calling' to his mate.

Says Biddy one day, "Tim," says she, "sorra doubt but you're a rale janius."

"I belave I may be," says he. "It's a wonderful gift," says he, "to have the right undherstandin' of music," says he, "an' maybe if I could go to London and play before the King on his throne, it's Lord and Lady Logan we'd both be, Biddy; for he's *be* to make us some recognisement," says he, "and foine ye'd look, Biddy, in a green silk robe, and me playin' to yez on a golden flute, instid of this owld wooden one," says he.

"Och," says Biddy, "sure we're happy enough as it is, and the only way to enjoy the present is not to luk back on the future before it comes," says she.

"Thrue for you," says Tim; "but it 'd be a mighty foine thing, all the same, to be the greatest fluter on airth, if only the rest of the world knew av it," says he.

A Cup of his Wife's Tears

Well, Tim got it into his head, by-and-by, that the janius that was in him was too big for his body, let alone being too big for the glen, and that that wasn't the right place for him at all at all, but that he might be making a mint of money out of his flute, wandherin' over the face of the airth. An' he began to get glum, and consaved that he was raly hindered, and from bein' hearty in his appetite he began to luk twice at his food before he touched it; an' 'twas little he put into his mouth at those times, and niver a word kem out av it. But Biddy stood by him like a jew'l, and niver a line crossed her purty face; but she'd just hand him his flute at the right time.

"Biddy darlint," says Tim one day, "you're a rale angel," says he, "barrin' that ye haven't got the wings," says he. "And that I'm not sorry for," says he, "for ye'd be to fly away from the likes av me one day," says he.

"Oh, go along," says she; "an' why should I fly away from the lovely music av your flute, Tim avic?" says she. "Sure an angel's harp 'd sound thin to me," says she, "if it wasn't Tim's breath that made the music."

"Lave your humbuggin'," says he, "I'll bid ye, for ye know yerself that all my chunes weary ye. I'll not be happy," says he, "till the wide world is listenin' to me."

Well, Ballykelly fair day kem round, and Tim put on his casthor, and Biddy barred the door, and away they wint down the glen to the fair, wid the flute stickin' out of Tim's tail pocket, but sorra

A Cup of his Wife's Tears

note did he play that morning, but the melancholy had hold of him, and there was notes in his heart too sad to be brought out av a flute, annyway. And so Tim strolled about at the fair without so much as a "God save yez" on his tongue, and the bhoys were afraid av him. And there was all manner of fun, but sorra a wink did Tim give to 't, but moped about suckin' the ind av his blackthorn, wid Biddy draggin' at his heels.

By-an'-by they came to a booth with one of these phrenologists (they call 'em) gotherin' away on an owld chap's head that he was examinin'; and sure says this chap, "I'll make a pint av tellin' your thrue kerreckthers, if ye'll step up," says he; "gintlemen, one shillin', leedies, eighteenpence, on account of the more numerous vartues resoidin' in the fair sex," says he. "I'll tell yez," says he, "more about your kerreckthers than ye iver dhreamt of, this rendherin' yez capable of seein' yourselves as others see yez, an' maybe showin' yez the short cut to fame and wealth. For how d'ye know," says he, "but hwhat there's a Gladstone or a Parnell, or maybe a Murphy, amongst ye? Full phrenological examination, one shillin'," says he; "and if ye wish for a private interview," says he, "yez can come inside, and for the consideration of a slight honorarium," says he, "I'll give yez advice, free gratis and for nothing, that'll last yez all your loife."

Says he, looking at Tim, "Excuse me, sir, if it wasn't an insult to a gintleman, I'd be afther askin' yez to let me examine your head gratis, for I can see it's a foine knobby one."

A Cup of his Wife's Tears

"Go up," says Biddy, givin' Tim a shillin', "and let him feel it;" and, thinks Tim, "Maybe it'll do me some good." And he sat down in the chair, but the flute in his tails bein' inconvanient, he tuk it out an' gev it to Biddy, while the professor went on feeling his head.

"Ye're a kind husband," says he.

"That's thrue," says Biddy, not heedin' the crowd.

"Gregariousness good," says the professor, "but ye've more aquaintances than friends, though."

"Thrue for ye," says Tim; "how did ye find that out?"

"It's all in the bumps," says the professor. "Here's another. Ye'd be a throifle stingy, if ye wasn't so generous. Humanity middlin', pugnacity good. Stop," says he, all of a suddint, "*is* this bump natural or acquired?"

"Is that the one ye got at the faction fight at Banagh?" says Biddy.

"No," says Tim, "for that was behind."

"Thin," says the professor, "ye've the biggest bump av music I iver encountered."

"Ah, luk at that now," says Biddy. "Sure, isn't it wondherful entirely?"

"Why, you're a very Orifice of music," says the professor. "'Twas he that could charrum inanimate things, but 'tis yourself that can make the stones to fly and the sticks to dance," says he, "if ye cultivate your talent," says he.

Well, Tim paid his shilling and kem away, an' "Throth," says he, "I feel the better already," an'

133

A Cup of his Wife's Tears

he began to hould up his head and sthrutted about all as one as a peacock. "Is it me," says he, "Tim Logan, wid the biggest bump of music on airth," says he, "demane myself wid caperin' about?" says he. By-an'-by nothin' 'd plase him, but he must go back to the phrenologist and axe his advoice.

So he an' Biddy went inside, an' says Tim, "Maybe ye could tell me, sor," says Tim, "how I'll become the foinest musician in the world," says he.

"D' ye wish to be famous, thin?" says the professor.

"Faith, I do," says Tim, "an' Biddy wishes it too, don't ye?"

"Ah, sure," says Biddy, "ye're famous enough for me already, an' I like ye fine as ye are."

"Fly away wid you," says he, "but you're not the lass I thought, or ye'd wish me to be at the top av the tree."

"Sure the twigs at the top is not the strongest," says Biddy, "an' maybe I couldn't climb afther yez."

But, says Tim, angered like, "Can ye not tell me of a charrum or a potion," says he to the professor, "that would bring the music out av me, an' make the wide world listen to 't?" says he, "for there's lashins in me," says he, "an' I'll be the biggest man on the airth if ye'll let it out," says he.

"I see," says the professor, lukkin' at Biddy. "Well, there's one potion that's often been taken by thim as has risen high," says he, "an maybe if ye

A Cup of his Wife's Tears

make up yer moind to dhrink it ye'll get there too," says he.

"Thin give me a pint av it," says Tim, "an' I'll take it now."

"That's impossible," says the professor, lukkin' at Biddy, "for I couldn't make it so quickly."

"Thin give me a description," says Tim, "an' I'll get it made up at a druggist's."

"Well, I'll do that," says the professor, "an' to show you that it's boney-fidey," says he, "if ye'll deposit five shillin's wid me, I'll guarantee to return it if the charrum fails; and there it is," says he, writin' something on a piece of paper. "Kape it for a fortnight," says he, "and thin thry it."

Well, Tim put the paper in the linin' av his casthor, an' was mighty particular not to lose it; an' when he got home he sent for Phil Mahoney, the schoolmasther, that had a power of larnin' an' could wish ye the tip av the mornin' in sivin languages; an' Tim showed him the writin'. An' Phil looked at it this way an' that, an' turned it round, an' says he, "I couldn't make yez undherstan' it widout logic an' tracheotomy," says he, "if I was to consthrue it into the vulgar tongue," says he, "for there's too many idiots in it," says he, "but it's rale sthrong Latin an' no mistake, an' if it's by way of a charrum, there's little harm can come to yez if ye kape it."

Well, in a fortnight Tim went down to Ballykelly again, and tuk the paper to the druggist's, and axed him for to make up the potion. An' the gossoon that was behind the counter could make nothin' av

A Cup of his Wife's Tears

it, but showed it to his master, and the master puzzled over it, and fetched down a big book, and says he, laughin', "We don't keep lachrymæ in solution," says he. "D' ye know hwhat's on this paper?" says he.

"Sorra a word," says Tim.

"Thin I'll thranslate it for yez," says he. "It says you're to drink a cup av your wife's tears, and ye may get hwhat ye want," and he gave the paper back to Tim.

Well, Tim was vexed as he walked home, an', thinks he, "It'll be a powerful long time before I get sillybrated at this rate," says he, "for in the natural coorse of things 'twill take Biddy years to cry a cupful," says he, "and that's what I don't like." And he detarmined not to tell Biddy; but when he got home he just sat and said nothin', but kep' lukkin' at her purty face, and wondherin' how in the wide world he was to get a cup of tears from her lovely eyes. For he'd be to have them somehow; and, thinks he, "If I tell her, she'll niver be able to do 't at all, but if I make her cry now," says he, "I can tell her afterwards that 'twas all for the description, an' no harm done." Howiver, he couldn't bring himself to damp her sperrits, let alone make her onhappy, an' so he was glum an' downcast for about a week; an' nath'rally Biddy was throubled too.

An' thin Tim began grumbling at her. "Ye're mighty glum, Biddy," says he; "maybe ye're not happy wid me, that ye keep so quiet," says he. "Maybe ye might have done better wid some other gossoon." An' Biddy said niver a word, though her heart was in her mouth, for she niver heard Tim spake so before, an' she wondhered hwhat had come over him. An' Tim was angry in himself bekase she wouldn't answer him, an' he kep' on every now an' again sayin' something to rouse her, as ye might say, but sorra a thing would Biddy do to carry on as he wanted, but gave him a look from her purty eyes that fairly squelched him.

II

THE HARP ON TARA'S WALLS

SO Tim, seein' it was no good thryin' that away, he cast about in his head for some other plan, and, thinks he, "I've heard av people cryin' wid laughin'," says he, "an' maybe Biddy could do that, and a pleasanter way it'd be." So he tuk down a newspaper in which he had spelt out all the jokes and larnt 'em by rote ; and that avenin' he made himself ter'ble pleasant wid Biddy, an' the likes av him was niver seen, an' mighty plased Biddy was, an' laft at all he said, an' axed him for to tell her "Driscoll's coortin'" wanst agin ; and, "Tim," says she, stoppin' him all of a suddint in the middle av it, "Tim, darlint, I wish ye wuz always like this, an' it's mighty happy I'd be."

"Why, thin," bellows Tim, disengagin' himself, "the mischief's got hould of you, I think, for whin I want ye to laugh ye begin makin' eyes at me, an' whin I want ye to——"

"What, Tim?" says Biddy, skeered like.

A Cup of his Wife's Tears

But Tim wouldn't tell her, bekase he knew that 'd be the wrong way to work.

"Faith," says Tim to himself next day, "I'll be to wallop her, I suppose, though it goes agin me to do 't;" an' he wint an' cut the tindherest stick he could find in the hedge, for he thought it wouldn't be the pain that'd bring the tears out of Biddy's eyes so much as his batin' her at all at all.

An' says Biddy, "That's an illigant stick ye've cut, Tim, but it'll be too light for the pig. Ye're too tinder-hearted, Tim," says she.

"'Tis not for the pig," says Tim, lukkin' at her sideways; but he put off usin' it till nightfall. An' he knew that Paddy Grogan, of Banagh, that bate his wife, did it whin he was drunk, so Tim wint to Murphy's shebeen that night, an' dhrank about a quart of potheen; but whin he kem home, bein' a thrifle heartier nor he intinded, he wint to the wrong ind av the room, an' began wallopin' the cow, till, my jew'l, she let out sideways wid her hind feet an' Tim was lyin' on his back before he knew it.

Well, Biddy nath'rally began to consave that the piece of paper that Tim had got from the professor was the rason of all his quareness, an' one avenin', while he was at the shebeen, she tuk it out av the linin' av his casthor, an' wint up to Father Mulcahy wid it, an' she showed him the paper an' axed him for to tell her hwhat was written on it, "For," says she, "'tis a charm that Tim got at the fair, an' maybe your hanner can tell me if it's a good or a bad one," says she. An' his hanner looked at it an' laffed, an' says he, "'Tis no charrum at all at

138

A Cup of his Wife's Tears

ll," says he, "but just a jingle," says he, "an' can't
do yez good or harm, more betoken there's some
thruth in it; for it says, if Tim would be a great
musician, he must first dhrink a cup av his wife's
tears; which is by way av bein' a figure of speech,
or po'thry, Biddy," says he, "an' manes that ambition
and janius may be the ru'n av domestic happiness;
but sure that can't be so wid you, Biddy," says his
riv'rince, lukkin' straight at her, "for I know well
that Tim is the kindest husband that iver walked,
and would niver bring the tears to your eyes."

"Indade ye may say that," says Biddy, an' she
vint home detarminin' to say nothin'.

An' afther a day or two Tim concaved that maybe
if Biddy thought he was dead it might onloose her
tears, an' that evenin' Biddy heard some whisperin'
outside, an' thin there came a knock, an' in walked
Paddy Grogan.

"Good avenin' to ye, Misther Grogan."

"The crame av the day to yourself, Widdy
Logan," says he, coughin'. An' Biddy turned a
thrifle pale, but she lukked at him again, an' she
lukked at the windy, an' she seen it was a thrick,
an' she said nothin'.

"The crame av the blessed avenin' to yourself,
Widdy Logan," says he, onaisy like.

"Ye've said that before, Misther Grogan," says
she, "an' it's mighty quare that ye call me widdy so
soon," says she.

"Well, I mane it," says he, for he was not one
who minded his words; "an' that's what I kem to
tell ye," says he, "that Tim's kilt!"

A Cup of his Wife's Tears

"Luk at that now," says Biddy, loud an' careless like; "criss of my crass, but that's mighty suddint. An' hwhat kilt him?"

"Sure we had a bit av a scrimmage down there," says Paddy, "an' Tim's head kem against a big stone that was flyin'," says he, getting up, "an' I wouldn't have come, barrin' that Tim axed me to tell ye he was dead."

"Thank ye kindly," says Biddy. "I wish Mrs. Grogan as kind friends," says she, "an' as much convanience in larnin' the news; for I'll not have to sit up to-night, now I know Tim's kilt," says she.

"He's been mighty fond av society lately," says she, "an' sure ye'll be after missing him at the shebeen."

An' Paddy Grogan was fairly conflusthered, an' wint out without a word.

Well, Tim had been listenin' outside, an' the way Biddy tuk the news pretty nigh sobered him, an' he wandhered up an' down like a spirit till about cockcrow, an' thin he wint in, an' there was Biddy sittin' by the ashes, pale an' determined, an' says she, "Good mornin', Tim; is it you or your ghost, for they told me ye were dead?" says she. An' Tim tuk th' opposite chair, an' sat glarin' at her, while she lukked down into her lap, an' said niver a thing. An' there they sat while the broad daylight kem in at the windy. An' whin Biddy began to go about gettin' the breakquest, says Tim, "Sit ye down, Misthress Logan," says he, "for I'll ate no breakquest till I have my supper, onless I tell ye what's on my mind."

A Cup of his Wife's Tears

"An' won't I make ye a cup av tay, Tim?"

"'Tis not a cup av tay I'm afther," says he, "but of something else," says he. "The charrum that I got," says he, "was that I was to dhrink a cup av me wife's tears, and it's thin I'd be the king av music-land. But if ye have no tears for me when I'm dead, Biddy, sorra a tear will ye shed for me alive. It's opposite sides av the road we are now."

"Ye'd a right not to tell me before, Tim," says Biddy, "an' I've kep' something from you," says she, "for I tuk the charrum that was in your hat to Father Mulcahy. An', Tim," says she, sittin' down, "do you raly wish to be the king av musicians?" An' Tim could say nothing. "Thin fetch a cup," says she, sinkin' back, wid tears rowlin' down her pretty cheek, an' before Tim knew where he was he was kneelin' beside her, an'——

'Dade they did, yer hanner. An' that avenin' Tim put the flute up on the wall, an', says he, "Hang there, you insidious implement av mischief!" says he, "all as one as the harp on Tara's wall," says he, "an' sorra a note come out av yez," says he, "an' may the breath av me that enters into you be my last," says he; an' from that day to this Tim has kep' his word.

An' that's his cottage across there, as I was tellin' ye; an' if you're goin' there ye'll find the front door behind, an' Misthress Logan 'll tell ye that the grunt av the gandher, an' the singin' av the kettle, an' the cry of the childer is music enough for her an' Tim.

"LOVE'S OLD SWEET SONG"

I

AN OLD LOVE

"WHÜP, whüp! Whoa-oa-oa! Steady
there, Bess! Steady, mare! Keep
thy legs out well afore thee! Pick thy
way, lass, pick thy way. I'll hold thee up, never
fear! Whüp, whüp! Steady, mare!"

Down the steep hill, through the silence of the
dark night; jolting here, jerking there, over the stony
lane, brushing in the gloom against the overhanging
boughs of great solemn trees; when Ben Mallock's
horse and cart, with Ben in the cross-seat, his legs
planted stiff and straight before him, as he pursed his
lips together and gripped at the reins with all his
might and main. The fierce mountain torrents,
swollen by the sweeping rains, had cut miniature
gullies and cañons in the rough road, and into these
the wheels of the homely cart jolted and bumped
ever and anon with a rattle and a whirr, causing Ben
suddenly to lurch from one side to the other.

"Whoa, mare! Steady, mare! Supper's afore
thee!" said Ben, as he held up her head.

In the very heart of the darkness, far up the hillside, a lonely light gleamed and twinkled.

"There be Jim Biddle's cottage," said Ben.

" Love's Old Sweet Song "

" Jim's candle-light ha' shone from among them there trees these fifteen years, rain an' shine. Well, well, how the time keeps a-going! It don't seem so many months since Jim came here. I minds it well, 'cos it was the same year as I put up my new chimbley in the kitchen. Fifteen years come next barley-mowin', that's the exac' time. Come up, mare, come up! You be gettin' as lazy a'most as old Trot! That there dog is about the cutest animal I ever knew. I s'pose all things gets cuter as they grows older. Now there's that Trot. It'd take a woman to be up to all his tricks and dodges. A man couldn't do it. You sends him off after the sheep, an' he rushes away barkin' fit to shake the mountain, an' as soon as he gets out o' your sight he sneaks through the hedge, an' lies down an' goes off to sleep. He's a reg'lar old sinner, an' thee be a'most as bad, Bess! But never mind, old gel! Thee an' me an' the dog, we be good friends, we be. We've lived together many a long year, an' we've never had a fall-out yet. Together we've bin, an' together we'll stay as long as it's God's will."

Ben, like most people who lead solitary lives, had fallen into the habit of soliloquising aloud. When his day's work was done, and he was jogging along homewards in his shaky old cart, he would indulge in long, low-toned monologues, now addressing his words to Bess, now to the dog, and now to himself.

So up the rough lane, until they came to the small gateway which led to Ben's farmhouse. The little thatched-roof building consisted of only one

"Love's Old Sweet Song"

story. On each side the door was a small window, and at the pine-end, under the creaking rain-pipe, stood a huge water-butt, almost as high as the house itself. All around ran a fringe of poplar-trees, under whose shadow, at the rear of the house, stood the paddock and stable.

Ben—having given Bess her feed of oats, patted her "Good-night," and padlocked the door, all by the light of a guttering candle—went round to the front of the house, and fumbled in the lock with a big key, to the tune of furious barking round the corner.

"Ay, ay, bark away, old rascal!" said he. "Thy bark is the biggest part o' thee. I'll wager, now, that the'st been sleeping thy head off up to this very minute. An' now thee wants to make me believe as the'st the savagest house dog in the valley. Get along with thee! I knows thee!"

The dog had fallen to bounding and yelping with delight, and Ben, before he opened the door, went round and set him free.

"Come along in, then," said he. "Thee and me's good company. Thee shall lie by the fire, and sleep to thy heart's content. Down, down, thee old rascal! Thee can't persuade me as thee's not bin sleeping!"

To light the fire in the huge, thick-barred grate, to cook the meal of bacon and potatoes in the frying-pan, and to sit before the simple fare at the small deal table, was but the work of a few minutes.

Ben had lived alone ever since his mother had

died, fourteen years ago, and had grown dexterous
in the performance of household duties. The fire
leapt and danced as he ate, casting strange gleams
and flashes upon the plates on the dresser, upon the
quaint old warming-pan which hung from the rafters,
upon the face of the old eight-day clock that ticked
slowly in the corner, and upon the small looking-
glass before which Ben every day brushed his gray
hair. At his side sat the dog, waiting patiently
for his share ; but Ben did not pay as much
attention to him as usual.

Ben was pre-occupied to-night. Mechanically,
and with an absent look on his face, he set the
dog his portion, brewed himself some tea, " cleared
the things away," and sat in the old oaken chair by
the fireside, slowly filling his pipe and sipping from
the cup at his elbow. The wind now and again
murmured outside amongst the poplars. The dog
stretched himself upon the hearth at Ben's feet,
and blinked at him with lazy affection.

But Ben heeded not. As he smoked his long
pipe, and looked into the glowing flames, he was
far away in a time eighteen years agone. Vague
memories, surely, must be those of eighteen years ;
dim and shadowy, and dulled of pain or pleasure
by the touch of time. Not to Ben. There are
some hearts as steady and close-locked as the heart
of the old oak-tree. It is the old things, the old
loves, the old friends, the old sorrows that live in
them. Ben's heart had fed itself for eighteen years
on a memory.

" Strange as I should think on it so much,

"Love's Old Sweet Song"

Trot! I thought on it last night, and night before, and night before that. Mos'ly I try not to think on it more 'n once a week—and that on Sunday night. It was on a Sunday night when I see'd her last, Trot. Eighteen years come a fortnight next Sunday. Bless me, but the time do slip by! I was only twenty-six then; and here I be at forty-four, a'most in the turn of a grindstone like. How well I remembers that there Sunday night! Well, well, what's the use of goin' over that again? There's no doubt as she gived me the go-by, and that's an end of it. But I don' bear her no ill-will for that. Very likely when she got to Lunnon she had a chance of marryin' men as could do much better for her in life than I could ever do. But I felt for a few years, Trot, as if there was no good in goin' on a-livin' in that weary, lonesome way— jes' workin' an' eatin' and sleepin', and then a-doin' it all over again—but I've got over that a bit now. All the same, somehow I could never take to any other woman, an' so here I be. It might ha' bin very different if she—but there's no good in vexin' about that. I sometimes thinks as we be wicked, darin' creatures, a fumin' an' frettin' and fightin' agen the will of the Almighty as we do. I wonder where she is, an' what she's a-doin'! I wonder is she married, an' 'as she got a good husband? I hope she have. I should be sorry to think as she'd got a bad man—a neat, smart, happy-minded gel like she was. Well, well, it's no good a-sittin' here all night. I mus' go out an' cut the chaff, an' then come in to wash up the things. Come along, Trot,

146

and give a look round—come on, you lazy rascal,
an' keep old Ben company. You an' Bess is the
faithfullest friends I've ever found, and we under-
stands each other all round, don't we, Trot? Come
along; it's no use for us two to be dozin' an'
dreamin' like this."

II

A DAGGER IN HIS HEART

BEN had been up early, and, after lighting the
fire and setting the kettle to boil, had gone out
to see to the wants of the little farmstead. The
mare stamped and neighed and rung her chain in
the stall, as she heard his footsteps.

"Oh, thee's glad to see me this mornin', is
thee?" he said, as he threw open the stable door.
"Thee knows it's Sunday mornin' as well as any
one, thee does! Thee knows as it's extra allowance
an' no work for thee! Come on, then; thee shall
have a good breakfast for thy welcome."

And as the mare rubbed her nose against his
shoulder he filled the manger with sweet hay from
the rough hurdle-basket above. Then he went over
to the fowls and ducks, who clustered and flapped
furiously around him as he threw to them their
Indian corn. He talked to them, also, in his quaint
affectionate style.

"Oh yes, thee's very fond of me, thee is, when
I brings along thy breakfast. That's what we calls
cupboard love, that is!"

"Love's Old Sweet Song"

The kettle was singing merrily as, with Trot at his heels, Ben entered the kitchen to prepare his own breakfast. How well they understood each other, these two! Trot sat patiently on the hearth, with expectant ears, as he saw the white table-cloth laid, and heard the musical rattle of the tea-things. He knew that his own liberal share was soon to be placed on the hearth,'as it had been placed every Sunday morning, year in year out. Surely there was never such a methodical man as Ben Mallock! Everything in its place, and a place for everything. Everything in the same order, even to the putting of the milk and sugar in the cup and the cutting of the bread and butter, while the teapot stood on the hob "to draw."

It was a warm morning, and the sun sent down a blaze of light upon the kitchen window as Ben sat at his breakfast. The robins sang lustily in the trees, and sparrows flitted about the eaves.

"Now then, Trot," said Ben, after he had washed the tea-things. "Let's have our usual sit-down on the wall. An' then I'll go to chapel, an' thee'll make believe to look after the house, an' go to sleep direc'ly my back is turned. Oh, I knows thee! Come along."

And putting on his soft felt hat with the wide brim, he opened the door, and sat on the low wall that ran in front of the house. The tall poplar-trees skirted it at regular intervals of six or seven feet. Ben rested his back against one of them, and fell to musing. Trot sprang up at his side and lay lazily in the sunshine, looking at his master with

"Love's Old Sweet Song"

half-open eyes. Thus they sat for half an hour in complete silence.

Ben suddenly broke into speech. It was his habit, now and then, after musing some time in silence, to continue the soliloquy aloud. "Ah, well," said he, "this here life of ours is a funny thing! It appears to me that it's just like this 'ere. The first part of it we're doin' nothin' but rammin' our head agen a stone wall—a chafin' an' a-frettin' for this an' that, an' never satisfied when we gets it. A few years later we are glad enough to sit contented and peaceful on the very stone wall agen which we rammed our heads. Every man has got to learn for himself. That's just where it is. It takes a long time for the sores and smarts to heal up, but, thank God! they do heal up at last, an' a man can go on his way quiet and restful. Well, Trot, it's time for me to get ready!"

In his high-crowned Sunday hat of hard felt; in his well-brushed suit of black, in his stand-up collar and his dark-blue tie with the old-fashioned pin in it, Ben was half an hour later trudging along through the beech-wood on his way to the chapel. A walk of twenty minutes brought him out upon the mountain top. Before him was the small weather-beaten sanctuary that had stood there for a century, surrounded by its grass-grown grave-yard, and beaten upon by every wind that blew. The congregation were coming in twos and threes from every direction, farmers, humble cottagers, mountaineers, and woodmen, and shepherds, most of them with their wives and children, and all dressed neatly and quietly, as befitted the day.

Ben, after his usual chat with sundry people who were standing around the wicket-gate, went straight to the square, high-backed pew in which he had sat since boyhood. He never once turned round during the homely service, and thus he did not see what every one else had mentally noted. There was a stranger amongst the congregation. It was an occurrence rare and eventful, and every one looked and wondered. Even the minister could not help speculating, as he peered over his glasses.

This unexpected member of the congregation sat in John Martin's pew, and John Martin's wife drew herself up with an air of gratified pride, as she saw furtive glances shooting in her direction from every portion of the building. It was not every day that Mrs. Martin had the opportunity of showing off as her guest a lady friend in a " Lunnon-made " dress and bonnet.

Meanwhile, under her veil the eyes of Mrs. Martin's guest were wet with tears. What memories, glad and sad, set a-ringing little bells of recollection, as the old scenes and the old days were brought back to her afresh by this visit to the mountain chapel! How altered were all the well-remembered friends, and yet how much the same! How many years older in face, and yet as steady-going and faithful and regular in their lives as they had ever been! It seemed to her that this return from the roar and turmoil of the fierce world to the rest and quiet of the old home laid a sweet peace upon her heart that somehow had its pain as well as its pleasure, and caused the tears to well upwards and blind her. After eighteen years! How cruel and selfish had she found the world! How cordial and kindly had been the welcome of the old friends, out of whose lives she had passed for eighteen years! And in a day or two she must return once more to the toil and moil and struggle of the selfish Babylon!

Thus she mused with swimming eyes, as the simple service drew to a close, and it was with a start that she realised the announcement of the closing hymn.

"Don't you remember Mary Howard?" Mrs. Martin said with proud excitement to half a dozen people at once, as they stood a few minutes later in the porch. "Why, bless me, you can't have forgotten Mary of the Mountain View Farm! That's right, I knew you'd remember her! Here, Mrs. Thomas, now who do you think this is? Here, Ben Mallock, now I wonder can you bear in mind an old friend?"

She stopped, for Ben's face was white, and his lips trembled, as he put out an unsteady hand towards Mary Howard. She too was pale, as she looked into his face.

"Well, Mary!"

"Well, Ben!"

There was silence for a moment, as they confronted each other. Then he said—

"It's many a long year since you paid us a visit, Mary."

They were simple words, and they came from a

simple heart, which had not a shadow of vindictive-
ness in the whole of its nature. But somehow,
to her, there was an implied reproach in the mild
tones, which caused her to colour slightly as she
replied—

"Yes, eighteen years is a long time, Ben, but not
long enough to make one forget old friends."

Then the minister came, and Ben passed on.
His lips were still trembling as he walked rapidly,
almost fiercely, down the mountain-road, hardly
knowing where he was or what he was doing. His
brain was in a whirl, and his heart seemed to be
bursting. The old sore had been torn open, and was
bleeding afresh with an aching indescribable. We
all know how a strong man can suffer, when forced to
look once more into the grave of a buried trouble.
All the wild agony comes back, all the unutterable
poignancy of grief, as keenly as though it were but
yesterday that it all happened. Ben had suddenly,
after many years, looked upon the face of the woman
he had loved. So long had his faithful heart been
locked with bolt and bar upon the old love and the
old pain, and now, in one moment, it had burst its
barriers with a passion uncontrollable. Oh, why
had she come here to stab him as with daggers—she
who eighteen years ago had thrown a blank desolation
over his whole life !

All unwittingly he had turned off the path, and
he came to himself, to find that he was striding
aimlessly among the thick undergrowth, four miles
distant from his little farmstead. He came to a
standstill, and wiped great beads of perspiration

"DON'T YOU REMEMBER MARY HOWARD?"

from his forehead. The fit of agony was over. He smiled to himself with a pathetic little gesture of shame, as he realised that he ought at that moment to be sitting at his dinner, with Trot at his side.

"Come, come, Ben Mallock!" he said. "This is fine goings-on for a man o' thy age! After talking so brave about it, too, all these years! Thee's no better than a child!"

And so he turned and walked quietly home, and bravely set himself to eat his simple dinner, and read the volume of old sermons in the afternoon, just as it had been his wont to do on other Sundays. It was at best a hopeless and weary attempt. Strive as he would, the day refused to be as other Sundays had been. He could not read; he dared not think. He went out instead, and wandered disconsolately round the house, while the poplars sang and crooned to themselves in the freshening wind. Now he would come to a standstill, and look sadly down the valley. Then suddenly he would pull himself up with: "Now then, Ben Mallock, now then! Thee's going at it afresh!" And then he would start walking again.

What pathos there was in those forlorn little attempts at humour, in that never-ceasing walk round the house, in that little soliloquy of his when at last he went indoors, and sat in his armchair before the fire!

"One thing's certain," he said. "Trot, old boy, one thing's pretty certain. Thee an' me's got to get over it somehow—thee an' me an' Bess. It's no good for us to vex. If she went away an' left us

"Love's Old Sweet Song"

—then she went away an' left us, that's all. I don't blame her for that. She ain't married, Trot, an' yet she's bin away all these years! It's all as plain an' simple as the day, an' what's the use o' frettin' about it? The day after to-morrow she'll be gone agen. I heerd Mrs. Martin a-saying it. What's the use o' us frettin', then, jes' 'cos she remembered to come here once agen after bein' so long away? We ought to be pleased at that, instead of vexin' about it like this 'ere. Anyhow, we'll keep out of the way till she goes away agen—thee an' me, Trot. What's the use o' showin' ourselves, an' a-forcing ourselves on her sight! I s'pose she'd a-hardly remembered me, if Mrs. Martin hadn' a-called my name out. Yes, it's the best thing we can do, Trot, is to keep out o' the way. I hope she's got a good home, anyways. Well, the best thing thee and me can do is to go an' give Bess and the others somethin' to eat, and then make ourselves some tea. Come along, old boy!"

III

SOME ONE'S A-WAITIN' FOR ME

BEN was up betimes, and before seven o'clock had struck he was plodding with horse and cart up one of the small lanes that lay hidden amongst the foliage on the other side of the valley. He was pledged for this Monday morning to commence a small carting contract for a farmer in the lowlands over to the west.

When he commenced his homeward way along

154

" Love's Old Sweet Song "

one of the silent by-roads it was already nightfall.
Ben sat in the cart with head bent forward, lost to
all around him, and Bess jogged on at her own
pleasure. Her master did not even speak to her
to-night. He sat, instead, ever lost in thought.
Occasionally he would lift his face towards the dim
gleam of the moon, and thus meditate. Anon he
would lean forward again in a fit of abstraction. So
was his mood all the evening. He did not even
speak to Trot, save to give him a friendly greeting
as he passed through the gate of the paddock. He
sat for an hour before the fire, forgetting even to
light his pipe; then he fell to walking to and fro
across the floor of the kitchen; then he sat down
again before the fire, and shaded his eyes with his
hand; and all through the long night watches he
tossed and turned and breathed uneasily in his little
inner room.

Tuesday morning set in dull and cloudy. It was
dreary, and Ben looked drearier still, as he stood at
the window.

"She's gone this mornin'," he said aloud. " I
expec' Farmer Martin drove her over to the station.
I hope she won't have rain, anyway, till she gets safe
on the Lunnon line. It don't matter then so much.
I s'pose there's plenty o' shelter as one can run to in
a big place like Lunnon. Well, Trot, old boy, it's no
good for you or me to think on it any more.

Nevertheless, he pushed his plate from him as he
sat at breakfast. "I can't understand this," he said,
wearily. "It's jes' as bad as it was eighteen years
ago. I'm worse nor a child, if I have n' got no more

155

" Love's Old Sweet Song "

strength of mind than this 'ere. What's the good
of worryin' about it? She's gone, and there's an
end to it!"

But if there was a lonely heart in the wide
world on this dull September morning, that heart
was Ben's.

Slowly he donned his rough work-a-day hat and
jacket, and slowly he harnessed Bess for the five
miles' journey across the mountain. The landscape
had looked gloomy enough in his own little valley.
It was more desolate still in the lowlands, where his
work lay. The mist had crept over them, and was
shrouding them in sullen melancholy. A drizzling
rain had commenced to fall, and the steady drip,
drip, of the trees and hedges fell with monotonous
regularity, as Ben filled his cart at each journey.
The afternoon was closing in rapidly towards twilight,
and Ben was on his "last trip" when—oh wonder of
wonders!—as he turned to secure the tailboard of the
cart, he saw Mary standing in the roadside near the
horse's head. He staggered, and caught hold of
the wheel as she came towards him.

"Well, Ben!" she said, holding out her hand.

There was a dead silence, while Ben, his head
in a whirl, stood staring at her with one hand on
the wheel, and the other pressed helplessly to his
forehead.

"You didn't expect to see me, Ben," she said,
coming nearer.

Ben hardly heard what she said. He only knew
that her face was looking kindly and earnestly into
his. It was the same face as of yore—pleasant

156

comely, tender, with sincere grey eyes, and sweet brown hair curling about the small ears. But how could it be Mary? Surely he was dreaming. Mary had gone away that morning!

"You didn't expect to see me, Ben," she said again. "You see, I have been staying here since last evening, and am going back to London to-morrow morning. I have watched you passing to and fro all day. I was obliged to come out at last, Ben. I thought I should like to say good-bye to you."

Ben was only just beginning to collect his senses.

"You—you've—been—here all day, lass!" he stammered.

"Yes, the Martins drove me over last night. But little did I think I should see you here, Ben. I have been wanting ever since the morning to come out to you, but I didn't know whether—whether—well, never mind that!"

There was another silence, broken only by the drip, drip from the boughs, and the voice of some one in the farmyard. Ben was still hopelessly dumb. Mary was looking on the ground, and a rush of colour had suffused her face. Ben's silence stung her like so many needle-points. Did he think she had come out to—to—

"Are you keeping well, Ben?" she asked, constrainedly.

"Ay, lass, well, thank God!" said Ben.

Again she looked down, and again she blushed hotly.

"It's many a year, Ben, since we've seen each other," she said at last.

"Love's Old Sweet Song"

"Ay, ay, many a year—a'most a lifetime," replied Ben, in an unsteady voice.

"Many changes have taken place since then," she went on.

"Ay, ay," answered Ben, "many changes."

Yet again there was a silence; for Ben's tongue clove to the roof of his mouth.

"Ben," she said, with a sudden effort, as she looked into his face. "Ben, tell me, what do you think of me? I didn't treat you well, I know; but I was young and foolish in those days. Ben, don't judge the Mary of to-day by the Mary of eighteen years ago! I have found what the world is since then, and have learned how to set the proper value on old friends. Don't let me go back to London to-morrow feeling that my oldest friend of all has not forgiven me!"

"Lass, lass, there's nowt I wouldn't forgive thee," said Ben.

"We were both young," she went on, hurriedly, "and we were both proud. I was a bit flippant in my ways—and you—you were always serious-minded, Ben. I knew you were right—I knew it as well as I could know anything—but my false pride would not permit me to acknowledge it until at last I wrote you that letter. And when you let it pass without even a reply, it did sting me—oh, Ben, it did sting me, to think I had humbled myself, only to be——"

"Letter!" exclaimed Ben; and again he caught hold of the wheel in a dazed way. "Letter! What letter? I received no letter from thee, lass!"

" Love's Old Sweet Song "

"You received — no — letter — from — me !" she echoed, putting her hand quickly on his arm. "Why, Ben, I wrote to you six months after I went away —and I never got the letter returned either. You must allow a woman to have a little pride, Ben. I waited for six months, hoping and yearning to hear from you. I wrote to your mother, in order that you might know my address. I couldn't do more than that, until, at last, my love for you broke all bounds, and I wrote to you direct. It was not a maidenly thing to do, but I couldn't help it. And when I received no reply, I was so stung that I took the chance of going away with the family to Italy ; and there I've been for seventeen years."

There was a long silence. They stood looking at each other, silent and awe-stricken, as the terrible truth was slowly borne in upon them.

"God forgive her !" said Ben at length, solemnly lifting his hat. "It was my poor mother as did it. She was allus jealous like in her ways, and set agen every girl as she thought might take her place. Lass, lass, this has bin a cruel thing for both of us !"

*　　　*　　　*　　　*　　　*

"Whoa, mare, whoa—oa—oa ! Steady there, mare ! Plant thy legs out well afore thee, and pick thy way ! Steady, lass, over the stones ! Supper's a-waitin' thee, lass ; an' some one's a-waitin' for me, with a bright fire a-burnin,' and a word of lovin' welcome ready ! Oh, think on it ! *some one's a-waitin' for me !* Eh, lass, but God is good—oh, God is good !"

159

THE PATIENT'S SECRET

I

A DOCTOR WHO LOVED THE POOR

GEORGE EASTON was a doctor, resident in London. He was a good man, and was possessed of considerable medical skill; yet Fortune had not smiled upon him, and his practice lay for the most part amongst the very poor, or those in rank just above them, so that his gains were small, in proportion to the time and care he lavished upon his practice, and it often seemed to him as though he should live and die a poor man.

His career as a young man had been rather brilliant, for he possessed considerable talent, and had taken many of the prizes and medals awarded to merit during his course of study. His friends had prophesied a brilliant career for him, but these dreams had never been realised. He had no fortune. He had not been able to take a fine house, or set up his carriage, or do any of those things by which men make a show at starting, and gain notoriety and observation. Moreover George had a very kind heart, and he had resolved from the very first that he would devote at least a part of his time to relieving the sad condition of the very poor, whose pitiful case often went to his heart.

The Patient's Secret

Altogether he was a contented man, in spite of his obscurity and poverty. He had abundance of work, he was intensely beloved and respected by hundreds in the city. At the end of four or five years' toil, he had married—not too prudently, perhaps, but very happily—a wife who was as brave to bear poverty as he was himself, and who loved him with all her heart and soul. They had one little son of five summers, and were as happy as heart could wish, the only cloud in their sky being the occasional difficulty there was in making ends meet.

The doctor sometimes made some very remarkable cures, but always amongst such obscure persons that nothing was ever known of them to the world at large.

"If only these people were rich, you would be famous and rich in a very short time," his wife would sometimes say, between smiles and tears. "And other men not half so talented thrive and grow fat before our very eyes."

"I have no wish to grow fat, my love," George would answer, "and I beg to state that my talents are known to a very great number of people."

"Yes, but only to the poor, who can hardly pay you even for the medicines you bring."

"Well, I call those the right kind of patients, very decidedly. Rich people have no difficulty in getting all they need, and they have plenty of choice of good physicians. We must be thankful, Anna, for the privilege of serving the poor."

"You are a saint, George," answered his wife,

The Patient's Secret

kissing him. "You make me ashamed. I cannot argue with you. But I think that God will one day bless you and reward you."

"He has blessed me already in more ways than I can count," answered the doctor, reverently, "and I think He rewarded me far above my merits upon the day when He gave me my brave little wife. I have received nothing but good from His hand all my life long; and if He thinks it well to withhold from me that worldly prosperity which is the portion of some—why, I can well dispense with it. A man's life does not depend on the abundance of goods that he possesses."

*　　*　　*　　*　　*

One cold winter's night the doctor and his wife were awakened by the sharp ringing of the night-bell. George got up, put on a few clothes, and then opened the window to ask what was wanted.

There was a short parley, and then he returned to the bedroom, and began dressing himself quickly.

"Oh dear!" said Anna, regretfully, "you are never going out this cold night?"

"I must, my dear. I am sent for."

"Who has sent for you?" asked his wife, who knew that he had gone very tired to bed only a few hours ago, and resented this untimely call.

"I do not know. Some new patient."

Anna roused up at that, and spoke in a different tone.

"A new patient, George? What sort is it? Is it one who will be any good to you?"

The Patient's Secret

"The point just now is, whether I shall be any good to him," answered the doctor. "I'm afraid he will not be the sort of patient you are always hoping to see at my doors, my dear. This man lives right away in the East End," and the doctor named a street in a very poor locality. "None but the very poor ever live out there, I think."

At this Anna roused up, and spoke impetuously.

"George, don't go. It is absurd for you to travel such a distance after a man who will probably not even be able to pay the cost of the cab—let alone any fee. Tell the messenger to go for somebody nearer. It is unreasonable to send out to this quarter. There must be many doctors much nearer. Don't go, George."

But the doctor was dressing himself all the while.

"My love, I must go. I did ask the messenger—who has now gone away—why it was he had come such a distance, and he said that the patient had particularly desired to see me."

"Oh yes, I can well understand that. The poor of the city know fast enough that in getting you they get the best professional opinion in all London—and get it practically for nothing! It is easy for them to make a point of sending for you; but if you make a practice of going all over the city at all hours of the day and night after every summons like this one—well, you will just wear yourself out before you are forty, and the world will not even know what it has lost!"

The Patient's Secret

" Come, come, little wife," said George, going up
and laying his hand on his wife's head, "don't make
a mountain out of a molehill. I am very seldom
sent for at night, and this is the first summons I have
ever had from such a distant quarter. I do not feel
justified in ignoring it. You know that I hold the
medical profession to be bound as sacredly by
unspoken vows as are ministers of the Gospel. If
a sick or dying person sent to one of these in his
hour of need, and he refused to come, we should
hold that he had disgraced and denied his office ;
and in the same way I hold that I should be unworthy
of mine, were I to refuse to answer such a call as the
one just received. You would not like me to be
unfaithful to my calling, Anna ? "

She held up her face for his kiss, her momentary
indignation soothed by his words and tone.

" I am not worthy to be your wife ! " she said,
humbly. "But you know it is because I love you so
much that I cannot bear to see you wear yourself out."

" I know it is, my love ; but I am a tough subject,
and in this case I shall not wear myself out, for the
distance is so great that I must take a cab. In
cases of urgency half the battle is getting there in
time."

" Yes, do not walk—and take the warm rug to
wrap yourself in," said Anna, solicitously ; and as
her husband left her she could not but heave a little
sigh. It was rather hard for the doctor to have to
spend his money on cab-fares as well as giving time
and medicine, and probably only the most meagre of
fees at the end—if any.

The Patient's Secret

George Easton strode out into the street, and his whistle brought up a cab, and soon he drove off.

"I will walk home," he thought, "after my errand is accomplished. But I must get there as fast as I can, lest the case be urgent."

The doctor's heart always yearned over the poor, wherever they were, and not even in his thoughts did he reproach the sick man who had sent for him all that distance.

"I may know him, after all. It may be an old patient of mine removed here," he thought, as the cab drove up to the door of a tall, narrow house, silent now, though probably swarming with life by day. He had ascertained from the messenger that the man he wanted lived at the top of the house, and the dark stairway was lighted here and there by the shafts of frosty moonlight that shone in, as well as by the faint but increasing light of a lamp that was burning upon the top landing of all.

"My patient has some consideration for my neck, at any rate," said the doctor to himself, and he knocked at the door by which the lamp hung suspended. He observed, also, that it was clean and well trimmed. "Perhaps he has a thrifty wife," was his mental comment.

"Come in," said a weak voice.

"I have come to visit Mr. Peterson," said the doctor, opening the door a little way. "Is this the right place?"

"I am John Peterson," answered the voice, and George entered without further parley.

The Patient's Secret

He found himself in a fair-sized room that was scrupulously clean, and well lighted from a lamp, the counterpart of the one that hung outside. Everything in the room was very plain, but beautifully clean, and though it was plainly the abode of poverty, there was no sign of sordid want. It was decidedly a better place than the doctor had anticipated, although it contained hardly anything but the bare necessaries of life.

Upon a bed in the corner lay a grey-haired man who looked about sixty years of age. He had the flush of fever on his cheeks, and his breath came in a laboured way.

However, there was a fire in the room, and the doctor was able, by means of the remedies he had brought with him and the hot water he was able to obtain, to relieve the patient greatly, so that he was soon able to speak without trouble, and give a little account of the attack of illness which had prostrated him.

He had no wife, he said, but there was in the house a woman who looked after his room and attended upon him a little. Any direction of a simple kind laid down by the doctor she would be able to carry out, and George told him what to do for the best, and prepared to take his leave.

"Are you pressed for time, sir?" asked the sick man, watching him with the intense gaze often seen in the eyes of the sick.

Easton looked at him, hesitated a moment, and then said gently, "Not especially so, my friend. I have no other case to attend."

The Patient's Secret

"Then will you sit down for a while and talk to me?" said the patient. "The nights are long and weary, and I have a fancy for a chat with you."

George seated himself beside the bed. It was no great act of self-denial to give up half an hour to beguile the tedium of the night for this poor man. The room was warm and comfortable enough, and there was something attractive in the aspect of the patient.

To his surprise, the man began to talk of books. There was a shrewdness and originality about his observations which showed an acumen and quickness of apprehension remarkable indeed in one of his class. George was beguiled into a long talk, and when he rose he found he had been about an hour in that room.

"Thank you, doctor, you have done me good," said his patient. "I am a wonderful deal easier than I was. You'll leave me some of that medicine, won't you? And you'll come again and see me to-morrow? To-day, I mean, for it's past midnight now, I take it."

The doctor had a busy day before him, and had had an almost sleepless night. It was a long way to come out again, and the case, though a genuine one of congestion, was not critical in its nature. But there was a look upon the man's face which he could not resist, and he answered kindly and readily:

"I will come again in the evening, but it may be rather late. I am a busy man, you know."

The Patient's Secret

" I do know it, doctor. I have heard about you," answered the sick man ; and then, seeing him about to depart, he drew an envelope from beneath his pillow, and held it out to him.

Dr. Easton was never fond of taking fees from the poor, but he recognised the fact that those who were able to pay for medical attendance ought to do so ; and this man, although poor, was probably in a position to pay a trifle for doctoring. So he took the envelope with a smile and a brief word of thanks, and, stuffing it into his pocket as he went down the dark staircase, speedily forgot all about it.

II

A RECORD FEE FOR THE DOCTOR

ANNA was asleep when he got home, and he himself slept soundly until morning. As they sat at breakfast, she asked him of his last night's visit, and shook her head, when hearing that he had walked all the way back.

" And talked an hour with the tiresome old man as well ! " she said, shaking her head at him with a smile ; " as though you had so much time to spare ! and never so much as a ghost of a fee—or the chance of one either, I'll be bound ! "

The doctor smiled, and, putting his hand into his pocket drew out an envelope, which he tossed over to his wife.

" You are wrong about the fee for once, my
168

dear; open that, and see what your husband has earned!"

"Well, at least it is clean!" said Anna, taking it up gingerly and opening it. The next moment she uttered a little startled cry.

"George! You never got it from that old man?"

He rose and came towards her, looking over her shoulder.

"Halloa!" he cried. "What can that mean?"

For the value of the note lying on his wife's lap was five pounds! Never in all his life before had Dr. Easton received such a fee.

"I can't understand it," he said; "I don't *think* it can be a mistake exactly. Poor people do not make mistakes of that sort. However, I am going again this evening, and perhaps I shall learn more. The man, though apparently poor, is not in want. It may be that he has saved up against a rainy day, and chose to give the fee at the outset, to cover the expenses of several visits, and medicine, and so forth. I confess I am puzzled. But I shall understand it all some day, I suppose. You won't resent my being called out at night another time, eh, little wife?"

"I'll try to be as good a wife as you deserve to have!" cried Anna, jumping up and kissing him; and that day was a happy one in the doctor's house, for this unexpected windfall came to them as a real blessing.

That evening Dr. Easton climbed the long staircase again, and found himself in the presence of John Peterson. The patient greeted him with a smile of

The Patient's Secret

pleasure. He was better, he said, but still ill enough to require care and medical skill. The doctor found that his directions had been intelligently carried out, but the cold was trying to the patient, and he set about devising two or three small means, whereby the draughts could be kept out and the room rendered more healthy. The sick man declared himself better already, and again asked the doctor to sit down and have a chat, as on the previous night.

When at length George rose to go, his patient again drew forth an envelope from beneath his pillow and held it out to him ; but this time the doctor withheld his hand.

"No, no," he said, quickly ; "the fee you gave me last time was sufficient to cover the expenses of your whole illness, which I am hopeful will not be a long one. I cannot take more."

But the patient still held out the envelope.

"But you must take it," he said, with quiet insistence. "I know the value of time and service as well as any man in the city. You will be doing a favour to me. You must not refuse."

There was something so earnest and pleading in the man's manner, something so quietly compelling in his glance, that the doctor felt it impossible to refuse him.

"In that case," he said, "I will gratefully accept. But you perplex me very much."

A smile lighted the face of the patient.

"I have perplexed a good many people before you," he said. "You will come again to-morrow, doctor ?"

The Patient's Secret

"Certainly," answered Dr. Easton, readily, and took his leave. When he got home he threw the envelope into his wife's lap. Again it contained money to the value of five pounds.

"George, what does it mean?"

"I know no more than you. The man lives in one room in a swarming house in the poorest quarter of the city. But he is one of the most well-informed persons I have ever met. I cannot understand it. But perhaps I may do so in time. I am to go again to-morrow. He is ill, and in need of medical attendance; but it is not a dangerous case. He will make a good recovery, I am sure."

For a whole week Dr. Easton continued his daily visits to his perplexing patient. On each occasion he was asked to sit and talk for an hour with the man before taking his leave. On each occasion the inevitable envelope was pressed upon him (his remonstrances being quietly but resolutely set aside); which contained the same amount as on the first occasion. After that first week he ceased his daily attendance, but went twice a week, always receiving the same handsome fee; and when his patient had really become convalescent he told him, with a smile, that he must now discontinue his visits—there was nothing more to come for.

"I don't think I agree with you, doctor," said John Peterson. "I am no longer sick; thanks to your kind care and skill, I am a sound man again. But I don't want to lose sight of you. I have not many friends, and friendship is pleasant. Will you let me ask a favour of you?"

The Patient's Secret

"Most certainly. I think you must know how deep a debt I owe you, and how gladly I should serve you if I could."

"Oh, that is nothing—a mere just debt of humanity that it is my fancy to seek to discharge in part," was the enigmatic answer; "but what I want to ask of you is, that you will pay me a visit once a week regularly. I have enjoyed the talks we have had together. I do not want to forego them."

"That I shall be most happy to do," answered George, heartily; "I, too, have had pleasure and profit from our intercourse. I should like to think that it would not cease."

"And he did not tell you anything more about himself?" asked Anna, as her husband recounted this interview.

"No, nothing; and, unless he speaks of his own accord, I can ask no questions. There is something very interesting to me in the man. He is not polished, he is not what would be termed a gentleman, and yet he is exceedingly well-informed, and has a noble mind and intellect; I confess a great curiosity as to his history. Perhaps some day he will unfold it."

"His illness has been a little fortune to us," said Anna, brightly. "I feel quite like a woman of substance—not a debt in the world, money in the bank, and all that we have long needed about the house bought and paid for. If we were to go on being so prosperous for a time, we should get rich patients coming to us. Nothing succeeds like success, you know."

The weekly visits to Mr. Peterson became a

The Patient's Secret

regular institution. But great was the doctor's astonishment when he found that this eccentric man insisted upon his taking every time the same fee as he had given him for medical attendance during his illness.

At first Easton revolted against this.

"You do me a kindness to take it," was his friend's rejoinder. "I am using no figure of speech. I tell you it is simple truth that you do me a personal kindness—a friendly favour—by accepting it. Then look at it another way. You give me several hours of your time weekly, and grudge neither that nor the fatigue of coming this long distance. To a professional man time is money——"

"Not always. I spend a good deal of time daily that brings me no return——"

"The greater the reason that some return should be made when it is possible. Humour me in this, my good friend. You will do me a true kindness if you will."

Then the doctor submitted, wondering greatly what it could all mean, and thanking God in his heart for this most strange thing that had come to him.

His wife had been right in what she said. Prosperity is a wonderful factor in life. Dr. Easton continued to live in a quiet way, but his home now wore an air of quiet prosperity which seemed the guarantee of professional success. He drove where once he had walked. He was able to buy presents for his wife and little boy. People observed the change, and said to themselves that Dr. Easton must be a clever man, to be getting on so fast. Rumours of his past successes were whispered about. He began to be called in by persons who had never thought of employing him whilst he was poor and obscure. Anna used often to meet him with beaming eyes and dimpling cheeks, and wave aloft a written summons to some stately house, where his services had never been required before.

Once admitted to these houses, the skill, kindliness, and acuteness of George invariably made its mark, and he never lost a patient he had once gained. He had to set up his own carriage now, for he was summoned to all parts of the quarter, and to other quarters too; and yet in the midst of all his success he would not neglect his poorer patients.

III

THE MYSTERY EXPLAINED

JOHN PETERSON took a great interest in George's work amongst the poor, was never tired of hearing details of various cases of deserving poverty and lack of work, and it could not fail to be observed by the doctor in time that some mysterious bit of good fortune again and again befell those of whom he had specially spoken to his perplexing friend and ex-patient.

At last one day he charged him with playing the unknown benefactor, and the man answered, with a smile:

The Patient's Secret

"Well, and if it be so, have you any objection? Are we not sent into the world to help one another as our means permit?"

The doctor drew his chair a little closer, and laid a friendly hand upon his companion's arm.

"My good friend," he said, "we have known each other above a year now, and I think there is no espisode in my life unknown to you. But you are almost as much of an enigma as upon the day when we first met. Of course I have learned a little of you and your circumstances. You are not poor. You must have large means. You have education, and are widely read. You have thought and studied much. Why, then, do you live like this—as a poor man amongst the poor? Your neighbours seem not to suspect you of what I am certain you must possess—a large fortune. You keep your secret marvellously well. But what does it all mean? May I not know?"

And Peterson answered readily:

"You may know all that there is to know. I have often been on the brink of telling you my story; yet there is so little to tell that I scarce knew if you would care to hear it."

"My curiosity has often been keenly stirred, but I feared to intrude—perhaps upon some sacred sorrow."

"No, it is nothing of that sort. What I do, I do from choice and conviction, not in any hope of escaping from the world and its cares or pleasures. I was born a poor man. In my youth I lived with my parents in just such a house as this. We were

The Patient's Secret

poor. We were surrounded by the poor. The only difference between us and them was that my father came of a better stock, had a fair education, and managed to give me a better one than his own.

"While I was still a child a stroke of good fortune befell my father. A small legacy unexpectedly bequeathed to him enabled him to set up in a small business. Fortune favoured him in a wonderful way. He became rich by leaps and bounds, took me into his business house, when I had finished the excellent education he gave to me, and throve in a way that amazed us all. We lived at Hull, and did a great export business, and my father lived to a good old age. He died fifteen years ago, and I found myself in possession of a very great fortune, as well as the thriving business.

"I scarcely know why it was, but after my father's death I no longer cared for the business. All interest seemed taken out of it. I was no longer young myself. My wife had died, leaving me childless. The sense of being alone in the world made life desolate to me. I sold my business, and increased my great fortune; but the question that haunted me all the while was—what in the world to with it all?

"I was musing in disheartened fashion one evening in my lonely house, when I chanced to lay my hands upon the Bible on the table, and, opening it almost at random, I read, half unconsciously, that passage where the Apostle tells how the Saviour of the world took upon Himself the form of a servant, and lived in subjection and poverty here below. Then a sudden thought came to me. If the Son of God found it thus expedient to live the life of humble poverty below, to do His Father's will, might it not be that now and again His servants might find they could best do *His* work of charity and mercy by laying aside their wealth and station, and living amongst the poor as one of themselves? Do not think, my friend," he added, quickly, "that I in any way confuse the thought of the work of a creature with that of the Redeemer of mankind; but the words I had read struck home to me, and I said in my heart, 'If I am to help the poor, I must live as one of them. That, and only that, is the way by which I can accomplish the task I have set myself.'"

"Ah!" said the doctor, drawing a long breath, "now I begin to see!"

"I left Hull, leaving no trace behind. I came to London, and I took this room in this house, where I have lived ever since. I have kept my secret. The people know, of course, that I have a little independence, that I can lend a helping hand to a very small amount to a suffering neighbour, and that I have time to give to those who want sympathy or counsel. They have come to think my advice good, because good results often follow it—they do not see how. I have my own ways of going to work. They do not think that the help they sometimes receive unexpectedly comes from me. I am to them as one of themselves, and I am no longer besieged by needy and greedy idlers, who come with specious stories."

"And you have not wearied of the life all these years?"

The Patient's Secret

"No. It is full of intense interest for me. I could fill volumes with the stories I have heard and seen. I have been far happier here than in that lonely mansion in Hull. I have all I need. I am a man of simple tastes. I love my countrymen, and I have been happy in feeling at last that I have been able to help them to help themselves."

"And how came you to hear of me and send for me as you did?"

"That is soon told. Several of your poor patients came into this part of the city, and I heard of you from them. 'That is a man worth knowing,' I said, and I made further inquiries. There was only one tale in the mouths of all. You spent yourself freely for the suffering poor, and you reaped almost no visible result from your labours. 'That must not be,' I thought in my heart; 'the poor are deeply in debt to this good man. They cannot pay him, but I will.'"

The speaker stretched out his hand, which George warmly grasped. That was all which passed between them. But the hearts of both men were full, and from that day the intimacy between them deepened rapidly, and the friendship became warm and deep and lasting.

For three years the friendship continued. Then John Peterson became suddenly and dangerously ill. Easton insisted on moving him to his own house; but his skill could not avail to arrest the progress of the malady, and the patient died peacefully and contentedly, surrounded by loving faces and tendered by gentle hands.

The Patient's Secret

Almost his last act was to draw from beneath his pillow an envelope, and place it in his friend's hands. It was not a fee this time, but a briefly executed will, leaving his entire possessions to his doctor, without condition of any kind.

Afterwards, Anna, looking over her husband's shoulder, broke into a startled exclamation of wonder ; but he looked very serious as he replaced the paper in its cover, and said slowly :

" It is a great trust ; but I pray that I may be guided to use it aright."

His wife looked at him with wondering eyes.

"What do you mean, husband?"

" I mean that we are rich already, wife, and that, having abundance, we must look upon this gift as a trust. It was dedicated by a noble heart to the alleviation of the sufferings of the poor. It must still be applied in great part to that purpose. Thankfully will I accept from our friend enough to make provision for you and the child, in case it should be God's will to take me away before I have done this myself. But the bulk shall be otherwise applied— to the object so near his heart. I look upon it as a sacred charge. We must pray to God that He will guide us aright in the discharge of that trust !"

Anna kissed her husband.

" I am not half good enough to be your wife !" she said. " But I will try to be your wife and help-meet in this thing."

BECAUSE I LOVE HIM

MISS AMY FINCH and her new friend, Mrs. Bagnall, sat in the window making the most of the fading daylight. The matron had just purchased at the annual cheap sale two dozen best pocket-handkerchiefs. It was obviously desirable to get them marked at once, and as Amy was justly celebrated for her ornamental letters, and had lately evolved a very prepossessing B, they turned into the spinster's room, and proceeded, one to mark and one to learn.

Suddenly Mrs. Bagnall looked up and said, "Amy, did you ever have an offer?"

"No," Amy answered, quite simply, "I never did."

"They say that every woman has had one chance."

"I don't know what became of mine, then."

"Some other woman got two, I suppose. Were you ever at all pretty?"

Mrs. Bagnall certainly was a most uncircuitous person. But she asked her blunt questions with a chirpy innocence that almost gave her the immunity of childhood.

"Yes," said Amy, stimulated to unconventional candour; "yes, I think I was."

Because I Love Him

"Ah," Mrs. Bagnall answered, "there's no telling. Of course," she added, "one need not be pretty to be pleasing. Yours, my dear, is a very good face."

That dry and belated crumb of comfort did not content Amy.

"I wish you would believe me," she said; "I tell you I really was."

She rose, and opened an old mahogany desk that stood upon the table.

"There now," she said, blushing rather prettily, "judge for yourself," and she placed a photograph in Mrs. Bagnall's hand.

It had been taken in London, fifteen years ago, during Amy's historic plunge into the deeps of fashion. An early example of some permanent process, it was quite fresh and unfaded. It represented Amy in a Dolly Varden dress—the livery of a certain splendid bazaar.

"Dear me," said Mrs. Bagnall, in hushed surprise. "What owls the men must have been! You were lovely, child—absolutely lovely."

"I certainly was pretty," Amy answered. "But you know there were troubles. Papa got into difficulties . . . and I had a long illness . . . and they made me wear glasses . . . and . . . it's all fifteen years ago. What with one thing and another —well, you see what happened."

Amy dropped a curtsey and laughed, but her spectacles grew misty all the same. She stooped down and poked the fire.

"My dear," said Mrs. Bagnall, "you are very well

Because I Love Him

as you are. And what, after all, are looks? Good looks do not make good people. We must not look at looks."

At this point Mrs. Bagnall became conscious of urgent claims at home.

"Come again to-morrow," said Amy, as she kissed her bosom-friend, "and we'll go on with the marking." The photograph lay upon the table. Amy took it up and looked upon it long. Then, moved by what thought who shall say?—in farewell or in assertion of identity still maintained; in sad surrender or in sadder clinging—Amy brought a pen, and on the white border of the picture inscribed her name. Her caligraphy was her greatest accomplishment. It suggested, as caligraphy sometimes does, delicacy and grace, which Amy's voice and presence quite failed to convey.

Having thus impressed her sign-manual upon the old portrait, Amy put it away, and, clearing her mind of cobwebs, took out the potted meat.

The next day, when Mrs. Bagnall returned to the charge upon the pocket-handkerchiefs, she noticed something unusual in Amy's manner. It was nothing very striking—only a kind of half-abstraction, and, once and again, the hovering of an inward smile.

"Amy," said Mrs. Bagnall, when her friend had lapsed into silence, "there is something on your mind. Are you in love?"

Amy started, "What do you mean?" she said, blushing a little.

"Dear me!" exclaimed her friend. "I meant

with your own picture ; but really, my dear, I shall
think it is with somebody else's."

"I was going to ask you a question," Amy
said, after a short pause, "but I think I shan't
now."

Mrs. Bagnall applied the expected degree of
cajolery, and Amy drew from a drawer a postal
wrapper. "It is mere curiosity," she said ; "but
should you call this a lady's or a gentleman's
hand ? "

"Oh, a lady's—no, a gentleman's. Really I
could not be sure. It is a very pretty hand, anyhow. Dear me, Amy, how interesting ! Would
it be discreet to ask how the correspondence
began ? "

"Oh, it is not a correspondence at all. We
arranged an exchange of papers through the 'Bazaar.'
She—— "

"Oh, Amy, don't let the romance ooze away
like that."

"Well, then, the person. The person sends me
'Black and White' in return for the 'Graphic.'
The only thing that matters is the address. It
would be very awkward to write Mrs. H. Austin,
if it really were a gentleman."

"You must be satisfied with 'H. Austin.'"

"But that sounds rude."

"Oh, never mind," said Mrs. Bagnall. "It will
goad him on to declare himself."

"Really, Emily," answered Amy, as she rose
and secreted the wrapper, "what things you do
say ! "

Because I Love Him

"My dear," said Mrs. Bagnall, "I only meant his identity."

From that time forward Miss Finch's unknown friend became a favourite theme of delicate banter.

Messages were entrusted to Amy, to be faithfully given when next she was writing to Henry, Hubert, Hugh, or Harold. The postman was made accessory to much circular archness relating to furnishing and to Continental tours. Volumes containing respectively "Mr. H." and "The Lang Coortin'" were pressed upon Amy's perusal. Altogether she enjoyed quite an Indian summer of matrimonial allusion. It happened one afternoon that Mrs. Sedgwick, having occasion to despatch her son Augustus to Amy's rooms with a basket of Jerusalem artichokes—a present wherewith she was wont inexpensively to promote the gaiety of her friends— thought she would greatly heighten the humour of her innuendo, and make the innocent youth the medium. Articled clerks, in Mrs. Sedgwick's view, were exceedingly innocent.

"Bring back the basket," she said, "and give her my dear love; and I wish she would lend me Byron's enigma on the letter H. Say it begins,

'It was whispered in heaven.'"

"It is not Byron's," said Gus; "it is Miss Fanshawe's. But what's the point of the allusion?"

"Goodness!" exclaimed his mother, amazed at the learning and acuteness that she had evoked— "what is the boy talking about?"

"Why, the handle's tied up with string," said

Because I Love Him

Gus, inconsequently. "Really, mother, I think this mission would be better discharged after nightfall. However, as you please."

With good-natured disgust the lad took up his mother's bounty and departed.

Asked to wait in Amy's room (while the maid threw the artichokes away), Augustus looked round for means of amusement. On the table lay the works of Charles Lamb. He took the book up, and it opened at "Mr. H." "Ah," he thought, " H. again. There's a mystery about this. More is meant than meets the—— Halloa!"

Gus's eyes fell upon a postal wrapper whereon the address was hardly dry. It lay upon a "Graphic" which had been rolled up, and then allowed to uncurl. It was obviously designed for the post. The address, in Amy's beautiful hand, was, " H. Austin, The Nest, Ripon."

"Oh, ho!", said Gus. "This lets the cat out of the bag. Good old Amy! What a lark! The Nest, too! That beats Jerusalem artichokes! Go in and win, Amy, and you'll have the little teapot that's spoiling in mother's box, and live very happy ever—— " Again the lad's meditation was cut off short. Half-hidden under a lady-like inkstand there lay a photograph.

"The plot thickens," he said, and dragged the thing out. "Well, I'm shot!" exclaimed Augustus, as he recognised the face. " I never suspected that old Amy had been a beauty in her day. If only I had been twenty years earlier in the field, I should have lost my heart. Where were the men's eyes, I

wonder?" He was just about to return the portrait
to its lurking-place, when a thought leaped into his
brain. Slightly curving the photograph, that it
might not resist the rolling that would follow, he
slipped it into the heart of the "Graphic," and
turned away from the table. Miss Finch, hurrying
in a moment later with the empty basket, found him
studying intently "The Monarch of the Glen."

"How kind of your mother!" said Amy. "But
she must not rob herself, you know."

"Oh, don't be afraid," Gus answered. "Mother
is very honest in that way. She gave me a message
for you, Miss Amy—it was—something about—never
mind. You can ask her to-morrow."

And, rather red and confused, Gus made for the
door.

"Oh dear," said Amy, "he has forgotten the
basket. I must take it up this afternoon, I suppose.
How queer he was about the message!"

Conscience had made a coward of the articled
clerk. Any reference to the letter H seemed like
a confession of the "Graphic's" secret enclosure.

That evening the young fellow encountered Miss
Amy at the post-office. She was forcing into the
box a stubborn and protracted roll. As he raised
his hat he reddened again, and felt an inward questioning.

Two days later Amy Finch stepped into Mrs.
Bagnall's drawing-room with the look of a woman
walking in her sleep.

"Emily," she said, "am I mad? Read this, and
tell me."

Because I Love Him

"Well," said Mrs. Bagnall, when in silence she had extracted the essence of a four-page letter, "that depends on the answer you mean to give."

"Then it is—it really is—what it seems to be?"

"That depends. If it seems to be an offer of marriage, there's no doubt it is what it seems. 'Hubert Austin.' You see I was right. Oh, Amy, I am so glad!"

"But, Emily, it is so sudden, so strange altogether."

"Why, you poor little thing, you are shaking like a leaf. Sit down here, and I'll rub your silly cold hands. Why, I dare say it is not so sudden as you make out. How long have you been writing to one another?"

"We have never written a word except our two addresses. The most that ever we have done has been to mark a passage that we liked."

"All about love, of course."

"You know, Emily, I wouldn't do anything of the kind. I should not have gone so far as I did . . . it was only criticism of books . . . if I had known for certain that it was a man."

"Well, you know now," said Mrs. Bagnall, "and that is enough. Of course you saw the line written across?"

"No," answered Amy. "What does it say?"

"Oh," said Mrs. Bagnall, "nothing of any importance, only 'I shall arrive to-morrow at 12.30.'"

"Oh, dear, dear!" said Amy, with tears in her eyes, "what shall I do?"

Because I Love Him

"First," said Mrs. Bagnall, "you will take a glass of cordial and a slice of cake. And then you and I will walk back to your house. Why, bless you, if you had only refused them once and twice a day, as I used to do in India, you would not worry yourself about an offer."

"Then I must refuse him, you think?"

"My dear," said Mrs. Bagnall, "we are not in India, and . . . we'll see. Give the poor man a hearing; I tell you, we'll see."

So they went to Amy's room and waited.

The knock came. Then Mr. Bagnall pressed her friend's hands and withdrew upstairs.

"Mr. Austin," said the maid, with awful curiosity rounding her eyes, and there stepped into the room a young man of twenty-eight or so. A pleasant-faced fellow, frank and kind; a gentleman all over.

The room was dark under the brightest conditions, and that was a day of cloud. Amy, sitting at its farther extremity, was only dimly visible from the doorway.

"Forgive me," said the young man, as, hardly sure of his way, he advanced slowly; "I ought to have prepared you. Say that you forgive me."

He stood, and tossing away his cap, held out his two hands.

Trembling and in silence Amy came to meet him. But there was such generous sweetness in the impulsive face that it made her feel she should not be long afraid. She put her hands into his, and let her eyes fall. Then she felt the hands that held hers close with a convulsive clasp.

Because I Love Him

She looked up, and fancied that the young man's face had grown a little pale. Then, before she could say anything, before she could even think anything, Austin was pleading his cause as ardently as the most exacting maiden could desire.

"Amy," he said, "it is not so sudden as it seems."

"Why, what could you know about me?" Amy said.

"Oh, almost everything," he answered. "Your handwriting told me a great deal. I have studied graphology, and a letter is like a living presence to me. As I read it I hear the tones of the voice and see the changes of the face. But your writing, Amy! —it is a perfect revelation of yourself. If you want to keep your secrets, you must employ a secretary."

"Do you really think that?" Amy asked, in some alarm. "Not, of course, that I have any secrets."

"Oh, you must not take me quite literally. But in soberest truth, there is a singularly personal quality in your hand. It has a perfume of its own. It made me think of violets."

"I dare say," Amy remarked. "Rhine violets."

"No, no; it was a purely spiritual suggestion. As a matter of fact, I hate the smell of violets—you might as well put mud upon your handkerchief."

"Oh dear," said Amy, "I got a new bottle to-day!"

"Why do you say 'Oh dear'? From this time forth you will not smell of violets, but violets will smell of you."

"I don't like compliments," said Amy.

Because I Love Him

"When the truth is a compliment, you must learn to bear it. But, Amy, it was not only your writing that made me love you. You talked to me in little crosses with blue pencil. I never knew such judgment as yours. You drink the spirit of a book like wine."

"I never drink wine," said Amy. "All our family are abstainers."

"Yes, yes," Austin answered; "but that is not the point. You are the very pope of critics, and infallible, whether you speak from chair or sofa. That made me love you, Amy—your amazing literary instinct—for good books are my life-blood. I want to write a good book myself. You will help me, won't you?"

"Oh dear," said Amy, "I am very slow, and dreadfully shallow."

"It is at your slow and shallow feet——"

"Oh, my feet are well enough," said Amy.

"Yes, yes; but figuratively. Let me sit at the feet of a good woman, while the critics snarl and wrangle. I believe in the wisdom of the pure heart."

"I think you are very impulsive," Amy said, after a momentary pause. "I think . . . if I were to . . . you would be sorry by-and-by . . . I have no money, except——"

"Money? If I had been a fortune-hunter, do you suppose I should have made no inquiry?"

"I only wanted to know how things are. And then I am older than you—a great deal older, I should think." Amy hesitated for a moment, and

Because I Love Him

then went on, with a little gulp of difficult resolution. "My birthday will be on Tuesday, and I shall be——"

"Don't tell me," broke in Austin; "I won't hear"; his fingers went up to his ears—"positively and absolutely I won't. Amy, your present shall be the engagement-ring."

"Nonsense," said Amy. "I will save you from your own rashness. Besides, *I* shall want a long time to think."

Yet on Tuesday the ring came—and stayed. For the two young people had met many times, and Mrs. Bagnall and Mrs. Sedgwick, having made searching inquiry, both of the lover himself, and also of lawyers, bankers, and a clergyman or two, had with one voice delivered their judgment.

"Amy," this emphatic pronouncement made; "if you don't say 'Yes,' an asylum is your place."

So the engagement was announced, and Kirkholm almost lost its head. "Never since Carry Whitworth 'went off' with that disreputable reporter had there been such talk. Excitement and tea ran high. Scones and wigs and apple-cake, pairs of fowls and ham with pink frills, made the hospitable tables groan —possibly also some of the guests.

But, groaning or gay, Mr. Austin made an excellent impression. He gave himself no airs, professed his devotion, admired the neighbouring scenery, and was exactly enough in love.

During this brief period the behaviour of Gus Sedgwick excited some remark. His mother and Mrs. Whitworth observed and denounced him. He

Because I Love Him

sat where he could watch the affianced pair, and chuckled. Now, as his affectionate friends justly remarked, that was not the way for a young man to behave.

In a month the festivities were over, and life paled down to its cold and normal grey. The tables lost their rosy trills; Mr. Austin was back at Ripon. Mrs. Whitworth had neuralgia.

But Amy? Oh, it was worth one's while to look at Amy. Her month of life had been put back. If this was not April come again, surely it was a time almost as fair, and tenderer and sweeter. The record of the pinching years seemed half erased. The hard and prim little lines softened into gracious curves. Her hair, almost rich and beautiful, caught a ripple and a gleam. Her light-grey eyes grew dark and full of dreams. Her very figure ripened.

Gus Sedgwick ceased to chuckle. He gazed at Amy still, but he gazed in a kind of awe. So might the conjurer gaze, from whose apparatus of deceit had sprung in very deed a gracious miracle. During Austin's stay, this singular change in Amy had been less obvious. Perhaps excitement overlaid it. Perhaps it needed time to strike its roots into the heart before it blossomed in the lips and eyes. Looking at Amy now, many a portly bachelor fluttered his watch-chain with a sigh, and said, "How blind I must have been!"

So time went on, and there was talk about the wedding—not as an event urging and imminent, but as of something that was surely stealing on. Already Mrs. Sedgwick's teapot had arrived, thoroughly

Because I Love Him

scoured, not to say scratched, and bearing this inscription : " Humble, I know, dearest Amy, but let me be the first."

It was in the late spring, when the engagement was about six months old, that Austin came to pay his second visit. Possibly he came to make arrangements for the great event. At any rate, Mrs. Whitwell leaped to that conclusion.

One day Amy, instigated by Mrs. Bagnall, gave her lover a little dinner. That friend was the only other guest, but still anxieties were deep and pitfalls many. There was the cracked soup-plate, and there was the landlady's temper, and there were Mary's thumbs. But all these difficulties were negotiated or surmounted. It really was going to be a very nice little dinner. Mrs. Lewthwaite (so was the landlady named) had come out with unexpected gusto. The dining-room, which she had generously lent, did exceedingly well. Mr. Lewthwaite's slippers were not obvious, and when it was certain that his lady would not be looking in again, Amy would run up and whip away the white embroidered antimacassars.

* * * * *

It was done. All was perfect, except the smell of baked plates.

* * * * *

It was over. Nothing could have been better. If Mary *had* nudged, to call attention to things that she was handing—that was an hospitable weakness.

Austin had been left to the enjoyment of a cigarette.—" Yes, and he did enjoy it too," said

Because I Love Him

Mrs. Bagnall, who had presented the case of cigarettes—Amy had not thought of them—and the salmon. "It was good, though I say it."

So there was a delightful flutter of congratulation, while Amy began to think of tea.

Suddenly she remembered something. Hubert had asked her to sew a button on his glove. The glove would be in his coat-pocket; she would get the thing done ready for his return.

With a strange sense of daring intimacy, Amy felt about in the many-pocketed masculine garment. Pockets, pockets everywhere, yet not a glove to . . . Yes; here it was. No! another cigarette case—or might it be a receptacle for gloves? There seemed to be no other possible lurking-place. She took the slender case into her hands, and glanced within.

A photograph. Well, she was not jealous; but whose picture did he carry about?

Not hers, anyhow, for Hubert had never wished to have it taken. She must look.

Guiltily, yet not without a sort of inward justification, Amy took the photograph out, and held it up to the hissing hall-light.

It was her own picture—that picture which, seven months ago, had so mysteriously disappeared.

How on earth had it come into Hubert's possession? At first Amy's mind had room for nothing but that wonder. Then the beauty of her own face mastered her, filling her with memories and wistful dreams. And then—swift and sure as a shaft of light—the truth smote into her heart.

Because I Love Him

Some one had sent Austin her picture, and he had fallen in love with that. And when for the first time he saw her living face, so altered by the trampling feet of fifteen pitiless years, he had felt the keenest stab of disappointment. That momentary falling of his countenance and that swift recovery had told all the story.

How gallantly, how chivalrously, he had behaved! Amy loved him better than she had ever loved him, yet now it was borne in upon her heart that Hubert did not love *her*. How plainly the road which had been traversed with undistinguishing eyes unrolled itself before her now! In that cocoon of self-beguilements whereby Hubert, intent at first on cheating only her, had finally all but cheated himself, she saw the spinning of every thread. When he looked upon the faded original of the picture, he had felt with instinctive nobility that one thing must be done. The ill-fruit of his romantic folly must be gathered by him alone. The woman must not eat of its bitter ashes.

"Never to tell her; not to let her know."

That line from Hubert's beloved "Enoch Arden," upon which his voice always seemed to tremble and break, rose naturally in Amy's mind.

He was so completely saturated with Tennyson, that his resolution, Amy thought, might have shaped itself to that piteous refrain.

Sometimes the part had been difficult acting, sometimes he had lost himself in his part; but he had never loved her. Well, the last lines would soon be spoken, and the lights put out.

195

Because I Love Him

"Oh," thought poor, desolated Amy, "if for one hour he had loved me, I could have borne it better. But the girl whom he loved was dead long ago. I was only her ghost. When he wanted to be fond of me, he had to read the picture into my face."

"Amy," came a voice from the stairs, "what on earth are you about? Mr. Austin and I are abusing one another like pickpockets; come and make peace . . . and tea."

"All right," Amy answered. "I had to do something." She replaced the picture and the case. Then she moistened her lips, and hummed a little tune, and ran lightly upstairs.

Act? Why, if it came to that, women could act as well as men. Better, perhaps; God help them!— they had more practice.

*　　*　　*　　*　　*

All through that sleepless night, salt with tears, acrid with humiliation, Amy groped her way towards a resolution. It was not the resolution to give her "lover" up, for that had been taken on the instant of discovery.

The mode of emancipation was the difficulty; for her slave would certainly refuse his freedom. All his chivalry and all his self-delusion would urge him to make jewels of his chains.

"Never to tell him; not to let him know."

Enoch Arden's resolution was capable of feminine adoption. She must save Hubert.

But how was it to be done?

Happily—for to Amy's direct and unimaginative

nature the burden of duplicity was heavy to bear—Austin was leaving Kirkholm the next day. To send him away without decisive settlement of the wedding-time was natural enough. In that matter to be indefinite is to be maidenly.

During the hours of their last evening she did not betray herself. Paleness and a few tears became the occasion well enough. When next day Amy waved from the platform, her lover never divined what gave the fluttering handkerchief its little touch of tragedy.

As soon as the sharpest need for deception was over, Amy's part was poorly played. At first her friends believed that Hubert's departure might well account for pale cheeks and swollen lids. But very quickly it became evident something was wrong.

Good Mrs. Bagnall burrowed gallantly towards the core of the mystery, but, somehow or other, always missed the way. There had been no quarrel; the engagement held, and Amy was only a little worried; and Mrs. Bagnall could not help her—save by leaving her alone. But Gus Sedgwick, as often as the chance occurred, stared at Amy. He did not chuckle, but often whistled meditatively.

One day, a month after Austin's departure, Augustus poured into a basket a quart of goose-berries, designed for the morrow's tart at home, and slipped out by the back door. The basket, he hoped, would give him the entrée of Amy's room, and there was something that he must say to her.

His plan succeeded. Amy came in looking so

white and fragile, so weary and old, that Gus's heart bled for her.

"I'm so much obliged," she said, holding out her hand, and calling up the ready, piteous smile. "What beautiful——"

"Hang the gooseberries!" interrupted Gus. "Miss Amy, I can't bear to see you like that. I thought once I had done such a mighty clever thing, and now—I wish I'd cut my right hand off first, that I do!"

"Oh, Gus," said poor Amy, forgetting her own trouble for a moment at the sight of the lad's distress, "you have not been betting again?"

"No," said Gus, "didn't I promise? Oh, Miss Amy, it was I who shoved it in. Just for a lark, you know—in the 'Mr. H.' days."

"Shoved what?" asked Amy, too much puzzled to reject the vulgar word.

"Why, the picture, Miss Amy—the confounded— I mean the beautiful picture."

"Oh, Gus," said Amy, pressing her hands together, "was it you? I think I must sit down for a moment. I don't feel quite well."

In a moment Gus was on his knees at her feet. "Miss Amy," he blurted out, with many sniffs and gulps, "I know all about it. You've had a regular bust-up, and he has chucked you, and it's breaking your heart."

"No, no," said Amy; "you are quite wrong."

"Bosh!" answered Gus; "you don't gammon me. It's just killing you; why, your hand"—he caught it in his own—"is like an eggshell. Well, look here:

Because I Love Him

as soon as I've got money for the fare, I'll go to Ripon and horsewhip the beastly sweep. I will—I declare I will: that's settled. And now, Amy, this is what matters most. Don't you cry. There are other fellows besides him. Amy—I don't mind a bit; upon my word I don't—*I'll* marry you."

For the first time during many days Amy's eyes brightened with a smile. Forgetting her propriety, she laid her hand on Gus's hair.

"Thank you, Gus," she said; "you are a dear, good boy."

"I suppose you'll like it to be soon?" he asked, stoutly, if a little ruefully.

"Well, no," she answered; "I am deeply grateful, Gus, but think I cannot——" Her speech broke off. The merriment in her eyes changed into resolution. "Gus," she said "I accept your offer——"

"All right," said Gus, buttoning up his coat. "Upon my word I don't mind."

"So far as this: I will be engaged to you for one week."

"What's the good of that?" said Gus. "Blest if I understand."

"Don't try," said Amy. "But, believe me, you will render me a great service."

Suddenly a keen look flashed out of the lad's eyes.

"You are going to humbug Austin," he said. "It is you who want to break it off."

"Yes," she said, solemnly, "I want to break it off."

"Why, Miss Amy?" he asked, moved by her manner. "Tell me why."

Because I Love Him

"Because I love him, Gus ; because I love him."

"Don't tell me any more," said Gus, reddening, and turned away.

Then he advanced to Amy with a soft brightness in his eyes. "Not because of our week's engagement," he said, " but . . . for other reasons . . . will you give me one kiss ? "

Amy threw her arms around him, and cried as though her heart would break.

THE WIFE FOR A RAILWAY MAN

"TALKING about them Waterloo 'ouses, old Billy Rogers was tellin' me he used to work past 'is own 'ouse, down Lambeth way, just a-level with the top floor where 'e lived."

"Well, that ain't nothin'," chimed in Dick. "Lots o' men does that. Why, when I used to work a night-goods, which I did every night for three 'ole years, I took an' put my missus an' kids into a one-pair back, as looked out on the line. Blow me if I'd 'a seen anything at all of the old lady if I 'adn't. A wonderful long shift it was; trip job, yer know.

"She worked out most of the day, and I was away all the nights, but there was always a light in the winder as I passed. Tell yer, I used to think as much of that light as I did of the points."

"You'd 'a stopped the train if it hadn't been there, I reckon, Dick."

"Oh, I don't say that. 'Company first's' the rule, yer know. By the way, any o' you chaps seen Mat Anderson lately?"

"Yes, I see 'im last year. He joined our club."

Dick laughed a long quiet lungy chuckle. "Oh, then," he said, "the chap's got married, 'as 'e?" and he shook with mirth. "You don't happen to know what sort o' gal the wife might be, do you?"

The Wife for a Railway Man

"No. 'E was keepin' company like for a long time first, I know that. You know what sort o' company-keepin' it is for us railway men. Take it when you can get it, and think yourself jolly lucky if you get it at all, and don't get shunted into a siding after all. Did you know Mat's girl afore he was hitched on?"

"Not exactly; but it was me that helped him to that there piece of luck, I reckon. 'E won't mind my tellin' on 'im. We was mates on an engine—old five-nought-two, you rec'lect"—("Ah," from the rest here)—"as used to take stuff up and down to Weymouth and them parts. We used to start down the hearly mornin', and be back again arter dark. We used to get through the Junction about six-thirty, as a rule, and then the line was clear for some way. Down Wandsworth way we went past the backs of some smartish villas. A long row there was of them, as like as cattle trucks, with long thin gardens running down to the line. I don't know what called my attention to it, but somehow, one day, I noticed there was a gal cleanin' the top winder in one of them, and, thinks I, that gal's rare and early up arter 'er work. A nice-lookin' gal she was, and next morning I noticed the same thing. There she was rubbing away with her duster—now it's no use your laughing, Tom, I was a married man then, same as I am now. There she was, rubbing away with her duster, and the glass so clean a'ready, you could see she was a good-lookin' gal. Same thing nex' mornin', and the next, an' settera. Seemed to me she was looking our way too. Thinks I, if that gal's

202

The Wife for a Railway Man

arter me, I'm sorry; but I looks at Mat for a few mornings, and, 'pon my word 'e was always mighty clean an' smart of a morning, and if 'e thought I wasn't lookin' 'e most generally took a quiet squint up at that winder, an' I noticed 'e kept a piece of clean cotton waste in his pocket, to give his face a rub with first, when we passed them houses.

"Now, you know, I didn't know Mat as well then as I do now. 'E's all right, but he don't say much, do 'e? Well, just to see how the points lay, I says to 'im one day, 'That gal 'll rub a hole in that winder one of these days.' 'Which gal?' says he. 'Why, the one you was staring at in them red-brick 'ouses,' says I. 'It's a good thing you an' me's both married,' I says, 'or else we'd be victims.' 'Why, *I* ain't married,' says 'e, quite surprised. 'Well, there,' says I, 'I thought you was.' 'Wish I was,' says 'e.

"That's a fact. 'Ed set 'is 'eart on the gal, and I reckon she'd set 'er 'eart on 'im, though 'ow they fust thought of it's more than I can tell you.

"O' course we giner'ly come 'ome in the dark, and there weren't no window-cleanin' and no squintin' to be done then, and Mat used to go 'ome sulky.

"'Look 'ere, Mat,' says I one day, 'why in the dickens and all don't you get hitched on? You must ha' been out with that gal every Sunday a sight o' months, and if you want a best man,' said I, 'well——' Mat smokes up, ''Ow in the dickens an' all am I to get married, when I don't know the gal's name, and never spoke two words to her?'

"'Well, I don't want to inter-bloomin'-fere,' says I. 'You never told me any of your precious secrets,

The Wife for a Railway Man

'ow was I to know? But look you 'ere, Mat,' says I, 'you might 've a worserer 'ead to advise you than me.' Arter that Mat let out pretty nigh everything he'd think about it, and I used to cheer 'im as well's I could. 'E'd been down there two or three Sundays, and hung about the place, but it weren't any good. The 'ouses was all mixed up that side, and, says 'e, 'If I seen 'er in 'er Sunday bonnet I shouldn't know 'er, for women ain't particular about showing their natural lights, and if she seen me cleaned up, I don't expect she'd know me, and I darsn't speak to her anyway.' There was a tramcar that ran along the road, and Mat told me 'e'd an idea of gettin' took on as a driver, so as to get round to the front of the 'ouse. But says I, 'No, Mat, you don't go so low as that. Besides, you ain't fitted for it. You'd be shovelling coals down the horses' throats, as like as not, and oilin' their shinin' shanks to make them go. No, what you've to do now is to write 'er a letter.' 'Letters want envelopes,' says Mat, 'and envelopes wants addresses. Sender's all right,' says 'e, 'but who in the dickens and all is the consignee?' 'Don't you trouble about that,' says I, 'once you write the letter, we'll get it to her per lump o' coal, or otherwise,' says I, 'at sender's risk.'

"Well, 'e come 'ome with me that Sunday, and I 'elp 'im to write the letter. I never see such a job in my life. We used up two pennorth o' paper before we got the wretched thing to bite at all. There were lots in it, all about Mat, and what wages he was gettin' and that, and 'ow 'e expected

The Wife for a Railway Man

to be shunted on to better work soon. I made him put that in to hurry 'er up. Then it ended by sayin' 'would she let him knows by signal whether agreeable or otherwise. If agreeable, signify the same by one white light placed in window arter 7.30 this evening. If points agin, please signal same by one red light; white light preferred.'

"Monday morning come, and there she was rubbin' away at that old winder in the sunrise the same as ever. Mat 'ad the letter tied to a goodish lump o' coal, with a rag to flutter a bit, and 'e waves it about at first till she nigh stopped rubbin', and then he flung it fair and square right into the middle of the lawn at the back of the house, and I give the whistle a screech, and orf we went.

"Well, Mat was a rum 'un that day. Seemed to me as if his boiler 'd bust. Sometimes 'e'd larf, and sometimes 'e'd look black. Tell you *I* 'ad to mind the traffic that day. 'She 'on't read it,' says he. 'Then she ain't a woman,' says I. 'Per'aps 'er missus is a woman too, and 'll get it fust,' says he, sniggerin'. 'An' if she's a widder woman, Mat,' says I, 'she'll put a white light in her best settin' room winder, and you'll come into a fortin'.'

"'Owever, we got startled up again. A bit late we was, and Mat could hardly stop when the signals were agin us. When we come nigh Wandsworth, 'e could 'ardly stick to the engine, stretchin' 'is neck out, to see what the gal 'ad put out. 'Well,' says I, as we drew near, 'is it red, or is it white?' 'It's *green*, by thunder,' says Mat; and sure enough it was. There, right up the top of the 'ouse, in a little 'winder as looked out of the tiles, she'd set a little lamp with a bit of green glass in front of it.

"'That's green enough,' says I. 'And so am I,' says 'e; 'she's foolin' me.' ''Old you 'ard,' says I, 'you're in too much of a 'urry; and that's what she means too. You know your lights,' says I, 'white's right.' ''Course I do,' says 'e.

> "White is right, and red is wrong,
> Green is gently go along."

"'What does she mean by "gently go along"?' says he.

"'She don't really mean "get away," Mat,' says I. 'That's only a woman's way o' puttin' it. When my old missus and me was walkin' out, that's what she says, too. I says, "Susan, will you hitch on?" She says, "Go along Dick, do," several times. I wouldn't give a 'andful o' cinders for a woman as'd stick up a white light the first time. That's a girl in a thousand,' says I, 'and she knows the lights too. She's the woman for a railway man,' says I, 'an' you're a lucky man if you git 'er. Mark you, she don't tell you to stop dead neither. When you see a green light, it means you go a little further, and see if you can get along, but have your hand on the brake, and don't be in a hurry—that's all. And that's what she means. Don't be runnin' into the terminus at sixty mile an hour.'

"Well, Toosday mornin' she was scrubbin' the winder agin, but this time she was settin' out with 'er back to the line, giving the outside of the glass

The Wife for a Railway Man

a turn. A nice little waist she 'ad. Mat never spoke a word the 'ole day, no more did I; but come night, and there was the green light agin, and Mat plucked up a bit. Wednesday mornin' she was very busy cleanin' the outside of another winder. 'Oh dear,' says Mat, as if 'e was 'urt, 'she's as white as a daisy,' and so she was, poor little creatur'. I reckon she 'adn't slep' a night or two. Thursday Mat chucks 'er another bit o' coal. 'E didn't tell me at the time what it said, but I reckon 'e was able to make himself understood. 'E was to be walkin' out by Wandsworth Cemetery all the Sunday, with a bit o' green ribbon in 'is buting 'ole. I know she met 'im right enough, and arter that they walked out reg'lar."

LOYAL HEARTS AND TRUE

I

AN UNGRACIOUS VISITOR

THE doctor was expected at Eolgary House. The lad, Duncan Campbell, had driven down to the pier in the trap, and had announced the news, which fell like a meteor among the folk of Barra. He was coming by this very steamer, said the lad, the steamer whose funnel they had been waiting and watching since early afternoon, though it was then near night.

They were gathered on and about the pier, these good folk of Barra, for the tri-weekly coming of the Oban steamer stood for them among the great excitements of life. It was their morning newspaper, their afternoon tea, their charity bazaar, their theatre. It furnished food for conversation in the between-times, news for neighbour to greet neighbour with, when they met on the lonely roads by the lochs with no man's house in sight, thought-material for a man at his fishing, and for a woman at her peat-gathering or harvesting. And when the glory of the arrival was enhanced by the presence of a visitor who had strayed from his path to Skye, or (what was a rare and almost unheard-of occurrence) of an actual inhabitant of the island, bedrid indeed was he who could bide at home. Even old Hughie, the blind and palsied, and Mary McCune, with her three-weeks-old babe scarce wrapped from the biting air, must needs trundle down to the landing; for was not the doctor coming back, to live in the great house at Eolgary?

Presently, well on towards twilight, the belated steamer rounded the point, labouring heavily through the ugly waves of the Minch; and as she came into the quiet waters of the bay, and steamed past the grey tide-locked castle, there was unfolded to the eager gaze of the onlookers from the shore the tall figure of the one passenger. He stood surrounded by a great mass of luggage, with his hands thrust deep into the pockets of his long brown ulster, and the collar of the same gathered close about his ears and chin.

Peter MacKinnon, the quay-master, felt that his position made him in some sense a host, and even as he stood ready to catch the rope he sang out over his shoulder to those immediately behind him: "It's a bit of a welcome I'll be giffing him whateffer, and himsel' wull no be the worse for't."

Accordingly, MacKinnon, not being shy, stepped up to the gangway, with an outstretched hand, and the air of one who owned the island, saying:

"Welcome to Barra, doctor! Ye'll not know me, I'm thinking, but my name's MacKinnon, Peter MacKinnon, at your service."

The doctor stood at the foot of the gangway without stirring or seeming to see the offered hand,

Loyal Hearts and True

"Aw—thanks," said he, with an unmistakable English drawl. He fixed his grey eyes, cold and impenetrable as the sea itself, steadily upon MacKinnon, whereupon that worthy shifted to the other foot, and actually retreated a step or two—to the unbounded amazement of all present.

But courage flowed back into him, perhaps through realisation of his very public position, and he continued boldly: "Och, ye'll be glad to come back again, doctor. There's a heap o' new people since your father's day, maybe ten or twel' families from Uist and Canna now, and the west coast; maybe, what with the bairns grown up and gone to the fishing, ye'll find things changed. Yet, what with the bad herring season, and nobody coming from the east coast whateffer, we're no the richer. But Eolgary's the same—just the same at all. Now I'm thinking it'll be a heap o' years since ye went away—a heap o'——"

"Seventeen," said the doctor, in a tone which cut through MacKinnon's smooth, soft drawl like a knife.

The quay-master stopped, disconcerted, and stared a moment, then said, more curtly:

"Dr. Craven, the folk here wass minded most friendly towards ye, and I'm thinking, if ye don't like us——"

Again the clear, sharp voice interrupted: "Ask somebody to take hold of my luggage, will you? I don't see my grieve."

But the steamer, having duly disburdened herself of Oban lading, and taken up the mail from Barra, was preparing to move on, and MacKinnon, with a red face, muttering in his beard, stooped to cast off the rope nearest him.

Meanwhile sundry officious hands in the background were pushing forward the lad Duncan, who would fain have escaped the notice of this new sharp-voiced master.

When the doctor understood that this was his grieve's deputy, he asked, frowning: "Where's MacCaskill himself?"

"Ow, sir, he will not be coming, since last night his foot iss hurt. He wass fall."

The boy spoke with the peculiar indistinct utterance and monotonous undertone which characterise the acquired English of Gaelic children, and the doctor did not fully understand, but still continued staring at the lad (perhaps he fell to thinking of other things), so long that Duncan looked as if meditating upon the use of heels. However, the doctor roused himself enough to command that his luggage be put into the trap, and transferred his stare to the vanishing speck of the steamer while the same was being done.

All the while he seemed quite oblivious to the presence of the interested audience, whose eyes duly examined, and, as far as possible, noted the contents of each piece of luggage as it was handled, and indeed developed a disposition to advise concerning its arrangement in the trap. This disposition the doctor discouraged promptly, by clambering into the vehicle, and without a word or even a look of greeting to any one, signing to Duncan to start the horse.

Loyal Hearts and True

There was a little silence in the motley throng which he left behind him. Before any one spoke, MacKinnon walked through the people into his box, with a singular gesture of rubbing his hands together, as if he were washing them. And then a man spoke —a Perthshire man, who still retained his dialect :

"Sall," said he, "the mon's no canny !"

The doctor and his lad drove the twelve miles or so between Castlebay and Eolgary without a word uttered. From time to time the boy cast furtive, half-frightened glances at his companion, who, for his part, paid no attention to him, being apparently wrapped in meditation, and that not the most cheerful.

Every foot of the road was as familiar to the doctor as if he had tramped it daily, instead of having never once seen it for nigh a score of years. Clustering about the door, in a dense cloud of peat-smoke, on a windy day like this, all the inhabitants stood and stared, parents and children, dogs and cats, ducks and chickens.

He knew it all so well; memories flocked in swarms, like bees among the heather, to the silent man by Duncan's side, and every sound and every smell brought up things which all the sun of India had not been able to burn out, nor yet could its rains wash them away. They seemed to awake in the doctor a man who had been asleep or dead these seventeen years.

And then, with a sudden turn, he was aware of the big dining-room window shining a welcome upon him, and, seen by the light streaming from the open

Loyal Hearts and True

door, the grey-headed grieve and several capped and aproned women servants behind him.

The old man began confused, eager apologies, but the doctor waved them aside, and with a curt, "I'll look at your foot to-morrow," stepped past the little group into the dining-room. They looked at one another in silence, until the grieve drove the women to the kitchen with sharp words, and when they had gone, shook his head sorrowfully, muttering, "His father wass a shentleman, he wass."

Meanwhile, the master standing within the door was realising that the whole scene corresponded in every detail to his mental image of it, formed seventeen years before. Nothing seemed to have been moved. His father's worn leather arm-chair stood on one side of the blazing peat-fire, and on the other, his mother's chair, with the white antimacassar with which, as a lad, he used to go fishing from the hair-cloth sofa. The family portraits, as sharp-featured and sour as ever, looked down upon him from the walls, from their places among Biblical engravings mottled with age. The very woodcut of a prize bull, once the pride of his father's heart, still held its place with unshaken majesty. The daguerreotypes on the chimney-piece had faded somewhat— that was the only change. The only one? No; the table was laid for one.

The doctor glanced hesitatingly at the two chairs by the fireside, and after a moment drew up a third. With a sudden movement he pressed the palms of his hands over his eyes.

Nevertheless, the maid who entered a moment

later with the supper found these same eyes watching her every motion. Whereupon, much embarrassed, she wrought sad havoc on the tea-tray.

"He glowered at me jist like a boghearn," she excused herself, sobbingly, when reproved in the kitchen.

"If he would only be scolding me," she went on, "but he jist looked, and looked."

The doctor, on his part, as he rose from the supper-table and walked to the window, asked himself for the twentieth time, "Have I done well to come?" He could see nothing but the reflection of the room, with its glow of lamp-light and fire-light upon the window-panes; but he seemed to feel the sea like a presence all around him, and the breaking of its surf mingled with the sound of the wind.

"If I were superstitious," he said aloud, with a nervous laugh, "I should think the ghosts of all the MacNeills buried in the graveyard yonder were howling about, to drive away the intruder. Yes—intruder—Sassenach intruder—that's what he called me, seventeen years ago!"

He fell into a gloomy meditation, and let the peats burn themselves into fine ash without adding to them.

II

A DOCTOR WHO DID NOT WANT PATIENTS

FROM the moment he stepped ashore it was evident that the doctor would not be popular. The whole island feared and disliked him, except, perhaps, two people—Peter MacKinnon, who, in spite of repeated snubs, maintained a sort of stubborn friendship, and old Dr. Mackenzie, as soon as he learned that his own practice would not be interfered with.

From the very first, Dr. Craven made it clear that he did not wish for patients, that he had come to the island solely on account of his health.

"He wull be very queer," one gossip would say to another.

"Ay, but India, where he's coming from, that wull be a queer place, I'm thinking."

"He wull not be on the island much when he wass a lad?"

"Nay, he wull be in school at Glasgie since seven years old, until he wull be going to India. Still, he wass coming up in the summers, whateffer."

"Hah, he's no' like his father!"

"Nay, it's no' like his father he iss!"

And such was generally the conclusion of the conversation.

Until the autumn rains came on, the doctor was to be seen day after day scrambling over the hills with his gun, or tramping about the lochs with his rod, or swinging along the shell-roads, or again galloping across the moors on his bonny yellow horse. Indeed, this pretty creature with the white-starred forehead seemed to be the only object of the doctor's affection, though he tolerated several fine dogs.

Eolgary House soon underwent a change, for though its owner did not touch the old-fashioned furniture, he filled the hall and every nook and

215

corner elsewhere with his fine scientific collections brought from India, and almost daily increased by some rare specimen from the island, and when the bad weather came he sat day after day at his big dining-room window busy with microscope and scalpel. Some days he would hum and mutter, "I was right to come, after all," but again he would drop his tools and gaze drearily out to sea, sighing, "But here I cannot forget, of all places in the world; here I cannot forget!"

He could not escape patients entirely. They were fairly thrust upon him as soon as the people discovered that a man who spent his days in study and experiment was more to be trusted than one who employed all his spare moments in alternately drinking and dozing. But his manner of receiving these unwelcome visitors does not stand to his credit.

One stinging night in December, as Dr. Craven was lovingly cutting the leaves of a new book which the last mail had brought from Glasgow, he was told that a man wished to see him. Very few of the islanders were known even by sight to the doctor; and this one was a stranger to him.

"Who are you? speak up!" he cried, impatiently, as the man stood dumb with embarrassment.

"Peter MacNeill, sir——"

"MacNeill, did you say?" interrupted the other, with a little start. "But this island is full of MacNeills," he added, recovering himself.

"O ay, sir, about seventy families of them," said MacNeill, with some pride.

Loyal Hearts and True

"Yes, yes. What do you want?"

"Peter MacKinnon, sir, wass been taken fery bad——"

"MacKinnon? MacKinnon?" queried the other, frowning.

"O ay, there's feefty families of them," said Mac-Neill, indifferently, adding with sudden pleading, "It's fery bad he iss, sir."

"Send for Mackenzie," said the doctor, with his fingers among the leaves of his book.

"But——" began MacNeill.

"Didn't you hear me? Go and get Mackenzie."

"But Misthress MacKinnon wull not be haffing the old doctor!"

"Eh?"

"Misthress MacKinnon wass saying it should be you, sir."

The doctor rose, and looked out at the night, but he could see only a white, dark-patched waste, and hear only the snapping of the sleet against the window.

"You know my terms are paid in advance?" he asked, grimly. It was one of his devices to keep patients away.

"O ay, sir," and MacNeill bashfully extended half a crown.

"That is Mackenzie's price—not mine. I ask five shillings a visit," said he, flushing somewhat, it must be admitted.

"But she wull not be knowing that," said Mac-Neill, distressed.

"So much the worse," said the doctor, once more

217

taking up his book. "Get Mackenzie," he repeated, and became apparently quite oblivious of his visitor.

MacNeill half raised his fist to strike, but his blaze of anger passed as quickly as it came, and he began rummaging his pockets in vain.

"Fery well ; I'll go back for't," he muttered.

The doctor nodded, only half hearing, and when the door closed reflected, "Rid of him, anyhow!" and called for his wine.

It was nearly midnight, and he was thinking of retiring, when he was startled by a long, heavy knock, and answering it, admitted the dripping, half-frozen figure of MacNeill.

"You again?" he cried, starting back angrily.

"Jist myself. Your five shillings," said Peter, gruffly, dropping the money in a little heap upon the table.

"Who wants the five shillings!" and he dashed them into the fire.

MacNeill made a quick movement to rescue it, stopped short, and said slowly :

"Misthress MacKinnon wass borrowing it for you, sir."

The two men eyed each other, until with a sudden gesture the doctor signified that he was beaten.

"Wait here," said he ; and presently MacNeill heard the sound of hoofs in front of the house, and the physician re-entered, equipped for the ride.

In silence they picked their way along the point across the sands, rendered dangerous by little frozen pools here and there, now that the tide was out, and into the main road which girdled the island. There the doctor spoke, shouting through the sleet:

"Where does this MacKinnon live?"

"At Borve," returned MacNeill, as they set their horses' heads in the very teeth of the wind.

"What is he?" shouted Craven again.

"You know him—the quay-master!" called Peter, reining up in surprise.

"Oh, that one!" The storm could not drown the doctor's contempt.

Thereafter they spoke no more until they alighted at Borve.

"His wife's a MacNeill," volunteered MacNeill at this point.

"You're a clannish set," returned the other gruffly, and walked in without ceremony.

A woman came out of a darkened inner room, shading her eyes from the sudden light, and the doctor, who was taking off his gloves, laid one hand heavily upon the table.

"Jessie," said he, and his voice died away before the word was uttered.

At this moment entered Peter MacNeill. "Is it anything more that I can do for ye to-night, misthress?"

"Ah, no, Peter," said she, with a look worth many words of thanks.

And when MacNeill had gone she turned her face to the physician quietly, as if she had not heard him speak. "Will you come in now to see my husband, doctor?"

"He your husband? Jessie!"

Loyal Hearts and True

But she lifted her finger warningly, and he followed her without protest into the sick-room.

When the examination was over, and the drugs had been prepared, and directions as to their use given, Craven went in for a last look at the patient, who had already fallen asleep, and returning to the anxious wife said: "He will do now, I think," and after a pause, "It's my turn now, Jessie."

"I don't call you George. My name is Mistress MacKinnon," she said, with gentle dignity. "What is it you wish to know?"

"How did it happen, Jessie—how on earth did it happen?" he groaned, not heeding her protest.

"What?" she asked, looking aside.

"This is a poor place for the last of the MacNeills," he began again, "and Peter MacKinnon is fit to—to tie your shoe—scarcely. Tell me how —how it happened!"

She rose and walked away from him.

"Understand," said she, "that in insulting my husband you insult me, and also that I refuse to answer questions put to me in that manner!"

"You love him, then—this drunkard?"

She did not reply, and he added, "Jessie, I have loved you these seventeen years and more."

She turned upon him then with a fine scorn.

"A pretty speech—that—to make to me! and I, sir, have been married for twelve years and more!"

He seemed insensible to her reproof. "I did not dream that you were here, Jessie——"

Loyal Hearts and True

"So little do you know of your own island, so little interest do you take in the welfare of its people. You don't know a dozen of them altogether."

"Not my island!" he retorted, bitterly. "I'm only the 'Sassenach intruder!' Ah, Jessie, Jessie, what a wreck it has made of my life!"

She started to speak, but checked herself, and with a touch of scornful smile, waited.

"Why did you send for me? You knew it was I."

"Yes," said she, "from the first day. But my husband's life hung in the balance, and was I to stop for sentiment?"

"No; and yet you broke our engagement for sentiment, and sent me off to India broken-hearted for sentiment. Perhaps you married MacKinnon also for sentiment."

The sneer cut her cruelly. Almost under her breath she said:

"It is time for you to go, Dr. Craven. It cannot concern you to know why I chose my husband."

"But it does!" he cried, forgetting that his patient was asleep. "When we knew each other in Glasgow, your father turned me off because he was 'MacNeill of Barra,' and I was a 'base interloper' a 'Sassenach intruder,' dwelling on lands that should be his!"

"Well, and you cannot deny that," said she.

"Cannot? Ay, but the land was bought, honestly bought, by my grandfather from yours.

Loyal Hearts and True

And when they drank together, if the one took too much, whose fault was it ? "

" I don't know the truth of the story," said she slowly, " but my father always believed——"

" Ay, ay ; and he believed that we burned the castle too, out of spite, that we might build our home upon its ruins. He believed that too, and everybody here knows that it was an accident."

" I don't know the truth," she repeated, slowly. " It is fifty years since, and Eolgary House stands on the ruins."

" You doubt my word ! " was the hot retort.

" To what end are we talking ? " she continued, with a weary note.

" This," said he ; " my life has been ruined. There is an explanation due. It is my right."

" Very well," she replied, " but I have misunderstood. I supposed that all was over between us. Did you then expect to come back and claim me, perhaps, after my father died ? Did you think that I would consider his wish less then, or cease to espouse his cause about Eolgary ? "

" But you loved—I thought you loved me," he groaned.

" Loved ? What is it ? Yes, perhaps ; I was young. But now——"

" Now you love this drunkard MacKinnon, I suppose," he said, rudely.

" I sent for you professionally," she said, in her lowest tone.

" But you—you were in Glasgow. Why did you come to Barra ? " he demanded.

Loyal Hearts and True

"Because my husband, who comes of a tribe that fought shoulder to shoulder with my ancestors, owned land, and held a post here. Good-night."

He picked up his gloves and whip, but still hesitated.

"Your husband is not out of danger."

"But you can save him?" she asked, all but her anxiety forgotten.

"Yes, I can save him, if he is worth it."

Even he quailed before her eyes, as the patient-faced matron was suddenly transformed into the Jessie of seventeen years before.

"Thank God that I was saved from marrying you! I can send for Dr. Mackenzie hereafter. He does not pretend to be a judge over man's life and death."

"But, Jessie——"

"Don't speak to me!"

"You wrong me. I am a poor excuse of a doctor, I know——"

"You are worse than that!" she flashed on him; "you are a poor excuse of a man! Having everything that heart could wish——"

"Not everything, Jessie."

"How do you treat your fellow-creatures? They are buzzing flies to you, to be brushed away, that's all. And you call yourself a martyr; you say you have been disappointed in love, and you waste your life."

She stopped suddenly, and he had no reply ready.

"Did you, or did you not, refuse to set Jim

Craddock's arm because he could not pay in advance?"

"I did; but——"

"Yes, when Dr. Mackenzie was in a drunken fit and helpless, and so the man had to lie groaning with a splintered bone for two days before he could get the money together."

"I did not know——"

"And when Annie MacTavish was so bad, did you not tell her to go to a hospital in Glasgow?"

"Yes, I could do nothing for her. I——"

"But she had no money, and so she died. You are a cruel man!"

His face was grey as ash as he stood staring as her. Suddenly, without a word, he left the cottage.

Her eyes filled with tears as she looked after him. After all, they had been young together.

"It was true what I said, and much more, but it was hard."

III

WRONGS RIGHTED

MEANWHILE, with loose rein and hanging head, Craven was riding away over the hills. The sleet storm had ceased, and the air was still and cold, dark moreover with the gloom that precedes the dawn. As he rode through the dimness, the words kept singing themselves in his ears, "You are a cruel man!" And every beat of his horse's hoofs

Loyal Hearts and True

kept time to the "cruel, cruel." But again, often as he crested a hill, and carefully guided his horse away from the rocky hollow bogs which kept pace with the roads, he would tell himself in a flash of defiance, "After all, my life is mine—mine to do as I please with, just as the house is mine, and the land. What right has she——" But then he must pause, for there was always another voice to urge insistently, "Is it? Is it?"

He reached the last hill, from which he could look down upon the bay.

"An interloper!" mused the doctor, softly patting the neck of his tired horse, who had stopped on the slope to breathe. "Ay, when it has been mine and my father's for fifty years, when I know and love every rock and every mound of turf, every scrap of heather, every cockle-shell upon the beach; love them so that they called across the sea to me in India, and made me home-sick with a yearning that brought me back."

All the while in his deepest consciousness a discomforting voice, which would not be silent and could not be stifled, was saying: "Ay, and you left your post and came away in search of health and pleasure. Not only cruel, as she called you, but selfish—selfish to the core!" He remembered having read or heard somewhere a sentence to the effect that a man who strove to save his own life should be the very one to lose it.

In this mood he rode down to the sands and out farther than need be towards the quick in-coming tide, to the great reluctance of his little horse.

Loyal Hearts and True

Roused at last by her trembling and snorting, and feeling her strong resistance to the rein, he looked up, and saw the danger in front, and for a moment, fascinated, let temptation assail him. It was so easy, so simple, just to stay where he was for a little while, and the problem of using and misusing life would be over.

Ah, but the horse was an obstacle. He could not hold her back much longer. She would speedily either bear him away against his will, or throw him, and leave him to solve the situation on foot. He laughed aloud at the absurdity of it all, and, giving free rein to his horse, allowed her to bear him away, fleeing like a fawn before the unknown terror of the sea. He looked back regretfully once or twice, and when he reached home and saw the red streaks of dawn shining on the black panes of Eolgary House, he said to himself, "It begins all over again."

For some days the island saw very little of him. He rode about on the most unfrequented ways, finally went away on business for a day or two, came back, and resumed his old habits of roving and riding.

One day he heard the postman shouting after him, and waited until that functionary came up to deliver his letters, rejoicing to be spared the long walk to Eolgary. The man's appearance attracted the doctor's attention. "You'll run that way once too often, some day," said he, not unkindly.

"Ach, I'm right enough, I'm thinking. Poor Peter MacKinnon!"

"Is he dead?" asked the other, quickly.

Loyal Hearts and True

"Wull, no ; but like to be. Dr. Mackenzie has give over going."

"The wretched idiot!" muttered Craven.

"What wass ye saying, sir?"

"Fine day. Good evening." And the doctor rode away.

But he did not go home. Half an hour later he walked into MacKinnon's cottage, to find Jessie with her face buried in the tangled hair of her youngest daughter, and the other children huddled round the fire and speaking under their breath.

She rose indignantly, but he put her aside. "I am come to cure your husband," said he, in a tone which admitted of no protest, and turned towards the sick-room.

"I have no money to pay you in advance," she said, bitterly.

He shivered a little, turned the movement into a shrug, and left her alone.

From that day on, MacKinnon began to improve. Every day the doctor met the wife, reported the patient's progress, gave a few brief directions, and left, as he came, without greeting.

One sunny morning in early spring, MacKinnon insisted that he was strong enough to go down to the quay, and when the doctor came his patient had fled.

"No matter," said he, smiling a little for the first time. "Make him rest when he comes back. Jamie," he continued to Jessie's boy, who was digging in the earth near by. "What are you going to be when you are a man?"

Loyal Hearts and True

The boy looked up startled, then hung his head embarrassed ; it was no everyday experience to be spoken to by the awful doctor.

" Fisherman ? "   Silence.

" Sailor ?   Captain ? "   Still no word.

" Doctor, then ?   Or shopkeeper ? " Jamie shook his head vigorously.

" You don't know ! "

" Yes, I do," said Jamie, his tongue loosened by defiance, " I shall have a big farm—as big as Eolgary —just as big, with horses and cows and sheep, and —— " he stopped, breathless.

Craven smiled a little, but Mrs. MacKinnon's face burned. She could not lift her eyes, but added hurriedly, as if to blot out the memory of those unfortunate words, "Won't you come in and rest a bit, doctor ? "

" Ay, that I will," said he, promptly, " I have a business matter to speak of. I didn't think you would ever ask me again, Jessie," he added, humbly.

" Nor did I," she admitted, in a low voice, " but you have saved my husband's life."

The subject was unpleasant to him, and he began hurriedly, " Jamie was speaking the truth just now, Jessie—about Eolgary, I mean. I have been meaning to tell you all winter, but I couldn't seem to—at least until your husband was well. I mean—— "

He stopped in confusion, and handed her a folded paper.

" Wha—what is it ? " she gasped.

" The deed to Eolgary, for Jamie.   Only let him

be MacKinnon-MacNeill. And then the MacNeills
will have their own again."

"But why?" she fluttered, "the property was
honestly bought up by your grandfather."

"Do you say that, Jessie?"

"Yes; but indeed, indeed, you must take this
back. I cannot—we cannot—oh, I don't seem to
understand!" she cried, pressing her hands against
her pale cheeks.

"The reason is very simple," he said, quietly, "but
it doesn't matter; you see I cannot use the property
in India."

"In India?"

"Ay, I return next month. I shall like to think
of you in the old garden, Jessie. I suppose you have
never seen it? It has all fallen into decay; I tried
to revive it, but it needed a woman's love. You will
succeed."

"George," she said at last, forcing the tears to
keep within bounds, "don't—don't go to India!
Stay on the island, I know you love it—love your
home."

"I love——" he began, "ay, I love it, but I must
go, and I shall like to think of you at Eolgary."

"But I will not go!" she cried, passionately. "I
shall be haunted——"

"By what? I think I was haunted there by the
spirits of your ancestors, buried in the old graveyard
yonder."

"By all the harsh words which I spoke to you—
now I see how unjustly!"

"They were not unjust—but true, every one.

Loyal Hearts and True

You cannot take them back. Surely you cannot refuse me this compensation. I am the last of my family. I shall not come back from India—whose else should it be, when I die?"

"It is not time to talk about that now!"

"Yes, it is," adding, "I shall live and die in India."

"But my husband?"

"Why not? He has always been friendly to me."

He stopped abruptly, and she added: "And you saved his life, and now——"

"Make me happy," he pleaded, and once more held out the paper. They looked at each other until his will prevailed; she put out a trembling hand and took the deed.

"Good-bye," said he, suddenly. "Ay, to Glasgow, by the 'Fiona,' to-morrow," he answered her unspoken question.

"I shall think of you in my mother's chair—and of MacNeill of Barra come to his own."

The next day was so wet and stormy that few of the islanders were interested enough to go to the pier to stare at the "Fiona." At the last moment, however, young Jamie MacKinnon fairly tumbled down the hill with a note for the doctor, who read the bit of paper as the ropes were being cast off, and then looked past the wee hamlet on the shore to the misty hilltops, with eyes as dim as they.

"Bless you for this, Jessie!" was his thought; "I never understood before, and I have been wrong. Thank God, there's still a little time, enough, at

Loyal Hearts and True

least, to start the other way, and thank God that I know her better, after seventeen years of bitterness —that she has been loyal, better than if she loved me. I think she must suspect—what I know—that my days are—well, no matter."

And as the hills of Barra sank slowly upon the horizon, he turned his face resolutely southward, and faced the blast, humming to himself a little tune.

"PASSING THE LOVE OF WOMAN"

I

THE TWO BROTHERS

A WINDOW, ivy-framed, was softly lifted to let a breath of the caller morning air into a sick-room.

"Ah—h!" came a long-drawn exclamation from the bed in the corner. "That's good, Steve! There's nothing that money can buy like fresh air, nothing. I'm thankful the day's come. The girls will be up and about soon, and they will make you a cup of strong tea; you need it sorely after the long night's watch, my lad."

"Never mind me, grandmother!" was the quick response from a tallish, broadly-built young man, who moved about deftly as any woman.

Old Mrs. Jennery, of Springholm, never had a daughter of her own, neither had her son, the father of the twin lads, motherless from their birth, whom he left to his mother's care when he died. "Granny" had had the uninterrupted bringing up of the pair. Of the two one was her pride, the other her puzzle. In Stephen, the elder twin, she recognised the vigour of her own strong character repeated.

"My lad's a proper strong lad!" she would

Passing the Love of Woman

mutter, and the keen old eyes would brighten, as she noted the stalwart youth tramp up and down the lands.

Then, her gaze swerving to the other twin, to Cyril, grew cold, and all pride died out. The languid, slenderly-built lad, with his mother's face, all lovely curves and vivid tints, his sleepy brown eyes and curling lashes, was a disappointment to the stern, self-repressed nature of his ancestress.

Cyril was no thoroughbred soil-tiller—not he. Stephen, maybe, had absorbed the physical strength that ought to have been divided between the two, leaving to his weaker half the finer, subtler brain essence, the seeing eye, the hearing ear for all things beautiful in nature and art.

Both lads had a good education, and when they came home, for all the world as though she had but held out on purpose, Grandmother Jennery failed abruptly—the human machine was worn-out.

" I wanted to see this day's sun rise, Steve, behind the uplands, because I've a feeling that my time will be come when it sets over the low meads to-night! " she broke the silence to say, equably, when the maids at length were heard stirring below, and Stephen had come back to her, after his cold tub, to bring her the good tea she craved from himself.

All that high summer day the dying woman lay watching the cloud-shadows stealing across the green slopes. Now and again there stole up from below a low, sweet wail from the Strad that was to Cyril another self. The sounds crept into her ears, but failed to stir up the old animus. What mattered it that the lad should idle thus? Perhaps God knew, and softer thoughts stole into the slowly-dying brain —perhaps Cyril's was, after all, the better part.

"Steve!" There was a hurried cry.

"I'm here, grandmother!" came the ready response from the window-seat, where tireless Stephen waited and watched the surely-ebbing life.

"I've been thinking, my lad, about Cyril's future. Lawyer Groome has got the will safe under lock and key; after what's coming is over, he will settle things as I've meant them to be at Springholm. You see it always worried me how two masters could bide here."

"That will be all right, grandmother. There's no need to worry over a trifle."

"'Taint a trifle, my lad. Oh, Steve, you've always been my lad—a chip of the old block—a true Jennery. But I've been a bit hard with Cyril, and it's all come home to me—now at the last; one sees so clearly now. And—and I'm sorry I did it, Steve!"

"Did what, grandmother?" gently questioned Stephen, coming over to the bedside and sitting down, to stroke softly the bent fingers that were ceaselessly clutching at the flowered quilt.

"Bend down close, my lad, and I'll tell ye."

The round, short-cropped, brown head came close down to the shaking lips, and a few words were whispered.

"You never did, grandmother!" Steve started back, staring at the hard, wrinkled face on the pillow.

Passing the Love of Woman

"I did so. And I'd the right. 'Twas my money that redeemed Springholm when I married your grandfather, though nobody outside knew it but Lawyer Groome."

"But, grandmother," broke in Stephen, "what has poor Cyril done?"

"Whisht! 'Tis not for you to question my right, Steve!" There was a spurt of the old dominating spirit.

As evening crept on the mistress of Springholm grew weaker and drowsy. Cyril nervously stole in to take his place beside Steve. There was an expectant hush in the quiet room.

"Cyril, come still closer. I can scarce see you. My lad, you may say that I've done you a hurt, but Steve will look after you—always. Say that you will, Steve? What I've told you will make no difference, promise me!" The bent fingers had stayed their clutches at the quilt to grip hard the slenderly-shaped hand—a true artist's hand—that Cyril half-diffidently extended.

"I promise, granny; have no fear!" Stephen stood up, a human tower, to put his arm across Cyril's sloping shoulders. "In all things and at all times Cyril shall be foremost. It will be my life-task to further him—at any cost to myself."

"Stay! Not that! 'Tis too much to promise!" cried out the dying woman, as the solemnly-spoken vow fell, clearly-syllabled, in the still, quiet room. "Take back such rash words, lad!"

"I have said them—and I mean to keep them!" was the terse reply.

Passing the Love of Woman

II

A NEW SPURT OF LIFE

SEVERAL years had slipped along since Grandmother Jennery abdicated in favour of the twin-brothers— years that had made a better man still of Steve Jennery. Cyril, on the other hand, had distinctly slipped back, physically-speaking.

"Rouse up, man," Stephen would say, briskly, a thread of anxiety vibrating through his energetic words. "What have you got to say to this new machinery fad, eh?" He would persist in asking.

"Oh, you know best, Steve!" was the indifferent answer. It was less than nothing to him that Stephen should pin *his* faith on the steam-plough while neighbour So-and-so would cling to the old-world implement. In him there was naught but a secret disdain for such practical matters as were only meant for the contemplation of minds of a lower plane than his own. He hugged to himself the belief that he was of another calibre from the sons of the soil; that he was, in short, a poet. This conviction served to isolate him from his human surroundings, and even in measure to separate him from good old Steve.

"Him'll never make old bones, look see," predicted the farm-folk about Cyril. "'Tis the old story, for sure. Never knawed a generation of Jennerys wi'out one on they dwinin' aff. Now, 'tis Muster Cyril, see if 'taint."

236

Passing the Love of Woman

Wilfully blinding himself to an evident fact, Stephen fought against the direful prognostications. Yet, with a certain contradiction, he privately waylaid and consulted old Dr. Scrope, as to Cyril's life-chances.

"Well, the truth is, dear boy," said the old man, laying a kindly hand on Steve's shoulder, "the climate here is dead against him. What he wants is a dry atmosphere, instead of this clay and dampness. And if you want to know where to put your finger on such, it's South Africa: not the coast, of course, but the interior; that would suit him down to the ground."

"Do you mean that—that to live on here would shorten his life?" Steve asked, with a forced calm, and he involuntarily straightened himself, as though to receive an expected blow.

"I'd give him two years!" half-absently observed Dr. Scrope. Then the old man brisked up, at a groan from his hearer who, abruptly turning on his heel, strode away.

"Poor chap!" The doctor twisted himself round in his gig, in order to watch Stephen's stalwart figure plunging heavily, with bent head, along the dusty white road.

"It would have been quite easy for me to die for him!" said Steve aloud. "I could have done it. Cyril is all I have!"

And Cyril it was, at that moment warm, living, and all unwitting, whose doom had just been pronounced.

"I will save him!" he said, fiercely, under his

breath. Steve did nothing by halves; his love for his twin-brother was a spendthrift outpouring in its lavishness. No sacrifice would he count as such to eke out Cyril's span. If South Africa really possessed such a high and dry climate on its table-land, a thousand feet above the sea, why, there was more than a reasonable hope of Cyril's health being rebuilt—there was a certainty. "The sooner you get there the better, old man!" decided Steve, with his teeth set hard, and a quite new look of pain in his honest blue gaze.

"How you do run on, Steve!" Cyril said, fretfully, then he coughed.

"Exactly. We've both got to run on, you and I!" he said aloud, cheerfully.

Then he unfolded his plan, all cut and dried, to the nervously astounded Cyril. Springholm had got to be let—that was the first move. There would be little or no difficulty about that. With a fat rent the brothers could take their pleasure leisurely for a time in the new country that was to build up Cyril, who listened limply enough to Steve's energetic castle-building.

"Seems to me that I should just perk up for a time out there, and then fall back as soon as we returned home," he murmured, hopelessly.

"In that case we need never return," steadily said Steve, after a little silence.

"What, give up the old country!" Cyril clung with a passionate love to his native land.

"It doesn't matter a rap, does it, whether the soil we tread is the stubbly *karroo* or the green meads of old England, so long as we are together, and sound in health?" asked Steve, sturdily.

A light flitted into the younger Jennery's eyes; then it flitted out again. Along with his body, his mind had grown strangely languid.

But when he had, by degrees, imbibed the full sense of the enterprising plan born in Steve's brain, Cyril felt a new spurt of life awake within him, as the sap stirs in the plant when the turn of the year has come. He threw himself into the preparations that followed Steve's decision with an energy built of new hopes.

Then came the rush of the winding-up; the breathless farewells to the old country; and before the two quite realised that they had broken away from the old home-ties, they were watching the fading English shores from the deck of a liner steaming down Channel, bound for the Cape.

III

THE DAWNING OF LOVE

IT was a hot, broiling December day. So long had the drought lasted that people forgot what rain was like. Up at the ostrich-camp the birds stood about, gasping, with bills wide open and throats inflated. The veldt was one stretch of hopeless brown. The sky overhead was a cruel, metallic grey, with never a grain of blue in it.

"Oh, for a big rain!" was the chorus in subdued

voices, throats being too parched for any but the briefest conversation.

It was the Jennerys' first experience of a severe drought. Steve and Cyril had made their way leisurely from Port Elizabeth to a large farm in the Karroo district, to the owner of which, Peter Langermann, they carried letters from old Dr. Scrope. He agreed to receive the Jennery brothers under his roof for a time, with a view to a partnership.

The household of Peak's View consisted of the farmer himself, his sister Anna, who reigned in his dead wife's stead as mistress—for Peter was a widower—and his daughter Daphne, an only child.

Daphne was a magnificent human specimen of Cape growth, a splendidly developed girl, thanks to the fresh, pure air of the karroo. As she sat in the verandah on the hot December morning, her slender fingers idling over some dainty lace-work, and by her side a little table, on which was a large dish of golden crimson-sided peaches, Cyril Jennery thought he had never beheld a fairer, sweeter picture—out of fiction.

He was lying back in a deck-chair, gratefully drinking in the hot dry air which, stifling others, was to his weak lungs an incomparable medicine. Cyril had mended from the moment he and Steve left the coast behind them. He flourished and expanded, to the joyful pride of the watchful Steve, whose heart beat with gladder throbs each time he heard Cyril's new light-hearted tones, and noted his springy step.

"That brother of yours is as good as gold, Mr. Cyril Jennery!" Aunty Anna put her smooth head out of the dim interior.

Passing the Love of Woman

"What's Steve been doing now?" enquired Cyril.

"Doing now!" echoed Aunty Anna. "Why, what he's always doing! Wearing himself out slaving after your fads. He's toiling up to the camp with that pair of ostrich-chicks you bought, and I expect all the thanks he will get may be a sunstroke."

Where Aunty Anna got her energy, and how she kept up its stream under the fierce sun of her country, would be difficult to say.

"Sit down and eat a peach, aunty," said Daphne, smiling indulgently at the volcanic little spinster.

"Sit down and eat peaches!" The suggestion was a match producing a further outbreak of energetic fire from this human crater. "And that piece of mischief January waiting at the back door to be dealt with! What do you think he has done now? Tied the last mail's *Punch* to the tail of one of the big ostriches, and the distraught bird is off like the wind into the next century—for I don't believe father and the 'boys' will ever catch up with it. They rode off an hour ago, and left January to me!"

Aunty Anna's print skirt swished round the corner of the verandah with the vigorous swirl of a kestrel "striking" down on its hapless prey, while the eyes of Daphne and Cyril met in mute laughter.

"That Kaffir boy January will catch it now!" said Cyril; and the girl sighed.

Day by day, Cyril Jennery and Peter Langermann's daughter were learning to love each other, not in idle, passing fashion, but with the strong, abiding love of man and woman which naught can change or lessen.

Passing the Love of Woman

Steve too was as happy as the day was long. His satisfaction bubbled over in ceaseless smiles and cheery words. Not even an obstreperous ostrich could disturb Steve's equilibrium, and one can hardly say more in praise of a man's temper in that part of the world.

"That elder Jennery's made up of the real stuff," Peter Langermann told Aunty Anna. "He suits me down to the ground. And if he will only fall in with this partnership scheme, I'll be a made man. I've taken to him as I never took to any lad before. That's the sort of son I'd have wished to have."

"He seems in no hurry to make up his mind about the partnership," observed aunty.

"His head's screwed on the right way. He is slow, but sure—what the Scotch call 'canny.' He's learning the land; learning our farming ways out here; learning to manage the ostriches up at the camp fairly."

And Peter Langermann was right. Steve had taken his time to master the bearings of an altogether new life. At last, satisfied that he knew his way about, he made the bargain between himself and the farmer.

There were other things that made the day brighter for Steve Jennery, all unconsciously to himself. It was hardly possible for any but a blind man to live under the same roof with so fair and sweet a human creation as Daphne Langermann and not be attracted. Apart from Daphne's lovely personality, Steve was stirred by the passionate affection between the girl and her father. It was akin to his own love

Passing the Love of Woman

for Cyril, so lavish was it, so altogether unexacting on Peter's side.

"She's all the world to the old man, that girl is!" he told himself, in full sympathy for the idolising father. That was at first.

Then two or three slight services he was able to do for Daphne aroused a feeling of individual interest in the serenely-calm, pure-souled maiden. The interest deepened into reverence for this

> "Perfect woman nobly planned."

It was a foregone conclusion that such reverence was but a step to another yet deeper feeling, and there came a day when Steve Jennery awoke to the knowledge.

He walked on air, in the secret exhilaration of his discovery. He thanked God aloud as he rode over the "lands" in the fresh, pearly, morning air. What had he ever done, he dumbly asked, that such good things should be showered upon him? There was old Cyril restored to health, a new man, likely to live as long as himself, and, perhaps who knew?—a man to be some day as happy as Steve!

Meantime there must be no talking of going back to the old country. There was, besides Cyril, that dearer, sweeter other to be cared for, watched over, and worked for in the new home of fair hopes that he was building.

Passing the Love of Woman

IV

A CRUSHING BLOW

STEVE was sauntering about on the *stoep*, waiting the return of Cyril, who had accompanied Daphne on her morning ride.

"Will massa come quick!" A voice broke in upon the day-dreaming. It was January, the Kaffir herd, and his face carried an exaggerated distress. An ostrich had just broken both legs, by madly charging at the wire fence. Steve was off like a shot to investigate the damage.

Half an hour later, when he came back from the ostrich-camp, Steve found the riders returned. Daphne was standing under a blue-gum tree, just as she had been helped off her horse. Her full-lidded eyes were downcast, her sweet mouth was trembling. Cyril, bending towards her, was speaking eagerly and low.

Steve halted abruptly. Something, he knew not what, tightened his heart-strings, and he clutched at his throat. The "deep waters were come in even unto his soul." Surely he was drowning, or was it that the vividly joyous hopes of the last few weeks were drowning? Suddenly Daphne raised her face. In the sweet, uplifted eyes that shyly met those of Cyril, Steve read the story of her heart, and the death of all hope for himself.

It was a strangely-aged man who crept away from the *stoep*, shrivelled as by a lightning flash. For days and nights after one picture was before

Passing the Love of Woman

his eyes, dreaming or waking—a girl, with pure, limpid eyes, standing under the blue-gum tree, beside one whom those sweet eyes told plainly was her lover.

"O God!" prayed this strong man, crushed, in his agony, "I said I would give up all—everything —to Cyril. I promised! But ask me not this thing. My 'flesh and my heart fail.' I cannot, even for Cyril!"

But no answer—then—came to the frenzied pleadings. With a starved heart crying out imperatively for its due, Steve watched the two who were dearest of all to himself in their new-found happiness. They, oblivious of the hunger in his envious eyes, believed they hugged their precious secret safe from all. When their awakening came, it was a rough one.

"Yes, you must speak to her father—the sooner the better!" Steve was saying, in a strangely deliberate voice, which Cyril was too uplifted to remark. The brothers were together, and Cyril had at last broken the news which was no news to Steve.

"Oh, I've no fear whatever of old Langermann's consent," rejoined Cyril.

"Her father will have to be told about grandmother's will, Cyril," Steve said, steadily. Himself, he would fain have kept it a secret that the dogmatic old mistress of Springholm had willed her little property and bit of money in the bank unreservedly to the elder of her twin grandsons, while to Cyril simply nothing was left.

*   *   *   *   *

Passing the Love of Woman

"You have the audacity to ask for my girl—you, a chap without a red cent to bless yourself with!" Peter's indignation was profound. And Aunty Anna backed him up. Their petted idol, their girl, to be thus cheapened in daring fashion!

"But, father dear"—Daphne's soft voice, unlike its usual serene evenness, trembled vibratingly—"I have heard you, a thousand times, wish God had given you a son. Will you not take him—my Cyril —to your heart as such?"

To have Daphne standing before him pleading with outstretched hands and entreating eyes for what he felt constrained to refuse, was new and painful for the worshipping father. But he steeled his heart.

"He could be no son of mine; he is a jack-anapes, with his idle fads! Now, had it been the other lad—oh! Daffy girl, why couldn't you set your heart on the right brother, a man whose equal it would be hard to find for worth, and whose pockets are not flapping empty, as are those of that brainless idler?"

"Father!" A hot flush flooded the maiden's face, and Daphne's voice hardened. "Even you shall not—must not—say such things about Cyril! Besides, a true woman doesn't pry into a man's pockets before she gives her heart away to him. You—my dear dead mother loved yourself, surely, without questioning the state of your purse?"

"That was quite different!" came the customary answer age invariably gives youth. "I tell you once for all, my dear, as I have told your would-be suitor, I'll have none of such as he. There's an end o't."

Daphne was astounded, stunned.

When at last she realised her father's grim, inflexible obstinacy, she collapsed in a passion-storm of grief. As for Cyril Jennery, he took his hurt— silently.

Shrinking into himself, he shunned even Steve— the man whose hurt was greater and deeper still. Yet it was Steve who, with his larger nature, pushed into the background his own sorrow, in order to compassionate what he humbly considered Cyril's greater need.

"Poor lad!" As a mother comforts her stricken child, he put his big, strong arm round the weaker man. Who could sympathise more fully with Cyril's loss, indeed, than Steve? Not that Cyril thought so.

"Ah! Steve, it's impossible to make you understand what it is to have, and to lose. You, who never had, never lost, cannot probe the depths of my sorrow!"

"I may, perhaps, guess at it, dear lad," quietly said Steve.

"Oh, guessing!" Cyril shook himself impatiently. "You can't know, I tell you, what it is to have set your heart on such a woman as my Daphne—and to lose her!"

Then Cyril lapsed into such rhapsodies as come natural to lovers in all ages, and Steve grew greyer, stonier. But he kept his arms round his brother's shoulder, though each word pierced his heart.

And presently, when the elder Jennery crept

away, it was with whitening lips that muttered: " In all things, and at any cost, Cyril shall be foremost . . . at any cost to myself!"

Cyril mooned miserably about, and grew conspicuously delicate-looking, startlingly thin, and Daphne obstinately kept her room. Peter Langermann, with a quite new perpendicular line between his eyebrows, came and went, a wretched man, while Aunty Anna audibly wished the Englishmen had never crossed the *stoep* of Peak's View.

V

A HEROIC SACRIFICE

THE clouds were massing up, as if a rain-storm at last were imminent. Steve glanced absently at them, but just so had they, again and again, deceitfully gathered—and dispersed—throughout the long-continued drought.

As he strolled past the larger dam belonging to the farm he stared vacantly at its dry, baked bed, full of cracks and fissures, while along its banks the very mimosas looked parched and hopeless.

" I fervently wish a rattling storm would come," sighed Steve. " Perhaps it would clear the air, and brace up old Cyril."

" We shall have the rains to-night, eh ? " he called out, with an effort to brisk up, as January, the herd " boy," crossed his path, going home to the kraal. But January's answer was only a blaze of white teeth.

Passing the Love of Woman

Then, with a flash of his rolling eyes, he shook his inky head sceptically.

But Steve Jennery was right and January wrong. Soon after midnight every sleeper under the roof of Peak's View sprang to the floor, flung out of their dreams abruptly by a roar overhead that reverberated with the fury of a hundred cannons in the near hills. Then, almost immediately, the darkness was as the noonday in the blinding blue flash that heralded a second and more appalling peal.

"The rains have come! God Almighty be praised!" The shrill, shrieking words came from Aunty Anna, who, regardless of her appearance in the rivers of white frills that constituted her night-gear, was rushing about the landings in expectant joy.

"Just the saving of us all, thanks be!" gratefully murmured Peter Langermann. "Get up, man, and lend a hand, will you?" he shouted into Steve Jennery's room.

But Steve was already outside.

"I'm off to look after the stock," he had hastily told Cyril, while he rapidly fastened on his *veldt schoon*. "You bide quiet, old man; no use for you to get a soaking"—and Cyril, whose nerves were not of steel, was quite willing to "bide quiet" amid such unearthly turmoil of the tropical elements.

By-and-by, when the thunder-clouds with their deafening clamours were stealing off, a new sound burst upon Cyril's ears, a volume of dull roars which Aunty Anna told him blithely was the *sluit* coming down.

Passing the Love of Woman

"Both dams will be filled! God Almighty be praised!" she ended, with a Dutchwoman's favourite exclamation. But Aunty Anna took care not to hint aloud that there was any possibility of the larger dams overflowing, for at her elbow stood Daphne, white-cheeked and wide-eyed.

While Cyril and the women-folk waited in the shelter of the farmhouse, Peter Langermann, aided by such of the Kaffir hands as had come over from the kraal, was occupied in seeing to the safety of the stock. Steve had volunteered to go to the upper ostrich camp with January, for more than one nest had come whirling down the sluits.

Suddenly a whoop from January and a few gasping words made him aware that more than the stock was in danger. One of the Kaffir's huts had been washed bodily down the largest sluit, and was rushing with mad velocity to the dam, on the banks of which a miserable, half-drowned Kaffir woman was shrieking wildly and waving her arms.

"What on earth——" Steve broke off, for his eyes had caught sight, in the lightening dawn already creeping up the sky, of a small black object bobbing in the seething waters. It was a child's head. A Kaffir babe had been swirled out of the hut, and was drowning before the eyes of its mother, who, rushing down stream ahead of the hut containing her infant, was shrieking out her agony on the bank of the dam.

Steve's heart bounded, then dragged slowly. With a brave man's instincts, he was for springing into the dam after that small bobbing black head. But—but life was cheap—Kaffir life, at least. Was one little dusky human object more or less worth the risk?

"Inasmuch as ye did it not to one of the least of these, ye did it not to Me." What could be less than the Kaffir babe? And why—why did those sorrowfully solemn words pierce his brain at such a moment?

"After all"—Steve was hurriedly throwing off the sacking that protected him from the steady downpour of the clouds, while thoughts jostled each other swiftly, as they do in the great crises of a man's life—"after all," he muttered, "why should I not? And if—well, old Cyril will get all, even her. God bless them both! Ah—h!"

The waters were cold—icy cold, as Steve plunged in. Across the heaving, tumbling waters that roared through the sluit into the dam he fought with a gallant frenzy, his chin above the eddying flood, his eyes fixed on his goal. At last he was within reach, and could seize the child by its hair. A long-drawn-out, sobbing shriek from the bank gave his flagging strength a new spurt, as he fought back with his burden.

By this time January's courage had attained sufficient proportions to incite him to venture into the dam. As the two men met and January's fingers clutched at the child, a larger body of water was precipitated into the dam. A sudden swirl wrenched the brave rescuer and his burden apart, sending Steve back into the middle of the deep waters, while the increased volume floated January and the child on to the banks.

Passing the Love of Woman

Hoarse shouts of dismay went across the tumbling waters, but no answering cries came back. There was nothing but the sullen roar of the torrent that was fiercely, pitilessly trying to suck down a brave man to his death. On the bank the Kaffir mother was deftly emptying the water out of her babe's mouth and ears, as if it were a slippery little black bottle. In a day or two the now still ebony form would be rolling over the mud floor of its home hut. But what of its brave rescuer?

*   *   *   *   *

Peter Langermann is more than content, nowadays, with the son-in-law whom he once spurned. Cyril Jennery, the sole owner of Springholm and the "bit of money," was worthy even of Daphne, decided the satisfied farmer. It is a contented family that dwells under the roof of Peak View, and since Daphne's baby-boy came to be its king the happiness of Peter Langermann and Aunty Anna is complete.

And that other—the one whose absent place makes room for all this happiness—what of him?

Under the blue-gum tree is a wooden cross, where in the dusk a crouching figure steals to croon, with shrill Kaffir wailings, a prayer. On the cross are the words:—

"HE LAID DOWN HIS LIFE FOR ANOTHER."

THE COVENANTER'S DAUGHTER

LITTLE Janet's home stood on the brow of a hill in Ayrshire, where heather, rocks, and mossy places stretched far around. These were days long before any one dreamed of railroads ; and her father's work was to carry to market the things that the country-people had for sale, and to bring them what they required in return ; and he had gained the name of the Christian Carrier.

It was a pleasant home-coming for John Brown to his comfortable cottage, his lively, cheerful wife, and his sweet little girl. Many a stranger, too, found a welcome at that bright fireside.

Among these were not a few wanderers, welcomed for the sake of the Lord Jesus ; for those were dark and sorrowful times in Scotland, and hundreds of good men were persecuted, and forced to leave their homes and hide in the mountains and moors, rather than sin against their conscience and do what they thought displeasing to God.

It was a dangerous thing to give food or shelter to any of these, yet John Brown did not fear to do so ; although on many a hill, and in many a moor near, the blood of some martyr had stained the ground.

One winter night John Brown was away from his home, at a neighbour's house, and his household were sitting round the blazing fire.

Suddenly the dog, which was lying at the fire, sprang up and rushed barking to the door. Janet

253

sprang up also, thinking it was her father, and ran to welcome him.

"Whist, whist, Collie!" she cried to the dog as she went to the door.

But it was not her father who stood there, but a stranger; young, worn, and weary-looking. He had a gentle, pleasing face; a shepherd's plaid was wrapped round him, and his shoes were very much worn; but he did not look like a shepherd. Janet led him in and placed him in her father's chair. She looked to her mother; but her mother did not know what to think. It was not impossible that the stranger might be a spy, who would bring danger and death on the house in which he was sheltered, so she left Janet to do what she would, and sang her little boy to sleep with a piece of an old song.

Janet took the stranger to the warmest corner, and helped him to take off his wet plaid, and did all the little kind things for him that she could, in the most winning way.

The stranger's face had been getting a little brighter as the mother sang to her baby; but now he burst into tears, and cried—

"May the blessing of him that is ready to perish be upon you, my dear bairn! Surely God has heard my cry, and provided for a place to rest my head for a night."

As he said this, John Brown entered the cottage, and, looking at him, greeted him with great respect. The weary-looking man with the shepherd's plaid was a persecuted minister, who wandered from place to place in peril of his life.

The Covenanter's Daughter

The persecuted minister had no home. He often slept in caves and woods; and sometimes he got one of the frail little huts in which shepherds slept in summer when they kept their sheep on the hills, but which were left empty in winter; and this he counted a very comfortable resting-place, especially when he and his friends could get sticks to light a fire.

Yet all through his trouble he had much joy in the dear Master Whom he served.

"Oh, let none fear a suffering lot," he wrote in a letter to a friend. "Enemies think themselves satisfied when we are put to wander in mosses and upon mountains; but even amid the storms of these last nights I cannot express what sweet times I have had when I had no covering but the deep curtains of night. Each star led me to wonder what He must be Who is the Star of Jacob, of Whom all stars borrow their shining."

When the household found that the stranger whom John Brown recognised was the faithful minister Mr. Renwick, every one was ready to attend to him. He remained with the family two nights; and it was a happy time for him and for them all.

Darker days came to the little household at Priesthill. John Brown was obliged to leave his home, and hide in a deep ravine. The pure white snow was stained one cold March morning, in the neighbourhood of his dwelling, with the blood of a pious man who bore the same name: and many days and nights of fear were passed by his wife on his account.

At length a day came on which poor little Janet had a terrible sight to see. Her father had gone out

The Covenanter's Daughter

one morning to work on some peat ground, when a party of soldiers, led by "bloody Claverhouse," as the people called him, came round him suddenly.

He quietly left his work, and walked before them, leading the way to the door of his own cottage. Janet's quick eye saw the troopers, and she ran to tell her mother that a great many soldiers were coming down the hill with her father. The poor woman cried—

"The hour that I feared is come upon me!" and she took up her own little boy, and wrapped him in a plaid, and taking Janet by the hand, went out to meet them.

Janet saw her father kneel down and pray; then he kissed his wife and boy, and last of all he kissed his little girl, saying—

"My sweet bairn, give your hand to God as your Guide, and be your mother's comfort."

Claverhouse ordered his men to shoot, but they were afraid: and he himself snatched a pistol out of his belt, and shot John Brown through the head. The soldiers rode away, and left the sorrowful woman and children alone with the martyr's body.

There is nothing more known of little Janet's story after the day that she saw her father shot dead before his cottage; but surely we can have little doubt that the father's prayers were answered, and that she "gave her hand to God as her Guide."

PRINTED BY WILLIAM CLOWES AND SONS, LIMITED, LONDON AND BECCLES.

The Alexandra Library.

A Series of splendid Gift Books for Girls; good bulk, well printed, admirably illustrated, handsomely bound. Large crown 8vo, cloth full gilt, 3s. 6d. each.

THE BOTTOM OF THE BREAD PAN.

By ELEANORA H. STOOKE. Author of 'Angel's Brother,' etc. With Three Illustrations by J. FINNEMORE, R.I., etc. Large crown 8vo, cloth gilt, 3s. 6d.

'An excellent story of domestic struggle, showing how a family of girls rose to the necessities of the occasion, and in the end were suitably rewarded. The plot is well conceived, and the story told with considerable skill.'—*Record*.

'It is a most admirable and well-told story.'—*Baptist Times*.

'An interesting story nicely told.'—*Dundee Courier*.

CARPENTER AND KING. By ANNA

MAXWELL. With Three Illustrations by E. BARNARD LINTOTT. Large crown 8vo, cloth gilt, 3s. 6d.

'A well-written story of the conversion to Christianity of a cultured and well-to-do young Jewess. The interest is sustained from beginning to end and the conversation will be found to be instructive without being wearisome. The ending is happy, for the conversion of a millionaire Jew (her twin soul) makes the ringing of the marriage bells a possibility.'—*Primitive Methodist Leader*.

'The story—an excellent one for girls especially, is told in a pleasant and effective style.'—*Glasgow Daily Herald*.

'The story has many picturesque elements, and is out of the beaten course.'—*Aberdeen Daily Press*.

BETTY TREVOR. By Mrs. GEORGE DE HORNE

VAIZEY. Author of 'About Peggy Saville,' etc. With Seven Illustrations by E. P. KINSELLA. Large crown 8vo, cloth gilt, 3s. 6d.

'We doubt if there are any more popular stories for elder girls on the market than those that have recently emanated from the pen of Mrs. Vaizey. This latest story is one of her best, and deserves to be widely used as a reward book or for the school library. The story is one that appeals to the finer susceptibilities of girls in their teens and will be sure to become popular wherever read. It has seven beautifully produced illustrations by E. P. Kinsella, and is handsomely bound in cloth gilt.'—*The Schoolmaster*.

'"Betty" ought to become as great a favourite as her predecessor, "Pixie O'Shaughnessy".'—*Christian World*.

'Mrs. George de Horne Vaizey has written a delightful story for young people.'—*Western Daily Press*.

THE RELIGIOUS TRACT SOCIETY, LONDON.

UNIFORM EDITIONS OF STORIES.

By ROSA NOUCHETTE CAREY.

The Stories by this gifted and popular author contain graceful, vivid pictures of girl-life. They abound in striking incidents, and the character-sketching is very true to life. The books are issued in a new uniform binding, in blue cloth, with author's autograph in gold on the side.

AUNT DIANA. With a Frontispiece. Crown 8vo, cloth gilt, 2s. 6d.

'Miss Carey is specially successful in her delineation of character and "Aunt Diana" contains many strongly marked individualities, full of life and colour. There is a strong love element in the story.'

AVERIL. With a Frontispiece. Crown 8vo, cloth gilt, 2s. 6d.

'This is a very interesting tale which will not be readily put aside by the reader until the end has been reached.'—*Leeds Mercury.*

'The figure is well drawn, and there are many touching passages in the story.'—*Scotsman.*

'The story is well produced and is edifying as well as interesting.' —*Rock.*

'The volume is very interesting, and quite suitable for girls young or old.'—*Yorkshire Post.*

COUSIN MONA. With a Frontispiece. Crown 8vo, cloth gilt, 2s. 6d.

The story of two girls suddenly bereft of their father—their mother died during their childhood—and their trials is told in Miss Carey's interesting and inimitable way.

ESTHER CAMERON'S STORY. A Tale of Life and Influence. With a Frontispiece. Crown 8vo, cloth gilt, 2s. 6d.

'Illustrates in a striking and beautiful way that the faithful discharge of ordinary domestic work is as really Christian work as visiting the poor, etc., and that attention to one form of Christian service does not justify the neglect of another.'

THE RELIGIOUS TRACT SOCIETY, LONDON.

UNIFORM EDITIONS OF STORIES.

By ROSA NOUCHETTE CAREY.

LITTLE MISS MUFFET. With a Frontispiece.
Crown 8vo, cloth gilt, 2s. 6d.

'This is a charming story of the conversion of a harum-scarum girl who got into rather more than the average amount of scrapes at first, into a womanly girl.'—*Rock.*

'One of the prettiest stories we have read for a long time. "Little Miss Muffet" is a charming heroine. From a wild unmanageable schoolgirl, she develops into a sweet and lovable young woman, proving that she only needed a loving and wise training to bring out the good that was in her.'—*Independent.*

'A healthy bright little book with plenty of "go" in it, and also sound spiritual teaching.'—*Christian.*

MERLE'S CRUSADE. With a Frontispiece.
Crown 8vo, cloth gilt, 2s. 6d.

'It tells how a young lady in preference to being a governess takes the place of head nurse in a wealthy family. If it were not for convention and what the world says, many ladies might be happier in such situations, especially those who are fond of children. The tale is certainly very interesting, perhaps a trifle highly coloured, but of a general good tendency. Of course it has the usual happy finish—evidently these story writers think matrimony the most blissful culmination possible.'—*Rock.*

'The charm of the book lies in the faithfulness with which they are sketched, and without any excitement the interest is sustained throughout.'—*Liverpool Courier.*

OUR BESSIE. With a Frontispiece. Crown 8vo, cloth gilt, 2s. 6d.

'A handsome gift book, and a thoroughly well written and interesting picture of a healthy and happy girl life. We might well give it another title and call it a vivid representation of the great power of loving influence. Well worthy of admiration and imitation of our young lady readers.'—*Freeman.*

'We can heartily recommend it as an appropriate gift book for young ladies. Its tone is thoroughly healthy; the story is interesting, and well told, and the binding bright and attractive.'—*Record.*

'There are many touching incidents in this excellent story which is one that girls will read with interest.'—*Liverpool Courier.*

THE RELIGIOUS TRACT SOCIETY, LONDON.

GIRL'S OWN SERIES.

THE BLESSEDNESS OF IRENE FARQUHAR.
By EGLANTON THORNE. Author of 'Her Own Way,' etc. With Frontispiece by ALFRED PEARSE. Crown 8vo, cloth gilt, 2s. 6d.

'The story of Irene Farquhar is delightfully told in this book. Irene is beautiful and happy in her home, bright and gay in society, and marked for a brilliant career. She has a fall from her horse, and becomes an invalid for life, as it is thought. Her entire circumstances are thus changed, and, although she is naturally downcast at first, she becomes resigned to her fate. . . . . The story brings into its chapters many recent and interesting topics, and as it is well written and engaging, it will form a useful volume for a prize or a school library.'—*Schoolmistress.*

'The book is both wholesome and entertaining.'—*Christian.*

'It is a pleasant story, and young girls will follow it with interest.' —*Record.*

BY LOVE IMPELLED.
By HARRIET E. COLVILE. Author of 'My Grandmother's Album,' etc. With Three Illustrations by SYDNEY COWELL. Crown 8vo, cloth gilt, 2s. 6d.

'It is a well-written book, and probably nearer to real life than the rosy-hued stories which we must admit that, for our part, we prefer to put in the hands of young people. Sydney Cowell's pictures are skilfully drawn, and the cover design is decidedly taking.'—*School Guardian.*

CYNTHIA'S BROTHER.
By LESLIE KEITH. Author of 'Ralph Ellison's Opportunity,' etc. With Five Illustrations by HAROLD COPPING. Crown 8vo, cloth gilt, 2s. 6d.

'The spoiled lad, who is the hero of the book, after getting into difficulties during a short experience of army life, emigrates to Matabeleland, and learns from his rough fortunes to value more truly the love of a noble girl.

'Cynthia's own love story runs side by side with her brother's, and, indeed, the interest centres chiefly about two girl friends.'— *Baptist Magazine.*

'A pretty story, charmingly told.'—*Guardian.*

HER OWN CHOICE.
By RUTH LAMB. Author of 'A Wilful Ward,' etc. With Frontispiece by ALFRED PEARSE. Crown 8vo, cloth gilt, 2s. 6d.

A charming story by a favourite writer.

THE RELIGIOUS TRACT SOCIETY, LONDON.

GIRL'S OWN SERIES.

MY BROTHER'S FRIEND. By EGLANTON THORNE. Author of 'In London Fields,' etc. With Frontispiece. Crown 8vo, cloth gilt, 2s. 6d.

Though written avowedly for girls, and consisting in the main of the story of a girlhood, this book will interest all young folk. The story grows upon the reader and has much in it that is stimulating and helpful. Though there is very little direct mention of 'religion,' there is a healthy tone throughout. Some of the characters are specially attractive, and though in one or two places there is a little improbability of incident, as a whole the book is true to life.

ONLY A GIRL-WIFE. By RUTH LAMB. Author of 'Of No Account,' 'Dear Miss Meg,' etc. With Six Illustrations. Crown 8vo, cloth gilt, 2s. 6d.

'A story by Ruth Lamb has always some useful morals unobtrusively mingled with its pleasant details. "Only a Girl-Wife" is not remarkable for sensationalism of plot or cleverness of style; it is simply an easy, sensible, readable story of a young wife's mistakes and how she learned a better way under good influence and the example of true Christianity. Girls will find this a wholesome and agreeable bit of fiction.'—*Literary World*.

'The tale is well-written and of good tendency.'—*Rock*.

A QUEEN OF NINE DAYS. By her gentlewoman, MARGARET BROWN. Edited and done into modern English by EDITH C. KENYON. With Three Illustrations by A. W. COOPER. Crown 8vo, cloth gilt, 2s. 6d.

'This is the pathetic story of Lady Jane Grey's short occupation of the throne. It is ostensibly told by her gentlewoman, Margaret Brown, and her simple and sympathetic narrative, touching many of the chief events and personages of the turbulent days of the early part of the sixteenth century, makes a bright and vivid story with a well-painted historic background.'—*Westminster Gazette*.

A LASS AND HER LOVER. By LESLIE KEITH. Author of 'Our Street,' 'The Deceiver,' 'Cynthia's Brother,' etc. With Frontispiece. Crown 8vo, cloth gilt, 2s. 6d.

'Not for some time have we read a story that contained so much good sense combined with real humour. . . . . To read this book is not only to be intensely interested, but invigorated in heart and mind. Unlike many books of its kind, it may be read through again and again with increasing delight.'—*Methodist Times*.

THE RELIGIOUS TRACT SOCIETY, LONDON.

THE GIRL'S LIBRARY.

REAPING THE WHIRLWIND. A Story of Three Lives. By E. F. Brooke. With Three Illustrations. Large crown 8vo, cloth gilt, 2s.

A story of school-girl life, of the loss of bank-notes, and the suspicion cast upon the innocent, and the blighting influence which for years clouded the youthful lives of the companions till at last confession is made. The misery brought about by the wounds of the tale-bearer is vividly and naturally portrayed.

MERMAIDENS. A Sea Story for Girls. By Sarah Tytler. Author of 'A Lonely Lassie,' etc. With Three Illustrations by Raymond Potter. Large crown 8vo, cloth gilt, 2s.

The story of Caroline Masham's youth, spent at sea on board her father's ship, written for the benefit of her descendants by the youngest daughter of the Rear Admiral, who was at the head of the Red Squadron—for these were the days when women and children might be seen on board His Majesty's frigates even in time of war. The "Sea Serpent" was attacked by two French frigates, and the battle in which the "St. Barbe" was boarded by ten English sailors, and in which Caroline's cool courage under fire received the doctor's commendation, is graphically described.

DEAR MISS MEG, and Other Stories. By Ruth Lamb. Author of 'Only a Girl Wife,' etc. With Three Illustrations by Victor Prout. Large crown 8vo, cloth gilt, 2s.

This volume comprises a series of capital short stories suitable for holiday reading. They are from the pen of Mrs. Ruth Lamb, whose circle of admirers is an ever-increasing one, and whose writings are of a character which makes them safe to recommend.

A WILFUL WARD. By Ruth Lamb. Author of 'Her Own Choice,' etc. With Four Illustrations. Large crown 8vo, cloth gilt, 2s.

The troubles into which the heroine falls by yielding to a very common temptation are well depicted by Ruth Lamb's skilful pen.

EIGHTEEN STORIES FOR GIRLS. By Rosa N. Carey, Sarah Doudney, Frances Lockwood Green, Mrs. Holman Hunt, Ida Lemon, Lady William Lennox, Isabella Fyvie Mayo, Mrs. Molesworth, and others. Edited by Charles Peters. With Seven Illustrations. Large crown 8vo, cloth gilt, 2s.

'This is a collection of readable stories by various favourite authors in an elegant and presentable form.'—*Christian.*

'These stories ought to win a warm welcome.'—*London Quarterly.*

THE RELIGIOUS TRACT SOCIETY, LONDON.

THE GIRL'S LIBRARY.

HER OWN WAY. By EGLANTON THORNE.
Author of 'Blessedness of Irene Farquhar.' With Three
Illustrations. Large crown 8vo, cloth gilt, 2s.

The title describes the book, in which the heroine discovers the
way of transgressors is hard.

**RAVENSDALE CASTLE. A Tale of
Elizabethan Times.** By L. C. SILKE. With Three
Illustrations. Large crown 8vo, cloth gilt, 2s.

This is a very charming story of life in Queen Elizabeth's days.
It has the interest that belongs to the portrayal, and to the evolu-
tion of a plot derived in the main from peaceful, social, and family
situations, yet with more than a spice of adventure, and at times
considerable strength of situation, occurring amidst its gentler elements.

'It is an excellent story for girls' reading, bound into a very
handsome volume. The illustrations have a delicacy of workmanship in harmony with the taste and spirit of the writing.'—
School Government Chronicle.

'There is a pleasant tone throughout the whole story.'—*School
Guardian.*

'This story will certainly please and entertain.'—*British Weekly.*

FINDING HER PLACE. By HOWE BENNING.
Author of 'Hope Reed's Upper Window,' 'Ursula's Begin-
ning,' etc. With Three Illustrations by ALFRED PEARSE.
Large crown 8vo, cloth gilt, 2s.

A well-told story of an orphan who, committed to the care of an
aunt and uncle, strives to find her place in life. The many trials
and vicissitudes she passes through are graphically told and she
emerges triumphantly at last.

SIR JASPER'S HEIR, and Other Stories.
By E. EVERETT-GREEN, LESLIE KEITH and other Authors.
Large crown 8vo, cloth gilt, 2s.

This is a collection of thirteen complete stories for girls by
popular writers. All the qualities of good fiction will be found
in this handsome volume—humour and pathos, brisk narrative and
sparkling dialogue. All girls and their mothers will be delighted
with it. The writers all employ their gift of story-writing to
worthy ends, and these tales not only immediately grip the interest of the reader, but stimulate to noble, self-sacrificing living.

THE RELIGIOUS TRACT SOCIETY, LONDON.

THE GIRL'S LIBRARY.

BRUCE HERIOT. By EVELYN EVERETT-GREEN.
Author of 'Alwyn Ravendale,' 'Barbara's Brothers,' etc.
With Three Illustrations by ADOLF THIEDE. Large crown
8vo, cloth gilt, 2s.

'A refreshing story for girls, told with the picturesqueness and
power of which Miss Everett-Green has so great a command. The
little lad—"Sonny"—who is introduced in the first chapter, plays
an important part in the story, and succeeds in bringing about the
reconciliation of two whom misunderstanding had parted. The story
has some clever character-sketching, and will be read with deep
interest. There are love-tales and love-tales : this is one of the
best.'—*Record.*

'A pleasant, healthy love story of modern life, which shows a
practised skill in the art of being sentimental without being sensa-
tional.'—*Scotsman.*

'As a present for girls the book is admirable.'—*Outlook.*

LOVE'S SACRIFICE. By MARY BRADFORD-
WHITING. Author of 'Wallaby Hill.' With Three Illustrations by SYDNEY COWELL. Large crown 8vo, cloth gilt, 2s.

'An exceedingly pleasant story of a young English governess, who
is stranded in Germany through the heartlessness of her employer.
A young German who loves her comes to the rescue ; but mis-
understandings arise between them owing to differences in national
customs. A thoroughly healthy story, giving a capital picture of
some aspects of life in Germany.'—*Sheffield Telegraph.*

'The story will please immensely girls of various ages, and we
can thoroughly recommend the volume as a gift book.'—*Record.*

'A charming story of an English girl's life in Germany.'—*Outlook.*

BY THE PATH OF THE STORM. By
DOROTHY BAIRD. With Three Illustrations by T. LIDDALL
ARMITAGE. Large crown 8vo, cloth gilt, 2s.

'This is another story for girls, written in a free, flowing style,
full of fine characterisation, and will be read with eager interest.'
—*Methodist Sunday School Record.*

'Here we have a fascinating and well-told tale. The motherless heroine is the daughter of a doctor. In his "fight with death"
he falls a victim, and out of radiant sunshine and joy Viola enters
upon the storm. But in the midst of perils and pathos of human
experience she learns the triumph over self and sorrow ; she drinks
of the fountain of human love, and attains at last to that Vision
of the Highest that deepens and enriches all. Our daughters will
delight in this story, and for their sakes the mother who reads it
will secretly bless the gifted writer thereof.'—*Presbyterian.*

THE RELIGIOUS TRACT SOCIETY, LONDON.

THE GIRL'S LIBRARY.

HONOR'S QUEST; Or, How They Came
Home. By LAURA A. BARTER SNOW. Author of 'Harold,' 'Ruth's Roses,' etc. With Three Illustrations. Large crown 8vo, cloth gilt, 2s.

'This is a pleasant, well-told story, chiefly concerned with Irish life, into which one, at least, well-known champion of the Irish Church Mission is introduced. The plot is well developed, the incidents well ordered, the characters naturally set forth. It is a good and interesting book for girls.'—*Church of Ireland Gazette.*

'There are many happy glimpses of Irish life which are cleverly portrayed. A thoroughly fresh and breezy romance, it is written in a captivating style, full of life and incident.'—*Christian.*

AUDREY'S OLD MAN. By DOROTHY BAIRD.
Author of 'By the Path of the Storm.' With Three Illustrations by J. FINNEMORE, R.I. Large crown 8vo, cloth gilt, 2s.

'This is a charming story for girls. Audrey is a lovable maiden, and her old man a most pathetic figure.'—*Record.*

'The story is well written, interesting, and in parts pathetic. For older girls it is a splendid story.'—*Schoolmistress.*

'Describes a girl's devotion to her widowed mother, and will inspire high ideals and noble ambitions.'—*Christian World.*

'"Audrey's Old Man," by Dorothy Baird, is very touching and tender. The course of true love does not run smoothly, but it calls out many beautiful and noble qualities.'—*Baptist Times.*

AN IDYLL IN VENICE. By MARGARET
SURREY. Author of 'My Hero,' 'Elias Trust's Boys,' etc. With Seven Illustrations. Large crown 8vo, cloth gilt, 2s.

'This is a very attractive and well-written book. The descriptions of "The Bride of the Sea," with the numerous excellent photographic illustrations, will revive pleasant memories in the minds of those who are acquainted with the beauties of Venice, and awaken a desire on the part of those who have not yet had that pleasure, to visit it. The "Idyll" is naturally and ably worked out, the tone is high, and the lesson impressive.'—*British Weekly.*

'The love story is well told, and the descriptions of Venetian life are done with great accuracy, and materially add to the interest of the book. The story is told with a good deal of literary charm, and will commend itself to adults as well as to young readers. It is illustrated by seven views of Venice.—*Record.*

THE RELIGIOUS TRACT SOCIETY, LONDON.

STORIES FOR BOYS.
By TALBOT BAINES REED.

The name of Talbot Baines Reed will always be associated with fascinating, healthy stories for boys, dealing with public school life, and early business careers. No writer has been able more skilfully to give his characters a real personality, or to portray more faithfully their failures, sharp struggles and final successes.

THE ADVENTURES OF A THREE-GUINEA WATCH.

With Seven Full-page and Sixteen other Illustrations in the Text. Large crown 8vo, cloth gilt, 3s. 6d.

A straightforward story of school-life, and of the duties and temptations of young men entering upon the work of life. The kind of book to rejoice the heart of the boy who gets it as a Christmas present.

THE COCK HOUSE AT FELLSGARTH.
A Public School Story.

With Seven Full-page Illustrations by ALFRED PEARSE. Large crown 8vo, cloth gilt, 3s. 6d.

A splendid story of school life. The rollicking fun of the juniors, the rivalry among the seniors, the school elections, the football match, are told in such a forcible manner that the tale will prove a source of delight to all boys—young and old.

THE FIFTH FORM AT ST. DOMINIC'S.
A Public School Story.

With Seven Full-page and Eight other Illustrations in the Text. Large crown 8vo, cloth gilt, 3s. 6d.

A lively story, abounding in stirring incident and in humorous descriptions. A thoroughly healthy tale to place in the hands of a boy. It ought to become popular both as a gift and prize book.

A DOG WITH A BAD NAME.

With Seven Full-page Illustrations by ALFRED PEARSE. Large crown 8vo, cloth gilt, 3s. 6d.

The story of a big ungainly youth who seemed fated to be misunderstood and to be made the butt of his comrades. His trials at school, and as a tutor, and the unsympathetic treatment by his guardian are delightfully told.

THE RELIGIOUS TRACT SOCIETY, LONDON.

STORIES FOR BOYS.

By TALBOT BAINES REED.

ROGER INGLETON, MINOR.

With Seven Full-page Illustrations by J. FINNEMORE, R.I. Large crown 8vo, cloth gilt, 3s. 6d.

The Guardian says:—"Mr. Talbot Baines Reed knows how to tell a story, and he does himself justice in 'Roger Ingleton, Minor,' in which he makes an excellent book out of the return of a long-lost half-brother who had gone out alone into the world, many years previously, after a bitter quarrel with his father. The discovery of the missing brother is not accomplished without many exciting incidents, out of which Mr. Reed weaves his plot."

The Aberdeen Free Press says:—"This story has a modern atmosphere. The plot is very skilfully constructed and the interest is maintained up to the last page."

SIR LUDAR: A Story of the Days of the Great Queen Bess.

With Eleven Full-page Illustrations. Large crown 8vo, cloth gilt, 3s. 6d.

The Guardian says:—"This stirring tale, which is played in the days of Queen Elizabeth, and tells of the wonderful adventures of a sturdy prentice-lad who contrived to crowd into a few years as much danger and fighting and hairbreadth escapes as would have lasted an army of ordinary folk for their whole lives. It is a capital book for boys which those who begin reading will have to finish. Mr. Pearse's illustrations, too, are very good.

The Aberdeen Free Press says:—"This is a stirring tale of adventure with plenty of fighting."

PARKHURST BOYS, and other Stories of School Life.

With Seven Full-page and many other Illustrations. Large crown 8vo, cloth gilt, 3s. 6d.

In this volume are brought together a large number of the miscellaneous stories written from time to time for the *Boy's Own Paper* by Talbot Baines Reed. The collection is prefaced by an appreciation of Mr. Reed as boy and man, and it contains some of his best work and his brightest wit. There are seven sketches of life at Parkhurst School; eleven character delineations of "Boys we have known"—such as "The Bully," "The Sneak"; twelve representations of "Boys of English History"; and seven other short stories of boy life and interest.

THE RELIGIOUS TRACT SOCIETY, LONDON.

THE BOY'S LIBRARY OF ADVENTURE & HEROISM.

WILD LIFE IN SUNNY LANDS. A Romance of Butterfly Hunting.

By GORDON STABLES, M.D., R.N., author of "The Shell Hunters." With Seven Illustrations by ALFRED PEARSE. Large crown 8vo, cloth gilt, 3s. 6d.

The Scotsman says:—"A lively story of adventure in butterfly-hunting, fighting bears and penetrating trackless jungles in various Oriental regions and some undiscovered parts of Africa."

The Daily Telegraph says:—"It is illustrated with seven vivid pictures by Alfred Pearse and is full of adventure all over the world with savage tribes of more or less appalling ferocity and hideous habits."

THE VOYAGE OF THE BLUE VEGA.

By GORDON STABLES, M.D., R.N. With Six Illustrations by ALFRED PEARSE. Large crown 8vo, cloth gilt, 3s. 6d.

"The Voyage of the Blue Vega," by Dr. Gordon Stables, is a yarn which all boys and many "old boys" will delight in. It is a tale of adventures in the Arctic regions, a quarter of the globe which has not been "overdone" in the way of fiction. The style of Dr. Stables—brisk, vivid, chatty, almost confidential, we might call it—carries the reader along as on a flood. There is plenty of adventure in this story, and there is also a romantic mystery pervading the whole. Everything comes all right in the end, as ought to be the case in a book for boys, but a great many threads have to be straightened out before that takes place. There lies the enthralling interest of the story. It shows convincingly that the hand of Dr. Gordon Stables has by no means lost its cunning.

COMRADES UNDER CANVAS. A Story of Boys' Brigade Life.

By FREDERICK P. GIBBON. With Seven Illustrations by ALFRED PEARSE. Large crown 8vo, cloth gilt, 3s. 6d.

A story quite likely to become the classic one of Boys' Brigade Life, just as "Tom Brown's Schooldays" and "The Fifth Form at St. Dominic's" are now confirmed favourites as stories of school life. "Comrades under Canvas" deals with the adventures of members of three Boys' Brigade companies during their annual camp. The interest of the story never flags for a moment, its style is breezy and healthy, and while there is nothing "preachy" about the book, the moral tone is keen and bracing. Boys have their characteristic temptations and failings, and this book, the sale of which ought to be encouraged by every Boys' Brigade officer and everybody interested in boys, will show lads how they may overcome their perils, and live noble, self-sacrificing, Christlike lives.

THE RELIGIOUS TRACT SOCIETY, LONDON.